INTRUSION

A KEENO ACTION NOVEL

INTRUSION

A Keeno Action Novel

by Réal Laplaine

ASTEROID
PUBLISHING

INTRUSION
A Keeno Action Novel

Asteroid Publishing, Inc.

Library and Archives Canada Cataloguing in Publication

Laplaine, Réal

Intrusion : a Keeno action novel / by Réal Laplaine.

Issued also in electronic format.

ISBN 978-1-926720-11-1

I. Title.

PS8623.A7255I57 2011 C813'.6 C2010-907654-0

PRINTED IN CANADA

INTRUSION is a work of fiction. Names, characters and events are the products of the author's imagination. Any resemblance to real persons, organizations or events is coincidental and not intended by the author.

Book cover by Maryna Bzhezitska

Dedication

To Eva Lena who supported the "starving" artist and believed that my writing would amount to something. To my many friends who encouraged me to keep writing with their feedback, enthusiasm, and even their critical remarks about my lack of grammatical skills.

CONTENTS

Foreword

The Keeno action series brings a new face to the literary world of Canadian icons.

Keeno (not KENO, which is a lottery), the main character of this new series, could be considered typical or representative of a "Canadian." If you haven't lived in Canada, you might be asking yourself right about now, "What the hell is a typical Canadian?" If you are a Canadian, you might be brought to a pause, wondering, "What is he talking about?" People I have met in my life have had different ideas about what a Canadian is. Some thought they were simpletons, others thought they were just nice people who lived over the border, while some projected an image of Canada as a snow-bound nation. Yet others seemed to hold onto some asinine image of Canada as a bunch of beer drinking idiots who wore funny hats, said the word "eh" a lot and watched hockey all the time.

I grew up in Canada. I started off in Montreal, bounced around different towns and spots in Ontario (and I do mean bounce, as I have no idea where the hell I lived, for the most part, until I was five years old). I eventually landed in Toronto, where my boat anchored, until I was twenty-one years old. In the mid-70s I headed south to America and left Canada behind, as a chapter of my life closed for over thirty years. But I never forgot about that nation or its people, and as the years progressed and I traveled the world and began my writing career, it occurred to me that something was amiss.

I am an avid movie watcher and book reader, and one day I sat down and tried to list all the Canadian action heroes, or for that matter, *any* Canadian hero that I could recall from the many books or movies I had read or seen. That's when it struck me. There was a huge chasm there. Here was a great country, yet it had so few iconic figures to thrust its name into the action-adventure genre. Where was that Canadian Superman, Canadian James Bond or Canadian Dirty Harry?

From that realization was where this story was born, and as such, I humbly present to you Keeno McCole. Some of Keeno's traits come from some deep well inside of me, and the rest of his qualities are borrowed from personalities I have known, along with a dose of imaginative license.

Keeno McCole is part Aboriginal, a Metis in fact, part English, part Irish and a dose of French .

Keeno heads up the anti-terrorist unit of the Royal Canadian Mounted Police, or RCMP. They are vested with the duty of keeping order in Canada, and have done so for generations. Canada is the second largest landmass in the world, and with only 30 million people, it poses an interesting challenge for the RCMP to deal with the criminal element in such a vast terrain. Traditionally known for their unique hats, blackjack boots and bright red jackets, and often seen mounted on horses the size of a house, they are a very well respected law enforcement branch within Canadian borders. Their motto is and always has been, "We always get our man," and stories abound of their adventures tracking down criminals in some of the remotest and loneliest places on this earth.

McCole and his small team are charged with the task of dealing with extreme criminal elements and terrorists. Each member of his team has been handpicked by Keeno himself, and each one of them possesses unique qualities that set him or her apart. Yet together, they are an effective weapon against terrorism.

Keeno McCole is a maverick. He wears cowboy boots, blue jeans and button-down denim shirts to work. He *tolerates* authority and has no inhibitions about telling bureaucrats and authoritative autocrats where to stick it. He is interested in one thing alone and that is stopping the bad guys. He survives more than his share of bullets and dances with death routinely.

It is my hope that Keeno and his adventures will entertain and excite you.

Réal Laplaine

Chapter 1

I

Every night it started the same way: alone in his room, sitting in a dark recess, staring at the crack of light that filtered underneath the door from the hallway outside. It was like a beacon to him. He could see it, but within his dark room, no one could see him. He would purposely slow his breathing, taking short shallow breaths, so as not to be heard. Inside was the omnipresent and growing anticipation, the incipient fear, the agonizing pain of knowing what was about to happen. Nearly every other night, it was repeated over and over, a living nightmare, a brutal reality that morphed a young boy's impression of the world and taught him that there were monsters out there. Ugly people who did ugly things.

Often he would sit there for an hour, sometimes two, huddled in his dark corner next to the door, with his knees pulled up to his chin. He would listen for every sound as the fear grew and became tangible, so real that it felt like a solid block in the center of his stomach. With it came the acid taste of terror. He couldn't describe it, but he knew what it tasted like.

More nights than not, the shouting would start, first with their voices rising in anger, then followed by insane, violent, irrational screaming that would shake him to the core. Finally, there would be the sound that sickened him; it was the dull thud of a fist landing against her body, or the sharp smack of a hand, followed by her muffled and agonized sobbing. The man's voice would bellow through the house, as if announcing his superiority. Then the brutal silence would ensue, broken only by the faintest sound of his mother whimpering.

Each morning he would wake, waiting in suppressed agony until his mother stumbled from her room, her eyes black and swollen from the beating the night before. He shuddered at the thought of what the rest of her body might look like. She would smile weakly at him, trying to hide her pain and humility while preparing his breakfast.

This scenario had happened so often that by the age of four he could no longer distinguish reality from his nightmares.

On his fourth birthday, his father stumbled into the house, drunken and crazed. She told the boy to go to his room. The ensuing argument quickly morphed from screaming to beating.

He stood motionless in the middle of his room, his small body shaking, not from fear but from anger. Something inside of him had snapped. Some dam had burst, and the young boy was suddenly transformed from a passive victim into that of an aggressor.

He stepped from his room and grabbed the scissors from the nearby bathroom.

From the kitchen, he could hear the man screaming insanely at his mother, "You fucking bitch, I'm gonna kill you."

The boy moved without a sound, entering through the kitchen door, where he saw his mother pressed back against the sink with blood streaming from her mouth. Hunched over her, with one hand squeezing her throat, was his drunken father. In the other hand he held a knife, poised above her. He screamed and ranted, saliva spitting out of his mouth as he did.

The boy closed the distance between them and without hesitation drove the scissors into the man's right thigh, pushing on them with all his strength. Blood gushed out, spilling on him and onto the floor. His father howled and screamed like a wounded animal and fell back against the kitchen table, which collapsed under his weight. He thrashed madly at his thigh, trying to pull the scissors from it.

His mother gasped as she took a breath. The skin on her throat was red and swollen where his hand had been choking the life from her. She stepped over the man and drove the heel of her shoe into his head and screamed, "If you ever touch me again, I'll kill you," and then she ran out of the house with her son. The police arrived only moments later, as fortunately, a neighbor had already called for help. His father was carted away but not before he had emitted a stream of obscenities and threats at the boy and his mother.

It was the last time he saw his father. It was also the last time he ever thought of him as anything but a monster, and he continued to have nightmares over the next years as he relived the incident over and over again. It became a part of his personal fabric, so much so, that it morphed him into someone that would one day become a criminal's worst nightmare.

II

The elderly man stumbled out of his small, ramshackle home, gripping his left arm as he did. He felt overwhelming anguish as pain filled his chest, like a sledgehammer being repeatedly smashed into his heart.

He tripped and fell to his knees as he staggered over to his beat-up '84 Ford pickup, fumbled to get his key from his pocket, and finally slipped it into the ignition. The battered and dented vehicle chugged to life, emitting a gray plume of exhaust as it did. He leaned into the steering wheel and pressed his forehead against it as he fought the agony. All he could think about was making it to the hospital in time.

He put the truck into gear, swung it recklessly in a wide arc, knocking over several garbage cans as he did, and pulled onto the road. Ahead of him, the dirt road cut a straight path through the Canadian Shield, heading for the small town that girded the inlet on Hudson Bay, just ten kilometers away from his lonely outpost on this remote stretch of barren rock.

He fought back the overwhelming desire to simply shut down and slip into unconsciousness, where he wouldn't have to feel the pain anymore. Instead, his survival instincts pushed him forward. He pressed down on the gas pedal and the old truck lurched and sped down the dusty road, throwing up a cloud of dirt as it did.

Unfortunately, Old Man Time showed up at that instant, as he always eventually does, informing the elderly man that his allotment of days on earth had just come to an end.

The man's eyes watered with tears as he tried to recall his life – the precious moments, his family, his friends – all in the flash of a few seconds. His heart, buckling under the brutal attack it had endured, suddenly stopped pumping and the man slumped back in his seat, dead. The truck lurched to the right and flew off the road. The sound of it crashing into the embankment was swallowed up in the vast, empty wilderness. The wind howled and screamed, as if in mourning for the man's sudden passing.

It wasn't until some hours later that another local drove by and saw the truck lying on its side with its engine still chugging and idling. He called it in to the local police and within the hour, a solitary police car arrived, followed by an unmarked white van. After the man was thanked for his help and given leave by the officer, two people from the van stepped out and walked over to the truck. Inside, they found the dead old man, his face wedged into the steering wheel and blood oozing out from several deep lacerations. They took him into the van, and after informing the police officer that they would take care of the matter, they abruptly drove off. The officer was more than happy to leave the matter to them so that he didn't have to do the paperwork. He made some quick notes on his pad and called for a tow truck.

Forty-eight hours later, the report that was filed by the Coroner's office was that fifty-eight year old Etsen Nakolak, a local indigenous Inuit, had lost control of his vehicle, swerved off the road and had suffered multiple fatal injuries to the head. No mention was ever made of the fact that he had endured a massive coronary meltdown, and certainly nothing was ever mentioned in the report about the micro-chips implanted in his left arm and the right side of his torso.

Understandably, it was a ruthless land, challenging and demanding, where death was not an uncommon occurrence. Then again, no one would have known that Etsen Nakolak was a test case, a human guinea pig, and that his heart attack had been intentionally induced, with malice and forethought – as part of a scheme that was about to be unleashed on Canada and the United States of America – and then the rest of the world.

III

Keeno was living alone with his mother in a small, unadorned apartment in Kingston, on the northern shores of Lake Ontario. His mother was struggling to make ends meet, working odd jobs and scraping money together. Yet, she still managed to buy him a birthday cake and a present for his fifth birthday. She had asked him what he wanted most and he told her, a compass. She found one in a second-hand shop, one which had been crafted nearly seventy-five years before he was born. Along with his ivory-handled knife, which he had found in a field near their home, he treasured it as one of his most important possessions.

The compass never left his side, and often he would sit in the sun on the sidewalk, watching its tiny hand as it pointed to the magnetic North Pole, imagining himself in different places around the world, mentally orienting to north, south, east and west. At night, he would sit in his room playing with the compass, looking at the sky to see which star clusters and formations matched the different bearings. It gave him a sense of security to know how to identify his location and direction anywhere and anytime. With his compass he could never be lost and with his knife he would always be safe. Security had become a byword to him. There had been no monsters in his life in the last year, but nonetheless, he was determined that he would never be caught defenseless again. Never!

His mother knew about his nightmares. She had heard him waking up, crying to himself and even screaming. She had taken him away from his father and gotten a court order that restrained the man from coming anywhere near them. But, she needed time to get more money to secure their future and to ensure her son's safety.

Keeno's full name was Kenneth Caliman McCole, but because he really hated the names Ken and Caliman, and wanted nothing that would associate him with his father, the monster, he made up his own name – something that would never remind him of the man, something that would erase his past. Although his mother never liked the name, she conceded to the strong-willed boy who was determined to keep it in spite of her challenges.

He was part Iroquois Indian on his mother's side, and because of this, he also had a given Iroquois name that translated to *Storm Bringer*. It seemed that the Iroquois people had some insight into where he was heading in life. He never really understood the significance of that name – not until much later when he came to realize that the Iroquois people had actually been pretty charitable about it. In the years to come, others would repeatedly call him a "shit-stirrer," although he preferred the Iroquois' interpretation which had a more poetic ring to it.

Shortly after his fifth birthday, his mother sat down with Keeno and explained that she had to move to the big city to make money to buy them their own house, and that in the meantime he would be staying on a farm with his uncle.

Uncle Lou was his mother's oldest brother. His farm turned out to be in the middle of nowhere, and from Keeno's perspective, it really was NOWHERE! In the ensuing three years he rarely saw another human being. The closest town was an hour's drive away, and the nearest major city, Ottawa, was a good three hour's drive east.

Uncle Lou owned a two hundred acre farm where he did some nominal cropping each year, and raised and tended to a small covey of pigs, chickens, a few milk cattle and a couple of horses. He was completely self-sufficient and only ventured to a store once a month, to purchase tobacco and the occasional case of beer.

From the day his mother dropped him off at that desolate farm with tears in her eyes, Keeno began to rise to a level of maturity that most kids only experienced in their teens. The lifestyle on the farm was stark and provided no luxuries whatsoever. The house was heated by an old turn-of-the-century wood stove in the kitchen and a wood-burning fire place in the small common room. They got their water from a well outside. The "shitter" was a small shack behind the farmhouse, where they took care of their personal business. Keeno had left behind the luxuries of civilization and had entered into a world that was completely devoid of any of the "soft" culture.

Uncle Lou introduced him to farm life, told him the schedule and what was expected of him, and from that point on he was up every morning at 6:30 a.m. hefting a shovel and a pitchfork, doing his share of the chores.

He came to admire his uncle and saw him as a good man. Although he was a loner, having lost his wife to a disease some ten years earlier, he had a quiet wisdom about him. He never spoke much and was known sometimes to say less than ten words in an entire day. Nevertheless, he became a mentor to the young Keeno.

Keeno learned most everything by watching and mirroring Uncle Lou. He followed him into the forest and learned how to hunt, track game, ride horses and handle his life in the wilderness of northern Ontario. His uncle showed him which wild plants he could eat and which ones would make him sick or even kill him. He showed him how to build a lean-to, in the event of sudden storms, and how to survive in the forest with just a knife and his wits. The lifestyle suited Keeno just fine. He enjoyed solitude. He'd had enough of human violence and insanity in the first four years of his life. He had his knife and his compass and these were his closest friends and allies.

He soon came to discover that Uncle Lou was a master at throwing knives. The man could flip a knife from its sheath, where it would seem to magically hover in the air, then catch it by its tip and throw it twenty or thirty feet, landing with deadly accuracy every time. It so amazed Keeno that he decided he would learn to do the same.

Uncle Lou had one other distinguishing characteristic, which Keeno found fascinating, though he had no desire to emulate it. Whether working the fields, milking a cow, shoveling shit or even shaving, the man always had a "rollie" cigarette dangling and burning precariously from his lower lip. It seemingly defied the laws of gravity, as it hung there with no apparent means of doing so.

Keeno began using his spare time to practice throwing knives. One day, after countless failed attempts, Uncle Lou stepped up next to him. Lou spoke with a strange kind of Canadian rural dialect that Keeno had never heard before. He never said the words *you* or *your*, but instead always bastardized them into *ya* and *yur*, with an elongated vowel sound that came out as a sort of drawl.

"I reckon that yur the most stubborn person I've ever met," he said lamentably, his rollie bouncing up and down on his lower lip. "Ya just won't give up on throwing that damn knife the wrong way." He pointed his huge leathery finger in Keeno's face. "Yur tryin' to throw a knife like it's something separate from ya. It's not. It's just like yur goddamn hand. Ya don't think about using that – do ya?"

Keeno shook his head.

"So stop thinking about the damn thing. Look at the tree, make an X somewhere and throw it like ya mean it and to hell with all this other stuff goin' through yur head."

Lou stepped off to the side, struck a match and lit up the short stub of his cigarette.

Keeno turned and faced the tree. He cleared his mind of any thoughts, focused on a spot, and let the knife fly. He watched as it spun in slow motion, hilt over tip. Even before it struck, he sensed the dynamics and the power in it – a sort of kinetic bond. It was as if he himself was moving through the air on the same trajectory. The blade sliced into the tree with the ease of going through hot butter.

Lou chuckled, "Now ya got it," and he walked away. That was the only day Uncle Lou taught him anything about throwing knives. Keeno practiced every chance he could. Over the next two years he brought his knife-throwing skills up to the level where he could strike his mark an average of nine times out of ten. But he wasn't satisfied with that – it had to be ten times out ten – so he kept at it.

By the time he was six and a half years old, his uncle had shown him how to load and fire a Winchester pump-action shotgun, a 33 Remington rifle, a Colt 45 handgun and a 22 caliber rifle – all of which he became proficient at using.

What Keeno didn't know, was that Uncle Lou was preparing him for life. Lou had known about the beatings and the abuse, including the incident when Keeno defended his mother against his father. When she had contacted Lou about having Keeno stay on the farm, Lou had not only agreed but had personally decided that he would help morph this kid and prepare him for his future. He somehow knew in his bones that Keeno would not be walking in the middle of the road.

Nearing the end of his stay on the farm, the one thing that Keeno had not yet mastered was throwing a knife with complete accuracy. There was always a 10% margin of error, which haunted him and reminded him that he wasn't perfect. One day, he stood out in an open field with a large oak tree in front of him, determined to break through. The tree stood as a symbol of weakness for him, a constant beacon taunting him that he had an Achilles heel. In some ways it reminded him of his father, the monster, something or someone that could beat him. He knew, somehow, that his future life was not going to be a walk in the park, that violence and insanity would not be a stranger to him, so there was no room for a ten percent, or even one percent, error.

It was a warm sunny day. The sky was blue, with only a few white cotton clouds floating by and the faintest hint of wind that rustled the leaves. The only other sound was the call of a distant crow. Behind him, he heard the telltale sound of a footfall, and turned to see Uncle Lou watching him from a short distance away. He was leaning against a fence post with no particular expression on his face, just the same old cigarette dangling from his lower lip.

Keeno pulled back his right arm and let his knife fly. The first throw was true to the mark. He walked over and pulled it from the tree and then repeated each successive throw with unvaried accuracy, until he had nine out of nine successes. How many times had he reached this juncture only to fail on the tenth?

He tried to convince himself that he didn't have to take it as defeat if he missed on the tenth throw, nine throws was still accurate and spectacular in itself. But no matter how he coated it, the truth was that he had challenged himself; that on the day that he could throw a knife ten times out of ten, without a miss, he would be a master and not a day before.

He stole a look at his uncle, who, with a small smirk on his face, raised both hands to display nine fingers. He had been keeping count. Keeno turned and in one swift motion he let the knife fly. It sliced the distance with silent beauty and cut into the tree with a thud that reverberated in the wide, open space. Ten out of ten – he'd done it! He turned to meet Uncle Lou's smile.

IV

They sat around a small, ornate wooden coffee table carved by craftsmen at the turn of the 18th century. The posh hotel room where they met was of similar design and quality. Located in Brussels, Belgium, it was a perfect meeting place. A special suite accorded only to the very wealthy and influential. It cost a meager five thousand dollars a night. Each pot of coffee delivered to the room was valued at two hundred dollars, and the small pastries they ate with their coffee were hand-baked by the best pastry chefs in the country; each one was valued at ten dollars a bite.

The men in that room could not have cared less if the room cost twice that amount, or whether or not each sugar cube was priced at one hundred dollars apiece. These men didn't count nickels. In fact, they didn't count because they had entire accounting departments that did nothing but track and monitor the millions of dollars passing into their private accounts every month. These were men who engaged in an entirely different order of wealth. While other people struggled to pay their bills, saved on groceries to pay for their kid's new sports equipment, or cut back on their vacation time to put a new roof on the house, these men never gave it a thought.

They existed within financial circles dominated by international bankers and financiers – circles that owned the major international, national and even private banking cartels, financing companies and their subsidiaries. They were men, and in some cases, women, who invested millions in companies and governments, and who made countless millions in return.

Their goal was not wealth, as that had long ago been achieved by them. Their ambition was control and power. Having owned a large portion of the gold, diamond and other financial markets on the planet, their objective was to perpetuate control through ownership of governments and its people. Money was power and with that power one could control through perpetuity.

They sat in a semi-circle facing the large bay window, trimmed with hand-crafted French curtains, overlooking the square below. Considered as "venerable and respectable icons" of their particular industry, these people represented countries such as Russia, Germany, England, France, America and Canada.

"You are sincerely ready to launch this operation?" one of them asked with a complete poker face, his German dialect heavily accenting each word.

The "old man," as he was known, even amongst this circle of elderly peers, nodded his head while sipping his coffee. He knew the protocols of such meetings – their questions were rhetorical. They weren't there to challenge him; they were there to make a statement, a show of confidence towards his plan, as well as a statement of their intent to support him. If they had truly wanted to challenge him, this meeting would not now be taking place.

No one in that room thought that his operation was fool-proof. They had all initiated their own plans and schemes, some of them successful, some not. The fact that the "old man" was taking an aggressive move of this nature was considered a little bit over the top by some, but no one was objecting too much, because in fact they knew, whether he succeeded or not, it would still plant a seed for their mutual and ultimate success.

"Naturally we wish you great success," the German said.

"You have looked at the consequences, yes?" the Russian piped up.

"Indeed – we have," the "old man" assured him.

The Englishman, one of the most powerful bankers in the world, smiled at him with conservative diplomacy, "I'm quite sure that you have taken the precautions necessary to avoid anything being traced back to you?"

"Yes."

The man smiled back at him, but his eyes studied the "old man's" face intensely.

Complete trust was not a quality that these men possessed. There was no one man in this room who had succeeded by being dependent on trust alone. In fact, trust was considered a weakness in this arena. There were formulas, predictive factors, credit ratings, mortgages and other protocols that assured them of success. All of them based on proven mathematical statements and rating systems. If someone reneged on their payments, one simply confiscated property, garnished wages, or employed other "legal" means to gain back more than their share of repayment. The system was rigged so the banks, the bankers and the financing companies always came out on top.

It was, by its nature, an industry that thrived off of the productivity of people, making them pay for their service as they did, and divesting them of their hard-earned wealth if they failed to make good.

V

Walking back from a short foray of hunting, Uncle Lou started a conversation, which he rarely did.

"We're gonna have to get ya ready for the big city. City folk don't take too kindly to guns and knives."

Keeno was staring at his feet, kicking up dust from the dirt path as they walked in the lazy warm sunshine. "I can handle myself."

His uncle made a small chuckling sound, none of which dislodged the thin rolled cigarette hanging from his lip.

"Ya remember that name the Indians gave ya – Storm Bringer?" He raised a brow.

"Yeah."

"When the Injuns name someone, it usually means somethin'."

"So I'm gonna cause storms – so what!"

His uncle smiled and waved a hand lazily at a few flies buzzing around his face, "No, smart ass."

Keeno wasn't taking any of this too seriously.

"Yur gonna find out soon enough the world out there isn't like here on the farm. There are people with different agendas – some of 'em really fucked up. Some of 'em don't like French or Injun; some just don't like "different," period. I think it's time I showed ya how to fight," at which Uncle Lou swung a huge hand straight at Keeno's head.

Keeno saw the movement in his peripheral vision and jumped back just in time to avoid the cruise-missile spearing by his head. It grazed his forehead much the same as scraping a sheet of fifty grit sandpaper over his skin. "What was that for?" he said as he rubbed his forehead.

"Just testing ya," Lou smiled.

"For what?"

Lou smiled and walked on.

Years later, Keeno would think about that moment, wondering if, in fact, Uncle Lou would have actually hit him if he hadn't moved. He came to the conclusion that there were no shades of gray with the man. If he hadn't moved as he did, he would have taken the full impact of that hand and Uncle Lou would have simply brushed it off, saying that he was too damn slow.

They sat down on a patch of grass under a nearby tree. Uncle Lou fired up the cigarette stub again and took a drag on it.

"Yur old man was an asshole, I guess ya knows that."

Keeno didn't answer, silence was his confirmation.

"There's few boys your age that would pick up a pair of scissors and stab a full grown man to protect his mom. I figure yur kinda special on that count." He took a drag on his cigarette. Keeno watched him as he did. It hadn't occurred to him that Uncle Lou even knew about the whole incident.

"Ya know why yur here, right?"

"Mom wanted to get her life together?"

Lou gave him a sidelong glance, "Ya can do better than that. Ya been with me for three years now, it don't take that long to get some money together."

Keeno bunched up his forehead. He hadn't actually considered that there was any other reason than what she had originally told him.

"Yur mom wanted to protect you from that father of yurs. She put ya here to make sure ya were safe for long enough to know that the man was out of her life and yurs."

Keeno let out a sigh. He suddenly missed his mother more than he was willing to admit.

"She was even willing to kill the man to defend ya."

Keeno nodded. "I know."

"Yur mom's a good lady, but she don't know that I taught you all this stuff on thrown' knives, shootin' guns and surviving. She don't know none of that."

"Why'd you do it?"

"Cause yur gonna need it boy. Yur walkin' a road already. Ya put yur foot on that road when ya was four years old. Ya showed that yur not the type of person to put up with any shit. I figured I'd best teach ya some tricks so that ya can survive."

Lou exhaled a bank of smoke.

"Cuz yur part Injun, part French and ya got those Injun eyes and black hair – some people are gonna treat ya different just because of yur looks. And ya got a definite 'don't fuck with me' look in yur eyes. If yur gonna walk through life with that face, ya better be ready to fight." He paused, dousing the cigarette as he did, then stood up and looked down at Keeno. "We'll be starting some fightin' lessons tomorrow."

Over the course of the next few months, Uncle Lou showed him how to fight and how to defend himself. He never asked how or where Uncle Lou learned the techniques, but the little he knew of the man was that he had done a stint in the Canadian Armed Forces before settling on his farm with his wife. What he taught Keeno was a mixture of martial arts, street fighting and kick-boxing.

Keeno felt daunted at having to face up to this huge figure of a man who stood over six feet tall and had hands the size of his own head. But as the weeks passed, Keeno's confidence grew. He learned his lessons well and he grew accustomed to facing a potential adversary who was over two times his own size.

When his mother showed up to take him home to the big city, it was a sad day for Keeno, who said goodbye to his uncle, suppressing his tears as he did. He had no better friend in the entire world than Uncle Lou.

Keeno never saw him again, as the man died a few years later, but he missed him dearly. Everything he learned on that farm would come to save his life and the lives of many others.

VI

It was a perfectly clear day, one of the few they would catch along the Hudson Bay shoreline. Winter was starting to show its face on the Canadian Shield, and conditions could become very rough, very fast, so they had a short window of time to get in and out. Storms could move in within minutes, and when they did, natural bearings and physical landmarks could disappear in seconds. There were countless bush pilots who had vanished in this territory, never to be heard from again.

The bush pilot snaked his plane along the coastline, looking for the telltale signs of the big boy, so that he could bring the plane down for a fast landing. His clients were from Chicago, having come this far to hunt down polar bears before they settled into winter hibernation.

The pilot tipped his right wing and glanced down at the terrain that slid beneath. It took only a few minutes to spot one of them standing on a rocky outcrop jutting into the bay. This was a big male chewing on some food, and for that reason, he would not be easily scared by the plane or the hunters.

The pilot swung the plane in a wide arc and brought it down on the waters of the bay. He powered down and slowly taxied the plane parallel to the shoreline, not two hundred yards upwind from where the bear was sitting. The animal watched them with one eye as it tore at its dinner with powerful jaws.

The pilot flipped open the door to his cockpit, stretched his legs, lit up a smoke and watched as the two hunters crept closer to the bear. He chuckled to himself. He had seen it before with city-folk, and he anticipated exactly what would happen with these two. They positioned themselves, took aim and let off one shot each. Both of them missed, of course. He knew the signs and he knew that these two would have a hard time hitting the side of barn with a shotgun.

He had taken many people out on the hunt and he knew from experience that when you hunted polar bear, it was best to kill them with a head shot if possible, which on this particular bear was a pretty small target at this distance.

To shoot such an animal in the body was to invite your own death, because many a bear had been known to take multiple hits in its fleshy body and still run down the hunter, tearing him to shreds before disappearing. A headshot was the only sure means of bringing it down fast.

As the bullets whizzed by, the bear seemed to pause, not quite understanding what was happening, but then suddenly it lurched forward, dove off the rock shelf and disappeared into the water. Its small head emerged a moment later as it swam with powerful legs and headed out into the bay towards a distant island.

The two hunters walked over to the rocky outcrop, probably wanting to satisfy their curiosity in the hopes that they could at least say that they had hit the animal. The pilot watched them. He was rooting for the bear, which by now had lumbered out of the water and climbed onto the distant shore. It shook the water from its body and turned to look back at the two hunters with disdain, it seemed. It had been robbed of its dinner and wasn't happy about that at all.

Suddenly, one of the hunters was waving frantically to the pilot, motioning him to come. The pilot slipped out of the cockpit and walked to the outcrop. Looking down at what the two men were standing next to, he saw the remains of a man's body. The face was badly marred and disfigured. The arms and legs had been chewed up. What little of the face remained was still enough for the pilot to recognize the man.

They retrieved heavy plastic from the plane, wrapped the remains of the body and flew back to the nearest town. The autopsy was carried out the very next day, revealing that the man had died of a brain aneurysm. The police report surmised that Jimmy Kinooka had probably been out hunting when the aneurysm occurred, and the rest was history. However, there was an important detail that never made it into that report: the fact that Jimmy Kinooka had two micro-chips implanted on each side of his lower neck. That small detail never saw the light of day, and disappeared into the ground where Jimmy Kinooka was mournfully buried by his family and friends.

VII

Keeno and his mom lived in a small house on the east end of Toronto. She had been true to her word, and had moved them into a home of their own. It was an area of town that was considered a bit rough, though in retrospect, Keeno would have described the people there as down to earth.

Moving to the big city had been a cultural shock for him. Accustomed to wide open fields and tracts of unpopulated forests for miles and miles, Keeno had to adjust to the fact that the rules of the game were different. Here, as an eight year old boy, he couldn't carry or shoot guns. He couldn't walk wherever he wanted and he most certainly couldn't take a piss on any street corner.

Every day, the concrete jungle reminded him of the relative freedom he had enjoyed for the past three years on the farm, and more so, it reminded him of how lonely his life felt without his Uncle Lou nearby. Silent as he was, Uncle Lou was the consummate teacher who had shown Keeno more about life and living than anyone or anything. Under his mentoring, he had matured mentally and spiritually well beyond his age.

Keeno sat in the empty classroom, doing his homework. He had lost a year or so in early schooling while living on the remote farm, and because of his age he had been put in this special class to catch-up. He preferred the solitude, the utter silence that filled the room. Here, he could collect his thoughts and focus on his homework, although he would have far preferred to be out hunting and practicing with his knife. He often found himself daydreaming in class, envisioning himself standing in that empty field with that singular tree in the center. He could sense the feel of the warm air, the sun caressing his skin and the weight of his knife in his hand.

He had his nose down, crunching numbers on some arithmetic when he was suddenly jolted from his concentration.

"Hey, mutt," the kid said as he leaned down on Keeno's desk.

Keeno looked up, "What did you say?"

"You're Injun and French – that makes you a mutt."

"And that's supposed to concern me?"

"We don't like mutts here," the kid said to him with a sneer. He was built like a bulldog with a thick neck and a head that reminded him of a watermelon. Suddenly the kid swung his fist at him. Keeno's left hand flashed up effortlessly and caught it mid-air. The kid's look of arrogance was quickly replaced with shock as he snapped his hand back and pointed, threatening, "I'll see you in the school yard," before storming away. Keeno didn't pay the incident much attention, and went on with his schoolwork. In fact, as the time passed, he completely forgot about it until he walked out of the school and found himself confronted by three boys – one of them being the same kid that had threatened him in the classroom.

"Where ya' goin', mutt?"

Keeno looked to his left and right, and saw other kids were gathering around to watch the incipient fight.

He stepped forward to go by but they pushed him back and he stumbled.

"Come on, mutt. Thought you Injuns were tough," the same kid provoked him.

Keeno stood there and looked the three of them in the eyes. He could tell they were getting edgy by the fact that he wasn't nervous or frightened.

"Gonna say something or you gonna cry?" the kid needled him.

"I'm not fighting you."

It seemed that eye contact was confrontational and generally meant that one was prepared to fight; it was a lesson that Keeno came to learn the hard way. True to his nature, Keeno looked them in the eye without so much as flinching and they took their cue and charged.

Keeno swung his book-bag into the nearest kid, clapping him in the side of his head and dropping him like a rock.

The one provoking the fight came at him undaunted. Keeno twisted his body, switching his weight to his left foot as he did and then snapped his right foot upwards at a 45 degree angle. The kid took the full impact in the chest, knocking him backwards and landing him on his ass.

As the incident unfolded, Keeno thought back to what Uncle Lou had taught him; "*If yur ever attacked by a group, remember they only got balls as a group. Single out one guy, preferably the leader, and nail him good and hard and the rest will run for the hills.*"

Incensed by the snickers from others watching the fight, the kid jumped to his feet and charged in once more. When he was less than a few feet away, Keeno faked a move to the left – a simple diversion which his antagonist fell for. Keeno shifted his center of gravity over to his right foot, twisted his body, and snapped his left foot straight into the kid's solar plexus. Keeno could actually hear the air as it wheezed out of his lungs, and with a pained look on his face the kid doubled up and dropped to the ground, gasping.

By now, the other two boys had long since packed it up and disappeared.

Keeno crouched down in front of the fallen kid and waited for him to look up.

"Look… if you really want to keep fighting me, I don't mind, but maybe we could try being friends," Keeno said, thinking to himself that anyone with this much balls was worth having on his side.

The look of pain in the kid's face, mixed with some sense of humiliation, slowly faded and he grabbed Keeno's outstretched hand.

"I'm Keeno."

The kid took a deep breath, "I'm Jake. What the hell kind of name is Keeno and where did you learn to fight like that?"

It was the beginning of a lifetime friendship between Jake Williams and Keeno McCole.

VIII

The man didn't look particularly different or special, and he certainly didn't stand out from the rest of the crowd. He was slightly balding with light, peppered hair. He had a noticeable paunch from a lifestyle of too many beers and too little exercise. He was wearing a brown suede jacket, blue jeans and a pair of brand new Nike running shoes.

As he approached the locker in the downtown Toronto Greyhound bus terminal, he nervously looked around to ensure that no one was watching, then opened up the locker and grabbed the briefcase inside. He quickly exited the terminal and headed for Bay Street, his destination being the University of Toronto. He had memorized the route so that he would know exactly where to go.

The man walked at a good pace, his eyes flitting nervously up and down the street, watching faces in anticipation of any trouble. He wanted nothing more than to get the briefcase delivered and out of his hands as quickly as possible. He sensed certain consternation just from knowing its contents and how important it was that he delivered it into the right hands, with no mishaps along the way. There was 25K waiting for him when he finished being their delivery boy, and that's all that really mattered to him.

Life seemed to have taken a bad turn for him in recent years, and so his circumstances dictated, it seemed to him at least, that he needed to do something drastic to change it. When the opportunity had come, a chance to make a wad of cash for just being a messenger, he jumped on it.

He'd never done anything like this in his whole life. He knew it was wrong. He knew that it could have disastrous consequences, but he was a desperate man, a junkie, hooked on his obsessions and without money to feed his habits, he was as good as dead. In his recent years he had fallen into gambling. He'd lost his home, his reserves and even his wife, who had left him because he had all but destroyed their lives. With the gambling, came the drinking, and eventually, the prostitutes. It was a deadly trio and he had long since given up trying to control the beast.

He arrived at the corner of Gerard and Bay Street, waiting for the traffic light to change, when his cell phone rang. "Yeah, I got it," he said. He looked at his watch, "I'll be there right on-time, no problem," he said, as he stepped out into the street with just a quick glance.

He was so preoccupied with his phone call that he failed to see the speeding car making the right turn onto Gerard Street. Although the driver scrambled to hit the brakes, the car smashed into the man with such force that it threw his body fifteen or more feet into the air as if it was a rubber ball. The man was killed on the instant of impact, but by the time his body had bounced and skidded to a stop, much of his facial skin was ripped off, his jaw was shattered, and there were bones extruding in several places. Blood pooled around his dead form as people nearby gawked in horror.

IX

Janene was reviewing some reports when her phone rang, "Yeah, be right up."

She made her way up to the CIC, the Command Information Centre – the heart and mind of the Royal Canadian Mounted Police. Although the official HQ for RCMP Ontario operations was located in London, Ontario, the Toronto branch was actually a strategic hub, with over five million people living in the Greater Toronto Area, representing 17% of Canada's entire population.

"What d'ya got?" she said to the Data Controller.

"Just got this in from the OPP," he handed her the sheet.

"Thanks."

Janene went back to her office, reading it on her way. If the Ontario Provincial Police (or OPP) were sending this report to the RCMP, it was because there was a serious possibility of terrorist activity.

Kelly looked up at her as she walked in, "Somethin' new?"

"Oh yeah," she dropped the report in front of her.

"Damn… that's kinda weird," Kelly said, after reading it. She looked up at Janene, lighting a cigarette as she did.

Janene and Kelly had been working together in the trenches of "RATU" for six years now. The acronym was short for RCMP Anti-Terrorism Unit. They considered themselves the "brains" of the outfit, while Keeno and Jake were the "brawn" who did the "James Bond" stuff – chasing after the bad guys.

Janene stood five feet eight inches in height. She was slim and curvy and had long brown hair that fell straight down past her shoulders. She had sharply defined features with high cheekbones, a slim nose and perfect lips – not pouty or overdone. She came from a family that hailed out of Finland, giving her slightly Asiatic features, mixed with the typical Scandinavian light skin.

She had come aboard with RCMP Anti-Terrorism Unit just months after Keeno had become the head of it. He had found her through a search of people who were particularly adept at investigative and forensic procedures. When he had called her in for the interview, he spent much of the time just listening and smiling at her. At the time she wasn't sure what to make of it, but later she would come to find out that he was actually paying no attention whatsoever to her answers and that after the first moments of the hour long interview he had already made up his mind to bring her on. He was simply enjoying looking at her the rest of the time.

Kelly, on the other hand, was diametrically opposed to Janene's refined features and attire. Whereas Janene always wore fashionable skirts, tops, and stylish high-heeled shoes and could have passed as a model any day of the week, Kelly came in from an entirely different spectrum. She was the epitome of a punk-rocker, with short cropped hair that was spiked with styling paste. It was mostly maroon in color, but sometimes, as in today, she had pink patches in it; other days she tried different color combinations. She usually wore blue jeans that were torn in all the right places, sometimes revealing a bit too much skin, sometimes bringing screams of protest by more conservative RCMP personnel. To add to the usual "go to hell" attitude that she flaunted at anyone who objected to her appearance, today she had on a tight t-shirt that said – GO AHEAD – BUST MY ASS.

While Janene had two stylish earrings, Kelly had four piercings in each ear, not to mention the ring through her left nostril. Amongst her many tattoos that seemed to cover most of her visible skin surface, Kelly's real prize was a green and yellow parrot, almost life-size, tattooed on the left side of her neck so that it appeared to be perched there, looking straight ahead. When she tipped or turned her head to the right, which she often did while smoking a cigarette, the parrot appeared be looking at you with coal black eyes. It was slightly unnerving to people who were in conversation with her.

Keeno had found Kelly in his search for a fourth member of their Anti-Terrorism unit. Though urged to pick people from within the RCMP itself, he had opted to do otherwise. He wanted people, like himself, who were new. He didn't want anyone in his office to quote him the rules or teach him RCMP protocols – especially no one that would bend to "the system." If he was going to fight terrorism, then he needed to do it on his own terms, and as such, he preferred a few rebels under his charge.

Despite appearances, Kelly was actually a genius in forensic investigations. She had excelled in every mathematical class through high school and college, and later in her forensics training. In spite of some objections from RCMP authorities who didn't like Kelly's outward appearance, insisting that it didn't live up to their "standards," Keeno got them to agree to let her aboard on a probationary status. That had been six years ago, and since then, Kelly had delivered up in aces and earned her wings as an official RCMP employee.

Jake Williams stepped through the door, balancing four Starbucks coffees in a tray in one hand and a bag of pastries in the other. " Uhh… a little help would be cool."

Kelly got up from her desk and grabbed the coffees. "Geez, Mr. Helpless. He can bust terrorists but he can't get through the door with some coffees. Poor boy," she needled.

"Stuff it," he said. The banter between the two was pretty much an institution at this stage.

"Hey, guys!" Keeno said as he walked into the office behind Jake. As usual, he was wearing blue jeans, a loose fitting button-down shirt, a black vest and black cowboy boots. He had long, coal-black hair that came down to the base of his neck. He stood six feet three inches high. His body was absolutely trim, hardened like a rock from a career that routinely challenged him to stay alive. His skin was slightly bronzed; he had a sharp chin, and high cheek bones. His eyes were deep brown and inset such that when he looked at you it could make you feel slightly uncomfortable because of their intensity.

Keeno smiled at Janene. It was a reserved smile, yet it had a hint of something else that they tacitly shared between them.

Jake shoved a coffee cup across the desk at him and dropped a bag with a giant bear claw next to it, "That stuff is the shit," he announced.

"You'll wanna see this," Kelly said, as she handed the report to Keeno. Keeno dropped into his chair and started reading while sipping on the coffee.

Finally, he dropped the sheet on his desk, "What do you think, ladies?"

"I think we should go down to OPP and check it out right away," Janene said.

"Check out what?" Jake mumbled through a mouthful of pastry.

"Uhh – a briefcase of shit found on a dead guy this morning," Kelly said, as she shook her head at him.

Jake was Keeno's closest friend and ally, and the person he most trusted in the world. After fighting in the schoolyard at the age of nine, they had become the best of friends and had grown up together in the east end of Toronto. They had joined the OPP at the same time, did a short stint as street cops, and when Keeno had been recruited into the RCMP, he insisted on making Jake his right-hand man.

Unlike Keeno, Jake was built like a wrestler, a quality which had been his trademark since they had first met in that school yard. He had muscles everywhere, a short neck and short, cropped hair. There wasn't an ounce of fat on the man and like Keeno, his body was trained and honed for survival. If you saw Jake walking down the street, his good-humored smile and casual appearance would seem to contradict the dangerous lifestyle that the man engaged. Nevertheless, he was lighthearted, insouciant and never took anything very seriously – at least not until the bullets started flying.

"I agree – you drive," Keeno answered back to Janene as he threw his keys to her. "I still have to finish this," he said, as he chomped into the bear claw and slurped up some more coffee.

When they arrived at the OPP office on Keele Street, they were quickly ushered down to a holding area where a team of medical examiners were hovering over the battered and bloody body.

Keeno briefly looked at the body of the mystery man, which was a mass of black and blue patches, exposed and broken bones, and dried and caked blood. "Geez," he waved a hand in dismissal and walked over to a table where the briefcase was being examined separately.

One of the female examiners looked up at him, "Who are you?"

"Keeno McCole, with the RCMP. What the hell is that?" he pointed inside the briefcase.

"We don't know yet but we think it might be a virus. One of these pouches is in the lab right now being checked out," she said through a surgical mask. Keeno bent over and studied the contents of the briefcase. He counted twenty-nine packages, if they could be called that. They were about the size of a golf ball, translucent green and seemed to have something else embedded inside them. He looked up at Jake, "Any ideas?"

Jake hunched his shoulders while still sipping on his coffee.

"Where's your lab?" Keeno asked her.

"I'll take you," she said and led them down a set of stairs into a lower level, passing through two security doors and finally arriving at a forensics lab, which was quite large and well equipped. "Lacie, this is Keeno McCole from RCMP AT," she introduced them to the lead technician.

A gray-haired woman turned and took off her mask. "AT, I assume, is *Anti-Terrorism*?"

Jake nodded. "That'll be us. When you've got terrorists, you call in the bad boys," he smiled proudly.

Keeno rolled his eyes at him.

"Any idea what's in that thing?" Keeno pointed to the green package that was sitting on a glass plate with an electronic microscope hovering above it.

"Not yet, but it's certainly like nothing I've seen before, that's for sure," she said.

"So you're gonna open it up?"

"No – actually, with our technology and that electron microscope, we should be able to analyze chemically what it's made out of without even touching it. Give me a few minutes."

She turned and put on her mask and then maneuvered her microscope into place with a joystick on a panel in front of her. As she operated the joystick, the microscope moved, producing a subtle humming noise. Chemical elements flashed up on a small computer screen in front of her and as they did she spoke into a hidden microphone, detailing her observations and interpretations. It all sounded like so much mumbo jumbo and went on for some minutes. Finally, she stopped and took off her mask.

"This is definitely a virus of some kind, but I've never seen this one before, and we have nothing in our records that matches it."

"How much virus is in one of those packages?" Keeno asked.

Lacie's face became more somber, "I'd have to analyze it more to say with accuracy, but offhand, I'd say there's enough virus to infect a couple hundred thousand people."

Keeno let out a deep breath. In his six years with the RCMP, they had handled bomb threats, death threats, hijackings and more, but never anything of this magnitude. It was times like this when he remembered back to the day when Uncle Lou had admonished him that there were people in the world who were screwed up.

Ironically, twenty-five years later, it was his job to stop the really messed up ones.

X

"What do you make of this?" Ross Fletcher, head of RCMP Ontario asked CC, his Operations Officer. Calvin Cole, or CC, as he was normally referred to around the RCMP, was Ross Fletcher's right-hand man. Wherever Ross went, CC could usually be found standing some feet away, certainly within earshot, so that he knew what was going on and could be one step ahead of the Director of RCMP's Ontario office.

CC was the epitome of an RCMP employee. He was experienced in all facets of RCMP Operations and he knew the nuances of nearly all RCMP activities, qualifying to effectively help oversee most Operations. He was also physically exemplary of their standards. His hair was always perfectly cut and combed. He was dressed impeccably, usually with a shirt and tie, or if not that, a blazer over a button-down shirt. He didn't look in any way formidable, but he was more than competent.

Seated at the large conference table situated at one end of the huge CIC, was the Director, CC and Keeno's team. One entire wall was lined with computer stations. Another wall, adjacent to the large conference table, had several large HD monitors mounted with satellite feed for media and other portals around the planet.

Ross Fletcher had started off as an RCMP Mountie at the age of twenty-one. He had seen duty in Ottawa and Montreal, patrolling the streets, riding horseback and getting his picture taken thousands of times by tourists who wanted to see a real Royal Canadian Mounted Policeman. Mind you, Mounties didn't just ride "horses" – they rode *huge* horses and were skilled at making them dance on a dime, and during crowd control or riot situations, Mounties could shave a man's face with the hind end of an eleven hundred pound horse while charging into the crowd.

Ross took over as head of the Ontario RCMP after the American debacle in New York City with the twin towers on September 11, 2001. Ottawa's power elite at the time had been concerned that Canada's anti-terrorism program was too weak.

Ross began his search for an ideal team, and to his credit was the fact that he eventually found and hired Keeno. Since its formation, RATU had effectively thwarted a number of attempted terrorists – or at least those who claimed to be such.

In the mainstream realm of "terrorism," Canada was not in the spotlight very much. Occasionally someone, following in the footsteps of the FLQ – the Front de Liberation du Quebec – would try to send up a flag of dissension by threatening some act of terrorism – but this was always rapidly quelled. Random terrorist threats, from bombings to threatened hijackings, had been attempted, but in every case RATU had succeeded in stopping them. Besides the battles waged in 1759, between England and France, over ownership rights to the second largest land mass in the world and the War of 1812, Canada had no other history of foreign aggression on its soil.

"Given that the dead guy had a briefcase full of lethal virus and that each package has a small air-driven detonator in it to ensure wide permeation, I'd say we're definitely in terrorist territory," CC responded.

"How does it work?" Keeno asked.

"From the lab analysis, it looks like a compressed gas bubble designed so that when the outer seal of the package breaks or disintegrates, the sudden air pressure causes the inner package to explode, spreading the virus. It's like an atomizer effect," CC explained.

"Any traces on calls?" Keeno turned to Janene.

"Not yet. Someone who saw the car hit the guy said that he was talking on his cell phone when he stepped onto the street. The phone got beat up pretty bad, so we're still working on it," she answered.

"Okay," Ross said, "any other leads?"

"There is one," Janene said, "his Nike shoes."

"Nikes?" Ross asked with a slight challenge in his tone.

"Yeah, I know it sounds lame, but I happen to be a Nike's fan. I keep track of the newest Nike's every time they come out with a style I like. My closet at home is filled with them. Those particular Nikes that the dead guy was wearing have only been released in the States so far. They weren't due to be released in Canada for another month. So that means he's either American or a Canadian who was recently over there."

"We'll know soon, when they run the prints on him," Ross said.

"Easier said than done," Kelly jumped in. "Whoever this guy was working for used a light acid on his fingers and burned his prints as a sort of insurance policy so that it would be harder to trace his identity. We have to go by dental records, but first they have to put his jaw back together. It got crushed during his free fall."

Ross nodded.

"While we were at the OPP today," Janene began to say, "I went through the dead guy's clothes. On the bottom of his Nikes was some yellowish stuff that was dried and caked on. I scraped some of it off and took it to our lab when I came back here," she paused to fish out a piece of paper from her binder, "and I just got this report back with an analysis of it." She slid a copy of the report over to Ross.

"Care to interpret that chemical mumbo-jumbo for me?" he said, with a slight smile.

"The chemical is not something you'd find on the streets of Toronto, or in fact, anywhere where normal people go. The main element contained in that substance, and I'll spare you the chemical details, is commonly used by pharmaceutical companies as the containing or holding agent for drugs they produce. In simple terms, when you take your headache pill, the actual drug is suspended in a gook or holding substance, which is the same stuff that was caked on the bottom of our dead guy's Nikes. It's proprietary territory of drug and pharmaceutical facilities. Very few other companies manufacture it."

Ross nodded, "Interesting."

"I assume there was no ID on this guy?" Keeno asked.

"None that was found," Kelly answered. "But, the OPP clean-up team found a ticket stub on the street not far from the body. It was covered in blood. It was for a bus that originated in Trenton, New Jersey, leaving 2 a.m. and arriving early this morning in Toronto."

"That stub could have been from anyone who dropped it on the street," Ross said.

"True. It's completely hypothetical at this point," Kelly agreed.

"It's something. Let's get on it," Keeno said, as he stood up.

As they left the CIC, Keeno grabbed Janene by the elbow, "See what drug companies are in the Trenton, New Jersey area. Maybe there's more to this than we think."

"And you?"

"Jake and I are going to go visit an old friend."

"Care to elucidate?"

"Not yet," he winked at her and then walked down the hall.

She watched as he walked away, thinking that as much as she secretly loved him, she felt he could be such a pompous asshole at times.

Chapter 2

I

The office was located on the 31st floor of the Bank of Montreal (BMO) building, one of the tallest structures in Toronto and visible from many miles on a clear day. Four men were present.

"Tell me what happened?" the old man asked, with an imperious tone that carried a subliminal threat.

"The contact was on his cell phone, right at the corner of Bay and Gerard, when apparently he stepped out on the street just as a car turned the corner and struck him. By the time he landed, he was dead."

"The briefcase?"

"In OPP custody."

The old man asking the questions was the head of the overall operation. The fact that their contact had been killed in the process of transporting the virus from the bus station to the University of Toronto, where it was to be prepared for distribution, was a major screw up – to put it lightly. They had elected to use a complete stranger as the delivery man, but now it was evident that the choice had been a poor one.

The old man stared out the window at the adjacent skyscraper and spoke without looking at the others. It was his way of keeping people slightly on edge and intimidated.

If he didn't make eye contact, they couldn't read him and that was leverage – something he had learned to use effectively in his ascent to wealth and power.

"What do you propose?" he asked with ominous venom in his voice.

"I don't know yet. Our sources tell me that the RCMP has been called in because of the terrorist ramifications."

"No shit!" the old man said, as he turned in his chair to glare at them. "It's supposed to have terrorist ramifications, but it's not supposed to be in the hands of the OPP or the RCMP." He stared them down long enough to get them worried. "Get the asset to figure out how to get that briefcase back NOW and then proceed with the plan. No more fuck ups," and he dismissed them with a wave of his hand.

The old man turned and stared out the window at downtown Toronto. In reality, the entire incident hadn't upset him that much, as the plan was still solid. Of course, he couldn't show that to these men, they had to feel his wrath and know the threat in his voice. It was his way of controlling people. He'd done it for nearly forty-five years now, and it came easy to him.

II

"Uhh, gonna let me in on where we're going?" Jake asked Keeno, as they pulled out of the RCMP parking lot in his Jeep.

"The University of Toronto, to see an old friend."

"Cool," Jake smiled. He saw no point in probing any further. Keeno had intuitions and you just had to trust that he was right. If he had learned anything in his last six years, it was simply this: check your gun, make sure you have a spare clip, and be prepared to dodge the bullets, because with Keeno they were coming!

By the time they arrived at the main University of Toronto campus, students were already pouring out of classes for the day. They found Ralph Ketchler at his desk, in his large but empty classroom. Keeno hadn't seen the man for nearly a year, even though he was a close friend to Keeno and possibly the only other man in his life that he considered on par to Uncle Lou. They had met years before, when Keeno was searching the U of T for some qualified people for his department. Ralph Ketchler had been the one who had tipped him off on where to look for some good post-grads, which led to finding Janene. From there they had formed a friendship and had shared many nights over pitchers of beer, talking about everything from genetic mishaps to the scarcity of good looking women in the day and age of "fast food cellular accumulation" – which was Ralph's way of saying that women today were getting "too goddamn fat" – completely missing the fact, of course, that he himself was the epitome of a cellular overload. Keeno enjoyed their times together and treasured the old man's flippant attitude towards what he called "crusty authoritarianism," his term for what he regarded society to have morphed into.

"Ralph!"

Ketchler turned and tipped his face downward to look over his bifocals.

"Look what the goddamn wind just blew in. Hell, we used to have some security around here but now anyone can walk in the goddamn door," he smiled as he lumbered up to Keeno to shake hands.

"How are ya?" Keeno asked with a friendly smile and a warm handshake.

"I'm good, just added a few pounds since you last saw me. Betty's been making too many damn good cakes these days," he patted his protruding belly.

"I can see that," Keeno smiled. "This is Jake, my partner."

Ketchler nodded and smiled at Jake. "Hmm, I've heard about you. No doubt Keeno's disease has rubbed off on you too," he eyed Jake inquisitively.

Jake wasn't sure how to answer.

"No women in your life either?" he eyed Jake over his spectacles. "Last time I checked on Keeno, he was living alone with that damn horse on his small ranch, like some monastic monk or something. Damn, if I was your age, I'd be out there hunting 'em down!" Ketchler said jokingly, taking the opportunity to needle Keeno about his love life.

"Yeah, I'm thinking of joining a priest hood, you know, celibacy and all that," Jake smiled.

"What about that pretty brunette in your office?" Ralph turned and raised a brow at Keeno, "She sounds like a good catch to me?"

Keeno rolled his eyes, "You're just a dirty old man, Ralph."

"Motivated and dirty are two very different things, my boy."

Keeno smiled. "Got a few questions for you, got a minute?"

"Sure, sit down."

"This doesn't go beyond these walls. A man was found dead today, in downtown Toronto, hit by a car. He had a briefcase filled with small pouches that were loaded with an unknown virus."

Ketchler bunched up his forehead, "How many pouches?"

"Thirty of them and according to the lab technician at the OPP, each pouch alone could infect a couple hundred thousand people."

Ketchler took off his glasses and rubbed his eyes, "Hmm… not good."

"You know something about viruses, so maybe you can give us some information."

"Like what?"

"Well, if someone wanted to hit Toronto with a virus attack, what are we lookin' at?"

"Well… if you want to debilitate a city with a virus attack, there are two ways to do it. An amateur would just go around spreading virus in a sort of linear or haphazard fashion, trying to cause maximal damage in one sweep. But if they're real pro about this, my theory is they'd go for multiple waves, or what we call *layering*."

"Which is?"

"Layering means just that; spread one strain of a virus, then hit them with another one before they can recover from the first."

"What would be the collateral damage – ballpark?" Keeno asked.

"In the first scenario, not much because a one-shot virus attack could be contained, but in the case of layering, one virus after another, you could cause an economic and financial melt-down that could domino-effect across the nation."

"Hmm," Keeno said.

"Are there different strains of virus in those pouches?" Ralph asked.

"No idea. They were still being analyzed at the lab."

"Let's hope that it was just one strain," Ralph said.

"What about deaths, what could we expect?"

"Again, first case scenario would probably be nominal, depending on how many get infected. In the second case scenario, with layering, you're looking at a dramatic increase in death potential. Nobody knows for sure with any virus, as each one has its own potency. For instance, when the WHO and the American government made a big deal about H1N1, we all thought the walls of Jericho were about to fall in. It turns out that the infection and death rates associated with H1N1, the Swine Flu, was practically in the same ballpark as any other influenza that passes through our society every year. Any statistic can be padded to make it look worse – even deaths from a flu. Someone just decided to make a big deal out of H1N1, probably to make money or to leverage some other advantage," he paused to wipe the sweat from his forehead.

He continued, "Thousands die of the flu every year and you never hear about those statistics. Most healthy people can beat any flu. The ones most prone to death are either very young and don't have the immune system set up to battle it yet, or are ill, old, or debilitated. People who are already at a disadvantage physically are the ones who can be hit hardest by any flu. But even a healthy body hit with repeated infusions of new strains could fold under that pressure."

Ralph paused as he collected his thoughts, "If they hit Toronto with enough viruses, especially with the layering effect, it would cause a titanic wave of fear. The system would be threatened. People's lives would be at risk. You'd have a government that would be watching billions of dollars going down the drain because productivity would be slashed. At the same time, the medical infrastructure would be taxed to the limit. Government costs would skyrocket. It would drive people to drastic measures to stem the blood-loss from a wounded society. Fear would be just as much a problem as the actual direct effects of the virus itself."

Ketchler wiped the sweat from his forehead and smiled at Keeno.

"One other question, do these viruses need special conditions to keep them alive?" Keeno asked.

"Yes, refrigerated conditions usually, but it depends on the strain."

"Where would you hide a virus, if you needed to keep it on ice until you released it?"

Ralph sat there for a long moment, contemplating the answer to the question, "Frankly, I'd bring it to the University of Toronto."

"Why?" Keeno asked, with some surprise.

"Because we have some of the best facilities in the country for virus research and control, our labs deal in it all the time, and we're probably more accessible than a private facility."

"What about security? Could someone really get stuff in and out of your labs that easily?" Keeno asked.

Ralph smiled, "Security is a matter of authority, you should know that, Keeno. He who wields the hammer, wields the power," Ralph said, with a sagely look on his face.

Keeno reached forward and slapped his old friend on the back. "You've been a big help Ralph," he said.

"Nah, you knew all this stuff already. You just wanted a chance to get out of that stuffy office at RCMP and check out our plethora of good-looking females on campus."

"You know me too well. We'll do coffee sometime."

"Indeed, and maybe you can bring that pretty little brunette from your office," Ralph smiled, with a leer in his look.

"The dirty old man reveals himself again." Keeno said.

Leaving Ralph's classroom, Keeno decided to do some more snooping around the U of T. He found a map of the campus, identified the labs and headed for the fourth floor wing.

III

Since mid-morning, when the briefcase had first shown up at her lab at the OPP, Lacie had analyzed twenty-three of the thirty viral packages. Each one came up with the same basic virus, with just one spin: there were five different strains so far. She also found a numbering system on the bottom of each package, which only showed up when she passed an infrared scan over it. *This*, she thought to herself, *must be how they identify which packages to release*.

She looked at her watch. It was nearly 7 p.m. She should have ended her shift nearly two hours ago and the lab was otherwise empty. She had already called Carol, who did the graveyard shift, to let her know that she was staying late, so Carol had seized the opportunity to take care of other business. Lacie was determined to finish analyzing all of the packages before going home.

In her twelve years working the lab for the OPP, she had never been confronted with viral terrorism of this magnitude. The sheer potential and destructiveness of these thirty pouches, if released, would be enough to sink Toronto into a serious economic slump, one which would domino across the nation. The potency of the infection would be such that the whole geographical zone would need to be shut off from the rest of the world, until the epidemic could be handled.

The only question that was not answered now was – how strong and virulent were the viruses?

She rubbed her eyes and carefully removed the package she had just analyzed from its perch under the microscope, placed it into a special container, capped it off, and then dropped it into the exit chamber.

She heard a noise behind her.

"Carol, that you?"

There was no answer, so she turned her head and was shocked to see a man standing several feet from her. She suddenly recognized him.

"What are you doing here?" she demanded. "This is a restricted area."

Before she could say another word, his right hand flashed upwards driving the blade deep into her midsection. He jerked it even deeper into her organs, ripping her wide open, while his other hand came over her mouth to stifle her scream.

Lacie jerked backwards in a violent reflexive action and as she did, her head slammed into the joy stick on the control panel. The killer held her with a steel grip as she shuddered and convulsed in her death throes. Finally, she crumbled to the floor and everything went black as Lacie died in a pool of her own blood.

IV

Keeno and Jake walked down a wing of the fourth floor of the University. It was dotted with labs in which students in white tunics and surgical masks were working.

One lab was labeled VIRAL DIAGNOSTICS.

"Hmm… good place to start," Keeno muttered.

They went into the lab where a student was stirring some green goop in a glass jar.

"Excuse me, " Keeno said, as he leaned on the table.

The student looked up over his face mask, "Probably not a great idea for you two to be in here when I'm working with this stuff," he said, with some disdain in his tone. Keeno motioned him outside.

"I'm Keeno, this is Jake. We're with the RCMP."

"Uhh huh," the kid said, with a nonplused attitude.

"Where do they keep viruses stored around here?"

The student let out a breath, clearly annoyed and pointed to the sign across the hall which said CONTAGIOUS VIRAL STORAGE. Then he slipped his mask back over his face and walked away.

"Wow, what an asshole!" Jake said.

Keeno smiled.

They went to the lab on the opposite side of the hallway, but it was locked. Like two kids looking at fish through a glass bowl, they peered inside the room until they heard footsteps approaching from behind.

"Can I help you gentlemen?"

Keeno turned and was faced with a stunningly beautiful woman, who stood about five and half feet tall and had brilliant red hair that fell to her shoulders.

"Well actually, we're looking for some information," he started to say.

"About?" she raised her brow with a smile.

"Contagious viruses."

She smiled, revealing a seemingly perfect set of teeth that made her face radiant.

"Well, that lab in there," she pointed, "is for the study of flu viruses, so you seem to have found the right place. But what exactly are you trying to find out?"

"We're with the RCMP. We're investigating a virus threat."

"Maybe I can help you. I'm Katherine Riggs, the resident teacher for microbial and viral diseases," she smiled.

"Wow, where were you when I was in school," Jake said.

She laughed at his forwardness.

"Can we talk somewhere?" Keeno asked.

"Sure, let's go to my office.

V

"I've never seen you so talkative," Keeno needled Jake as they got into Keeno's Jeep an hour later. "Wouldn't possibly have anything to do with the fact that she has a set of legs to die for?" he leered.

"I have no idea what you're talking about," Jake said, with a large smile.

"You spent a lot of time looking at all of her, and I do stress ALL."

Jake let out a deep sigh, "I have to admit that is one woman I would love to meet again."

Keeno's cell phone rang. "Someone got into the OPP, killed the lab technician and got away with the virus," Janene said.

"Shit! That means we're dealing with an inside connection. No one gets into a secure OPP lab without connections," he said, as he put the Jeep into gear and raced back to the RCMP.

Twenty minutes later they arrived to the office.

"When did they find the dead technician?" Keeno asked, as he charged through the door.

"About ten minutes before I called you, so… about 7:45," Janene said.

"They moved fast to recover that virus, so we can only assume that they intend to use it very soon, maybe tonight," Keeno speculated out loud .

"I think we should start with water treatment plants," Kelly said.

"Why?"

"Water will get them the biggest bang for their buck. Air would disperse the virus and lessen the chances of making a big impact. Water is a better carrier in this case."

"Hmm."

"I'm already putting together a list of all the big venues in town, as well as water filtration plants," Kelly continued.

Over the next few hours they postulated different scenarios, trying to get a clue of how and where the virus might be released and where.

Ross Fletcher walked in as everyone was huddled over the small conference table.

"Bad news guys, we just found out that Trillium hospital in Mississauga has admitted some cases with strange new flu symptoms."

Keeno looked at Janene and Kelly, "We're already behind the eight-ball. Jake, you get out to the nearest filtration plant in Mississauga and check it out. See what you can find."

Jake was up and out the door.

"Let me know," Ross said, as he turned and left.

Janene looked up from her computer at that point.

"Since we did find that bus stub near the body this morning, and there was that yellow substance on the dead-guy's Nikes, I went ahead and checked for any pharmaceutical plants in the Trenton, New Jersey area, and there is one. They're called FAB-MED," Janene said.

"How big are they?" Keeno asked.

"They supply some of the big-boy pharmaceutical companies in the US and Canada and they definitely manufacture that stuff we found."

"OPP checked with the bus drivers who do the Trenton to Toronto route, and one of them vaguely remembered a guy who looked like our dead boy. Forensics have almost got his jaw reconstructed with what bits and pieces they could find of his teeth, so we should be able to get a match on dental records soon," Kelly added.

"Book me a flight to Trenton, will ya?" Keeno blurted out, as he grabbed a travel bag from under his desk.

"Just like that?" Janene challenged him.

Kelly smiled. She knew by the tone of Janene's voice that it wasn't Keeno's impulsiveness that bothered her. They all knew that when he got a feather up his ass about something, he was going to do it, whether others agreed or not. Kelly could tell by Janene's expression that she was worried about *him* personally. When Keeno went off somewhere, it usually meant that he would get involved in trouble and would probably come back with another bullet hole or knife wound to add to his ample collection of scars.

"The only way to beat these guys is to find the source. Trying to find who is dropping the virus, and where, is going to be like trying to find a needle in a haystack right now," Keeno said as he pulled out his passport and RCMP ID. He slipped his knife from his back pocket and packed it into his small luggage case, which he kept in the office for such contingencies. Airlines simply didn't take too kindly to passengers carrying throwing-knives with four-inch blades.

"See if you can get me on a flight in about two hours. I'm going up to see Ross," he said as he walked out of the office.

"I hate it when he does that," Janene fumed, as she angrily tapped her computer to book the flight.

"Chill out, girl, he always comes back alive."

"Yeah, but how many lives has he got left and how many bullets can one man take?"

"I don't think Keeno has any concept of dying. He throws himself into the winds of life and challenges it to beat him," Kelly said, as she lit up a smoke.

"Yeah, that's what worries me," Janene said, as she finished booking his flight to Trenton. Once again she had procrastinated on telling him her feelings, and now she'd have to sit it out and just hope that he came back alive.

VI

Harold James sat at a large mahogany desk in the Canadian parliament in Ottawa. In his hands was a package that had been carefully prepared for him. He had rehearsed the speech several times to make it sound eloquent and compelling. He had also practiced his facial demeanors, like an actor, so his body language would resonate the urgency of passing the proposed legislation.

He was going up in front of the Canadian legislature to present an emergency health bill, one which would herald in a new age for Canada. If approved, it would also net him a big boost in popularity ratings.

Harold James was a member of the NDP, the New Democratic Party of Canada. He loved the political spotlight. In particular, he loved hearing or seeing his name in the media. It was an orgasmic-like thrill for him.

Several days ago he had been selected by the party head to present this piece of legislation. He was directed to put the bill onto the "conveyer belt," as they called the legislative process.

The fact that the bill would open the door to making Canada a police-state didn't concern him at all, he was just the messenger.

VII

By 7 a.m. the next day, Keeno was pulling out of the airport parking lot in a rental car in Trenton, New Jersey.

Ross Fletcher had sent him an SMS while in the air, letting him know that he had cleared his trip to Trenton through Homeland Security. Ross admonished him that he had no jurisdiction in America beyond that of intelligence, but Ross knew he was deluding himself and that Keeno would do whatever he wanted to do. He had learned to live with the fact that his maverick style was both unpredictable and uncontrollable, but he also knew that with Keeno, the results were inevitable.

Keeno drove west on the 95, then turned southward onto the 295. FAB-MED was a few miles down the highway, located near the Hamilton Marshes, just across from the Delaware River and Pennsylvania.

He thought about the article he had read in the in-flight magazine on the historical background of Trenton, NJ. Once a thriving industrial town, it was now a place of less than 80,000 people. Probably unknown to most people, Trenton had once been the nation's capital following the revolutionary war against England. George Washington himself had won a critical battle on these very shores. It seemed, as he drove through the city, that it was now just a shadow of what it once had been.

From the information Janene had given him on his way out the door, FAB-MED had established Trenton as their headquarters fifteen years earlier. It provided washed or clean chemical constituents, the base elements that were used by the big pharmaceutical companies for their main drug products.

He arrived at their parking lot, easily the size of two city blocks, and parked amidst the ocean of expensive high-end cars. "Drugs are lucrative business," he thought to himself.

Stepping into the huge reception area, he quickly eyed the wall showing pictures and names of company executives, and chose one of them. He walked over to the nearest receptionist. She looked up at him with a smile.

"I'd like to speak to your Operations Manager."

"Whom may I say is calling?"

"Keeno McCole."

"Is he expecting you?"

"No he isn't. Tell him I'm with the RCMP," he smiled.

She looked a bit miffed as she picked up the phone and spoke into a receiver to someone, "A Mr. McCole from the RCMP to see Larry Egens."

"Larry Egens will be here momentarily. Would you like some coffee?"

"Thanks, but no," he said, as he thought back to the gook they had served him on the flight, which was still burning a hole through his stomach.

A man in his late forties, partly balding but in good physical shape, came bounding around the corner with a snap to his walk and extended his hand, "Mr. McCole?"

"Yes," Keeno shook his hand.

"I'm Larry Egens, Operations Manager, let's go to the conference facility." He led the way down a hallway, which was wide enough to line up two football teams in a line of scrimmage. They entered the huge conference room. In the center was a Titanic-sized conference table with a bank of computers down its center.

"Drugs do good business," Keeno said.

"Unfortunately, Americans consume pharmaceutical drugs like candy," Larry said matter-of-factly. "What can I do for you?" he asked, as they sat down.

"I'm doing an investigation," Keeno said, as he watched the man's eyes. It was one of his trademarks and one that his uncle had warned him about years back. Keeno could look at people with such intensity that it had a tendency to bring out the best and the worst in them. When they squirmed or flinched, he knew they had something to hide. Larry sat there nonplused, a good sign in Keeno's books.

"Can you be more specific?" he asked.

Keeno pulled a paper from his coat pocket, "Here's a chemical analysis of some substance that was found on the bottom of a dead guy's shoes. According to our forensics people, this substance is used by drug manufacturers in making over-the-counter drugs."

Larry read the report, "Yes, that's correct. It's a compound that we manufacture and distribute to our client companies."

"How many companies manufacture chemicals like that?"

"Oh, roughly four or five others in the United States, but we're probably the largest."

"Do you have security protocols?"

"Absolutely. Employees wear industry rated suits and masks that prevent contact with any substance. Before they leave, the suits are discarded and they have to shower down. No one walks in our plant in civilian clothes."

"That's assuming that your protocols are all enforced," Keeno said with a challenging tone.

Larry paused for a moment and thought about it, "Yes, of course," but the question left him miffed.

Keeno fished into his coat pocket and pulled out a photo of the dead guy. The picture was pretty grotesque, as the man's jaw had been crushed from skidding along the concrete and much of the skin on one side of the face had been scraped off. "Do you recognize him?"

As Larry looked at the picture, his facial muscles tightened and his eyes grew large, then he hastily put the photo on the table.

"I've never seen him before."

Keeno was watching Larry's eyes and for the first time in their conversation, he knew that he was lying.

"You're sure?"

He shook his head. "Don't recognize him," he said, as his eyes flitted nervously at the photo.

"Okay, can I see your processing plant?"

"Sure," he said, as he stood up, happy to get off the subject of the dead guy.

The tour of the plant took less than twenty minutes, during which Keeno counted twelve security cameras, several of which were swiveling and following them as they walked through the facility.

He thanked Larry as he left but he'd already decided that he was coming back later that day. As he approached his car, he glanced back at the building and locked eyes with a man staring at him from an office window. Then the man turned and faded into the background.

"FAB-MED had secrets – that much was for sure," he thought.

VIII

Kelly was reviewing local news and media stations for any information that might help in their investigation. It wasn't as if CBC or some other station was about to give them any substantial clues, but sometimes in the investigative world of the RCMP, a small fact or salient point, could help to string together a whole puzzle.

As usual, the media was filled with sensationalism, celebrity gossip and forecasts about stocks and the economy, but one thing did catch her attention and she clicked on it. A doctor in Oakville had been interviewed about a sudden and unprecedented number of flu cases showing up at their hospital.

She pulled up the list of hospitals in the West end of the city and made a few phone calls. Thirty minutes later the picture was clear; even more hospital waiting rooms were filled with a sudden flu outbreak.

She dialed up Jake.

"Yeah, what's up?" he said, in his usual blasé tone.

"I just called a few more hospitals and the figures of flu cases showing up are friggin' scary."

"Damn."

"What did you find at the water treatment plant?"

"Nada. I checked with the Systems Operation Manager and floor technicians for all three shifts and no one saw anything out of the ordinary. I cruised their security-cam footage until 4 a.m. – not a thing."

"Maybe you should go to the hospital in Oakville and interview some people. See if there's any common denominator with them."

"Any word from Keeno?"

"Nah, he's in Trenton checking out this drug company."

"Ok, call ya later, after I've inhaled enough of the virus at the hospital."

"Funny!" she hung up but for a brief moment Kelly was worried. She was accustomed to having Keeno and Jake chasing down guys with guns and bombs, but an unknown virus – that was uncharted territory.

IX

Tom Sneider, Vice President of FAB-MED, watched as the stranger walked across the parking lot, then suddenly turned and looked straight at him. For a brief second they locked eyes before Tom backed away from the window.

He pressed his intercom, "Stacey, get me Larry please," he asked his secretary.

Moments later Larry Egens walked into the office. He had the look of someone who had a secret he didn't want to tell anyone about. Larry still had the picture in his mind of the dead man. Despite what he told the RCMP officer, he did know the man and it scared the shit out of him that he was dead.

"Who was that guy you toured through the plant?"

Larry cleared his throat nervously, "Keeno McCole, he works for the Royal Canadian Mounted Police."

"The RCMP, in Trenton – that's odd."

"He said they found some suspension substance on the bottom of a dead man's shoes in Toronto."

Tom cocked his head, "And…?"

"I read the forensic report that he showed me and confirmed that we did make that substance. I also told him that it was manufactured by other facilities too."

"So why the tour?"

"I think he was interested in our security protocols," Larry answered, but he was hesitant and withdrawn.

Tom nodded his head slightly, "Did he tell you who the dead guy was?"

Larry took a deep breath and got a pained look on his face. He was still reeling from the sight of the man's battered body. "It was Arnie Norton."

"You're sure?"

"Yes."

Sneider paced behind his desk for a moment, thinking as he did and then he looked up at Larry, "You seem upset about Arnie, so go home early today. Take it easy tonight and don't talk to anyone about this until I've had a chance to look into it myself."

As Larry walked out of the office, Tom selected a number on his cell phone that only he knew about.

"We've got a problem!" he said to the man who answered.

Keeno found a Denny's restaurant and a Starbucks further down the 295. After a good breakfast, he slipped over to Starbucks and engaged a large cup of coffee. He loved sitting in coffee shops, sipping on coffee and disconnecting from the world of terrorism, if only for a few moments. It gave him a sense of peace to be able to log-off, collect his thoughts and get focused for his next round in the fighting ring.

He called Janene and brought her up to speed. She told him the latest news on the growing flu statistics and what Jake was up to. Things were not looking good in Toronto. Naturally, she inquired about him and he assured her that he was on his best behavior.

As he stepped out of Starbucks, a young girl who was squatted against the wall looked up at him, "Got a buck? I haven't eaten since yesterday morning," she said. Keeno placed her around sixteen or seventeen at most.

He crouched down next to her and looked her in the eyes, "You a run-away?"

She turned her head, avoiding eye-contact and his question, but he knew he had struck a chord. He reached into his pocket and handed her an American twenty-dollar bill.

Her eyes went wide as she slowly reached for the money, hesitant, as if he was going to pull it back.

"Get some food," he smiled.

She stood up, "Thanks."

Keeno turned and walked to his car at the far end of the parking lot. As he approached his car, he heard a scream from behind him and turned to see two men snatching the money from the young girl.

"It's mine," she screamed and then began to cry. They just laughed and walked away.

The picture suddenly conjured up a part of his past. They were memories he had long since buried, memories that flashed from his subconscious, reminding him of why he had chosen to fight criminals as his career.

He turned on his heel and walked straight at them.

"Hey, assholes, give it back," he commanded.

Both men, larger in size than him, turned. "You fuckin' crazy, man?" one of them said as he flipped a switchblade out of his pocket. "Get the fuck out of here before I cut you deep."

Keeno smiled, "Ooh, big man with a knife." He stepped closer. "Look, give the money back to the lady and walk – ok?"

The guy with the knife came at Keeno waving it menacingly, "I said – FUCK OFF! Are you fucking deaf or just stupid?"

"A little of both I'm afraid," Keeno said, while staring him in the eyes.

The guy swung in with his knife-hand, slashing at Keeno's face. Keeno caught his arm mid-air, snapped his wrist back with a popping sound that signaled a breaking bone and then speared his right toe into his groin. The guy hit the ground like a sack of potatoes, squirming and moaning.

Keeno picked up the guy's knife, turned and let it fly at the other guy who wasn't sure if he should run or attack. The knife sliced the air just centimeters from his head and thudded into a pole behind him.

"Take your friend. If I see either of you guys near her again, you won't be walking," he said, as turned back to the girl. He handed her the twenty and told her to get some food. When she stepped out of a nearby fast food place, Keeno insisted on driving her home.

"What's your name?" he asked her, as he pulled in front of her house twenty minutes later.

"Annie."

"Take some advice Annie, there are two types of people in this world, those who make something of their lives and then there are the losers, like those two jerks back there. You need to make a choice which camp you're in."

It was nearly 2:30 p.m. when Keeno got back to FAB-MED. He pulled in at the far end of the parking lot and waited. He didn't have to sit for long when he caught sight of Larry Egens coming out of the building through a back door, getting into his car and driving by him.

He followed Larry down the highway. Fifteen minutes later, Larry parked in front of his home and as he did, Keeno pulled up next to him.

"Larry, let's talk," he said, as he stepped out of the car.

Larry was shaking at the sight of Keeno again. He had not been able to get rid of the image of Arnie Norton's dead body; it was haunting him. "I'm not supposed to talk to you," his voice quivered as he spoke.

"You can talk to me or," he pulled out his cell phone, "I contact Homeland Security and we start a more painful interrogation process."

"You can't do that."

"Wanna bet?" He started dialing a fake number.

"Hold on, damn it!" Larry exclaimed, while looking over at his house with a worried look. "Ever since you showed me that photo I can't stop thinking about it."

"Who is he?"

Larry stared at the ground for a moment, "Arnie Norton. He used to be a shift manager at FAB-MED."

"And?"

"We weren't particularly close, I was his boss. About five months ago he quit the company. I know he had issues, but he held his cards close to his chest when it came to his personal affairs."

"When did you last see him?"

"Week or two ago, he came to the company."

"What was he doing there?"

Larry shook his head, "Don't know."

Keeno stared him in the eyes, tacitly demanding more information. Larry was hesitant.

"What else?"

Larry shook his head, fighting the impulses inside. "When Arnie was leaving the plant last week he wasn't suited up. He should never have been inside the facility like that."

"So why'd you lie to me this morning? Are you protecting someone?"

"No," he said with pleading eyes. "I just don't want to get anyone in trouble."

Keeno folded his arms across his chest, "Larry, get a clue. Arnie is dead. He was found carrying a briefcase of viruses. A technician in Toronto was murdered by someone who stole that briefcase from a secure lab and now, that virus has been released and a lot of people are sick. How many deaths do you want on your conscience by not telling me everything you know?"

Larry let out a deep breath. "All I know is that Arnie had gambling issues. When he quit the company, it was just after his wife left him. His life was in shambles. He lost his house and most of his assets to gambling. Someone told me he was drinking a lot and engaging prostitutes."

"Sounds like a good mix for a dupe," Keeno said.

"What do you mean?"

"Guys like Arnie can be bought off. They're junkies, they need money to keep up expensive habits like gambling and whores. He was probably just the messenger, trying to make a fast buck. I need to find out who was behind him, pulling his strings."

"That's all I know," Larry said, with resignation in his voice.

"What happened after I left this morning, anything?"

"The VP, Tom Sneider, called me to his office and wanted to know about you."

"So he knows everything that you know, right?"

Larry nodded.

"Here's my card. Watch your back and call me if you think I should know something."

Keeno drove off and found the nearest restaurant, ordered a meal and called Ross at the RCMP. He downloaded everything he had found out so far and asked for more info on FAB-MED, as well as on their VP, Tom Sneider.

He could smell the snake now. The trick was getting it to stick out its head long enough to cut it off.

X

Jake was trying to stay clear of the constant hacking and coughing as he navigated his way through the hospital waiting room. The idea of catching the flu simply was not appealing to him. He talked to different people, trying to ascertain some common denominator, some clue behind the sudden wave of sickness.

He walked over to a young couple holding hands with their heads pressed against one another. Their faces were ashen and lifeless. He eased up to them, trying to stay up-wind if there was such a thing, to avoid getting the bug. He flashed his RCMP badge at them.

"Seeing as both of you seem to have the flu, did you do anything or go anywhere specifically in the last day?"

"We went to the game at the Rogers Centre last night," the woman answered.

"What time?"

"'Bout 6:30," the guy muttered weakly and then started hacking.

"Ok guys, thanks."

He walked over to two kids who were sitting on either side of a woman. Their faces were pale and their noses were running. "Ma'am, I'm with the RCMP and we're working with the hospital. Can you tell me if your boys were recently someplace where they could have caught the bug?"

She nodded, "They were at the game last night."

"You mean at the Rogers Centre?"

She nodded again.

He suddenly realized that he was onto something. He went to three more batches of people, two of whom confirmed that they too had been at the game and while the third man hadn't been there himself, his brother had gone. Jake raced to his car, dialing Keeno as he did.

Chapter 3

I

"It matters very little what the RCMP finds out. Soon Toronto will be engulfed in a storm of internal disorder that will make it impossible for them to pursue any investigation on us," the man's deep, sonorous voice proclaimed with a tone of arrogance.

"In any case, I will call our assets into play to deal with this RCMP agent."

"Do that! We don't need him making undue trouble for us," the voice said, and the line went dead.

Malcolm McDonald sipped on his hot tea while looking down at the main road that skirted the harbor. Directly across from him ran the Ma Wan Channel, its waters embracing a small island with one of his favorite dining establishments in Hong Kong. He savored the idea of going there again.

He felt a sense of pride about the operation which he had helped to contrive, and while things were moving along, his guard was piqued. The unexpected death of the messenger carrying the virus in Toronto, and the fact that the RCMP was snooping around FAB-MED didn't help matters.

In spite of this, he gloated because where others had chided him for taking too many precautions, McDonald knew that his ascension up the ladder of wealth included never depending on one tactic – he always had a back-up plan and he always had an escape clause built into his schemes.

In anticipation of this very problem, he had hired an anonymous agency to remove undesirables from the playing field. The stakes, being the highest he had personally ever played, dictated carrying a fully loaded, yet concealed gun.

He briefly looked at the picture of the RCMP agent on his mobile phone before pressing the SEND button and passing it over to his contact at the agency. Soon enough, Keeno McCole would be dead.

Besides, he thought to himself, he had more important matters to deal with, namely the seventeen year-old girl waiting for him at his apartment. It was time to unwind, as things were going exactly as planned.

II

The next morning, as Keeno was coming out of the shower, his cell phone rang. "What's up Jake?"

"Looks like they dropped the virus at the Roger's Centre last night." He went on to explain what he had found at the hospital.

"Good find," Keeno muttered.

"But where to from here? We could spend a week combing that stadium and find nothing at this point."

"That's what they want us to do. Go back to the office and work with the girls, see what you guys can come up with."

"How's things in Trenton?"

"I found out that our dead guy is an American. He worked for FAB-MED up until about five months ago. He was here last week, that's how he got that stuff on the bottom of his shoes. So far, all roads are leading to this company."

"You need any help?"

"Not yet, I'll buzz if I do."

"Ok, later."

Keeno got dressed and then slipped his knife into his back right hand pocket.

Although trained on most types of weaponry, his two favorite forms of self-defense were his hands and feet, and his throwing knife. Ever since his days on the farm, where he had perfected his knife throwing skills, it never left his side. It was a double edged throwing knife, 5.5 inches long, made of solid stainless steel from tip to hilt and there were a few dead terrorists and criminals who had felt its sting.

He left the Hyatt Hotel in his rental and twenty-five minutes later pulled into FAB-MED's parking lot. He stepped up to the same receptionist as the day before: "Tom Sneider, please."

She made a quick call and a moment later a young blond was escorting Keeno to the VP.

Tom Sneider, slender and trim, six feet two inches tall, had dark brown hair with gray patches on each side.

"Mr. McCole," he extended his hand, but Keeno didn't reciprocate. "What can I do for the RCMP?" Tom asked with a superficial smile, to cover up the uncomfortable moment.

"I spoke to your Operations Manager yesterday, Larry Egens," he said, while looking Sneider in the eyes, "about some chemicals that were found on the bottom of a dead man's shoes up in Toronto."

Tom nodded with perfunctory concern on his face and played out the role as if he knew nothing about the matter. But Keeno already knew from Larry that Tom had been told everything.

"We're trying to establish why a dead man, carrying some lethal virus, would have this chemical base on his shoes. Any ideas?"

Tom canted his head, "it's a good question, but unfortunately, I have no idea where you're going with this. Surely, we're not the only manufacturer of such chemicals," he deflected.

"Do you recognize this man?" Keeno handed him the picture of Arnie Norton, but Sneider didn't so much as flinch at the mangled remains of Arnie's face.

"That looks like Arnie Norton, used to be a plant manager here. You say he was found dead in Toronto with a briefcase of virus?"

Keeno smiled, "Was Arnie here recently?"

Tom's eyes glassed over, quickly retreating for the right answer to the question. However, his evasive tactics were transparent.

"I did see Arnie up here last week, and from what I remember, he was in seeing our payroll department."

"Would it have been possible for Arnie to get down to your plant in civilian clothes?" Keeno asked. He was purposely baiting the trap for him, to see whether he would deflect, sidestep or retreat in response.

Tom shook his head. "It's possible, of course, if he violated protocols. It's difficult to do, considering we have security measures and a team of security personnel monitoring who goes in and out of the plant."

"So then that makes your security suspect?"

"Are you accusing my people of involvement in this virus you found?"

Keeno locked his eyes on Tom's. "This is not a legal process."

"It's beginning to sound like you've already made up your mind about this," Tom deflected.

Keeno smiled, "When, and if, I make my mind up about this investigation, and if you or any of your people are involved, you'll know about it – believe me."

The air snapped and sizzled hot between them.

"Why did Arnie Norton stop working at FAB-MED?"

"We don't inquire into the personal motives of employees, but I heard he had some issues."

Keeno nodded subtly, "Such as?"

"Gambling."

"So maybe he needed money and someone gave him an offer he couldn't refuse?"

"Sounds plausible, but what are you suggesting?" Tom probed.

Keeno folded his arms and stared at him, "I'm only suggesting that a former employee of yours, with a gambling problem, showed up in Toronto with enough virus to incapacitate the city."

Sneider was getting unnerved by the man's forthrightness. "I'm afraid that I cannot account for Arnie Norton's activities, and as to the suspension substance on the bottom of his shoes, who is to say that he didn't get that caked on when he was still working here six months ago?"

Keeno smiled. "First of all, I happen to know that Arnie not only came here last week, but that he was seen leaving from your processing plant and he wasn't wearing a protective suit. Secondly, the Nike running shoes he was wearing in Toronto were just issued in the States in the last month, so that means he couldn't have had that shit caked on them from months ago."

"And lastly," Keeno said, as he stared him in the eyes, "I never said anything about Arnie having the virus in a briefcase. I only said that he was carrying the virus. How did you know he was carrying a briefcase?"

Sneider suppressed his impulse to tell Keeno to leave.

"You've made your point, but it's all hypothetical."

"You're right, just the crazed conjectures of an RCMP anti-terrorism agent. Give me a bit more time and I'll see if I can get you something more tangible," he said, walking out of the office.

Tom glared at Keeno as he left the room, and then he dialed up security, "Find Egens and tell him I want to see him now!"

Keeno got into his car and pulled out of the parking lot. He went around the bend, just out of sight of FAB-MED, and parked on the side of the road.

His cell phone rang. "How's it going?" Janene asked.

"Can't complain– how about you?"

"Considering that Toronto is a zoo right now, nothing out of the ordinary. There have been about a thousand admissions to local hospitals with this mystery virus, in just the last hour. The news is hitting the media pipeline, which will fan the flames even more. To make matters worse, Harold James, the NDP motor mouth, just went live with CBC announcing his proposed emergency health legislation to parliament, mandating nation-wide flu inoculations."

"Sounds like fun," Keeno joked.

"Indeed."

"Did you find anything juicy about FAB-MED?"

"Their VP, Tom Sneider, is your classic corporate man: big classy house, a boat, goes on vacations every year all over the world, a wife, two kids in college, and he keeps a mistress or two in other countries judging by his expense accounts. As far as FAB-MED goes, they provide the clean chemicals for the big pharmaceutical giants. They have millions in assets, a very wealthy company."

"What about their Board members?"

"There is one old-geek that caught my interest, his name is Malcolm McDonald. He's a founding board member and trustee, and he holds partnerships with several off-shore companies. He's practically Jurassic and probably most of the employees at FAB-MED have never even heard of him, but he's active behind the scenes with the company."

Keeno was digesting what she was saying while keeping an eye out of his peripheral vision for any sign of Larry Egens. "Ok?"

"How about you?"

"I've got a snake by the tail. I'm waiting for him to bite."

"I knew it," she mumbled.

"Knew what?"

"Sending you down there alone, you're bound to get into trouble. Can't you just do the reconnaissance work and then let Homeland Security deal with the rest? It's their jurisdiction."

"No way, and miss out on all the fun?" he teased her.

Janene took a deep breath to control herself, knowing full well that she was getting nowhere with him.

"Ok, I'll call you if I find out more on FAB-MED. Be careful."

He remained parked there for a few more minutes when he saw a black Saturn approaching from behind him. The car was moving slowly, like a shark combing the waters for its prey. It came parallel to his own car and as it did, the driver turned and looked him in the eyes. It was not the casual look one might expect. The man studied Keeno's face with an intensity that sent up an alarm. Then he drove past.

In his years of fighting crime and terrorism, Keeno had learned how to read people through their eyes. As he watched the Saturn disappear around the curve, he knew one thing for sure – those were the eyes of a killer.

He put the car in gear and followed the Black Saturn. As he came around the corner, he saw the FAB-MED plant ahead. The Saturn had disappeared, but at that instant Keeno saw Larry Egens pulling out of the lot. It suddenly dawned on him that the guy in the black Saturn might be after Egens. Maybe Larry knew something he wasn't supposed to know, and judging by the fact that Sneider let slip that Arnie Norton was carrying the virus in a briefcase, it was pretty much a given fact that FAB-MED was involved. The question was, how deep and who was pulling their strings?

He followed Larry onto the 295 highway, and was so preoccupied with watching his car in the distance that he failed to notice the one approaching in his blind spot to the right. The shot exploded through the passenger side of his rental, smashed into the gearshift and shattered the handle. Luckily, it deflected the bullet downward and instead of cutting a wide path through Keeno's abdomen, it cut a gash into his right thigh.

Keeno winced as the pain streaked through him, but he knew that he had only seconds to act. He twisted the car to the left, hitting the brakes as he did, yet the shooter's car stayed with him.

He slashed his car to the right and jabbed it into the shooter's, trying to force him off the road. The man deftly eased back on his gas and slipped out of his clutch. Then he surged his car parallel to Keeno's again and aimed his gun straight at him.

In that split second, before the fatal shot could be delivered, Keeno jerked the wheel hard to the left, careening the car over the median. The bullet intended for his head cut a path behind him, shattering the window and scattering glass into the car.

In the next few seconds, his car ramped upwards, like in some Las Vegas daredevil act. It flew over the median, angling across the oncoming traffic, and landed straight in the path of an oncoming truck. The truck driver, seeing a car spearing across the freeway in front of him, jerked his vehicle to the left and managed to avoid a full-scale collision, clipping the car on one side only.

From Keeno's perspective however, it felt like a train had just head-butted him. The impact sent the car spinning in midair. It then crashed onto the road and screeched along the asphalt top. When it hit the shoulder, it flipped and soared over the ditch. He watched as his world spun and then he felt the bone-jarring thud as the car slammed into a tree.

The force of impact plowed his forehead into the steering wheel. Then, as if that wasn't enough, the 2500 pound car dropped to the ground on its hood, where his head took another beating.

It took him a minute to reorient himself. He shook the daze from his head and felt a trickle of blood running down his cheek, pooling onto the inside hood.

Keeno crawled out of the open window and wiped the blood off his face, feeling the sting from the cut on his forehead as he did. His right pant leg was wet with blood where the bullet had cut into the skin.

Looking back towards the freeway, he watched as the shooter's car approached. There was no doubt about it, he was a pro and he was coming in for the kill.

Keeno faded into the forest.

III

He stood about five feet eleven inches in height and was of medium build, but beneath his loose fitting clothes was a body honed like polished steel, conditioned as a lethal killing machine. He had dark black hair, closely cropped to his bullish shaped skull. He was wearing sunglasses, a light gray windbreaker, a pair of black pants and black leather shoes. In effect, there was nothing about this man that stood out or made him particularly noteworthy in any crowd – which is exactly what he intended.

He made his way along Lakeshore Boulevard, which skirted Lake Ontario, pretending to be on a casual walk. In truth, he was heading for his next target.

In the distance was the Canadian National Tower, standing like a monolith, heads above any other structures in downtown Toronto. Once the tallest man-made structure in the world, the CN Tower now took back seat to the Burj in Dubai, which speared into the sky, half a mile above the

Red Sea. He eyed the CN Tower like a wolf might eye a stray sheep. He would have loved to have made his mark on that tower. Unfortunately, the winds at that level would disperse the pathogen and reduce its usefulness to practically zero. Instead, the people who paid him to do his deeds had chosen another target for sabotage.

He amused himself as he walked along, thinking about the hysteria that was growing in Toronto. Just the day before, he had slipped relatively unnoticed into the OPP lab, killed the lab technician and recovered the virus before anyone could find out about it. Without wasting a minute, he had jumped into a cab straight to Rogers Centre in downtown Toronto, picked up a ticket for the game, and joined the nearly 49,000 people who piled in. The sell-out crowd was typically composed of people from all over southern Ontario, even as far as Buffalo, New York. When the game was well into the second quarter, he had made his way to the main engineering unit, slipped past two technicians who were too busy talking about sports to notice him, and placed two of the packages into the main air circulation pump line, puncturing them as he did. By morning, his sources had informed him that the virus had taken effect and hospitals were already reporting a sudden influx of illness showing up at their steps.

He spotted the gray block building ahead. It belonged to the city of Toronto Water Works Department and pumped fresh filtered water into the west end of the city. It was a small building, not itself a water treatment center, just a pumping station. Such facilities were locked down, security coded, and were checked once or twice a week to assure that everything was in operating order.

He waited until no one was in sight, then pulled out the special key he'd been given, unlocked the entry door, de-activated the alarm system using the code provided to him, and walked into the main pump room. Under normal circumstances, no one except authorized personnel and engineers would have been able to accomplish what he had just done in a matter of seconds. However, the people paying him were obviously well connected, and as usual, money could buy anything – including treason.

The inside of the station looked like something from an old sci-fi movie, with retro-style pumps and machines hissing and thumping in an endless rhythm as they propelled fresh drinking water into the west side of Toronto. He traced the main pump line and found the small access door, then punctured and dropped two pouches of the virus into the holding tank. As he exited the building, he reset the alarm.

After walking five blocks, he jumped on a city bus and rode towards the airport, then switched to a cab that took him to his hotel.

He planned to order a good dinner, watch a movie and wait for the media to report on the next wave of illnesses. Everything was going as planned and Toronto was about to experience a meltdown of Biblical proportions.

IV

As he faded into the trees, Keeno knew he was at a disadvantage. The cut in his leg hurt like hell and it was leaving a trail of blood for the shooter to follow. Not to mention the fact that all he had to defend himself was his knife, against at least one gun. The only advantage he could add to his arsenal was that he was back in his domain, the forest, where he had first learned to hunt and survive as a young boy. Here, he could call on skills that most men didn't have or didn't use, considering that urban life didn't demand survival-smarts in the wild.

He moved deeper and deeper into the trees, weaving as fast as he could. He pulled out his knife as he walked, found a long piece of wood and quickly honed one end of it to a sharp point. Looking over his shoulder, he caught the faint glimpse of the shooter moving into the tree line.

He slipped behind a tree and worked over another piece of wood. When he was done he had two spear-like weapons, each about three feet in length. He moved back deeper into the woods and as he did he heard the telltale signs of his tracker behind him. It was the subtle crack of a twig, the immeasurably tiny sound of a footfall against a backdrop of the whispering wind and the light rustling of leaves. Fortunately, his ability to distinguish man-made sounds from those of nature had not been lost to him in spite of his years of city life. It was this subtle skill that separated the hunter from the prey in this domain.

He found another large tree and settled behind it, easing the weight off of his throbbing leg as he waited. This is where the fight would have to come to an end.

He knew he was outnumbered in terms of firepower, so in order to beat the killer he'd have to use another tactic. It was yet another lesson he remembered from his days on the farm when he had been hunting with his uncle. Uncle Lou had taught him that the Iroquois learned by watching injured animals that would appear to be dead, but when their attacker came near, they would lunge at it. Keeno's tactic was to make the shooter think that he was unarmed and defenseless, then hopefully, he would let his guard down.

He waited until he could hear the escalating sound of footfalls behind him, and then he peered around the tree from the left, catching sight of the shooter some fifteen feet away. He let loose one of his sharpened sticks at the man. The shooter easily dodged the pathetic weapon, and as he did, he fired on him. The bullets tore huge gouges into the tree.

Keeno barely slipped back behind the tree as the shots pounded into the solid oak. There was a deathly silence that followed. If he moved, if he exposed himself the wrong way, he knew he'd be dead. He listened to every sound in the forest, waiting for something to give away the shooter's position. Then he heard it, the sudden crack of a twig just to his right. He turned and saw the shooter bolt around the tree. Keeno surged to the left, dove to the ground, and rolled twice as shots plied the dirt around him.

He came up onto his good leg, and in one smooth motion, he let his knife fly. It cut the air in silence and impaled the man in his left thigh before he could get off his next shot. For a moment the shooter cringed in pain and lowered his gaze from Keeno to see what had hit him. This was the moment he had been waiting for, the one brief lapse in time when the shooter's guard was dropped. Keeno stood up and lanced the second roughly hewed spear, like a javelin. As he did, the shooter took his next shot, paying no attention to the piece of wood traveling his way. Keeno dove to the ground, but not before the bullet had grazed his left shoulder.

He waited, anticipating the killing shot, but there was nothing. Finally, he looked up and saw the shooter clasping the make-shift spear, which had impaled him through the base of his throat. He gasped as blood frothed from his mouth and then seeped from the wound.

Keeno found no joy in watching any man die, and he had certainly seen more than his share of death. The man's cold eyes locked on his for a moment and then he fell to one side, dead.

Keeno looked at his shoulder. Blood was staining his shirt where the bullet had grazed the skin. He put his hand over the wound and then went over to the dead shooter and collected up his knife, as well as the man's gun and cell phone.

Making his way back through the trees, he suddenly found himself confronted by a crew of emergency responders, ambulance personnel and several police officers who were all huddled around his wrecked car. His rental car looked like a piece of junk.

He pulled out his RCMP badge and held it up in front of him. "Anyone got a bandage?" he smiled disarmingly as he approached them.

V

"You're where?" Jake and Ross Fletcher asked almost simultaneously, as they listened to Keeno's call on the conference phone in the RCMP CIC.

He grimaced as the doctor applied a pad to the burned flesh on his left shoulder. Meanwhile, a nurse was sewing up the cut on his leg and padding it with antiseptic.

"I'm in a hospital in Trenton."

"Care to elaborate?" Ross asked, while thinking how he was going to run damage control on this with Homeland Security.

Keeno was balancing his cell phone between his ear and right shoulder, "Well, how about we talk in a few minutes when I'm sewn up and I'll explain it to everyone."

He hung up just in time to let out a yelp as the nurse shoved a needle into his leg with a good dose of pain-killer. She smiled, subtly reminding him of the contract killer he had just left for dead.

"Thanks," he said, as he gingerly flexed his right leg.

"Try to take it easy," the doctor said.

Keeno slipped off the gurney and smiled at the doctor. "Unfortunately, taking it easy is not part of my life, but thanks for the advice."

As he walked out of the room, a man approached him. "I'm Steve, with Homeland Security in Philly, and you're supposed to have a conference call with someone from the Department." He followed the agent to a small private room in the hospital and within minutes he was speaking to Ross Fletcher and a table of people at his end, which included Janene, Kelly and Jake, as well as Frank Cairn from the Philly office of Homeland Security.

He downloaded the full story since arriving in Trenton, and summarized his suspicions so far.

"So basically," Frank Cairn said, "you're saying that FAB-MED is linked with this virus attack in Toronto and that this contract killer was sent to kill you?" The man's voice had a certain edge to it, a sort of incredulousness that was already beginning to piss Keeno off with its challenging tone.

"Yeah, that's what I'm saying, Frank," he responded. His fuse was short after the showdown with the shooter. He simply wasn't in the mood for any bureaucratic bullshit from some suit and tie geek.

Jake could hear the angst starting to build in Keeno's voice. He knew what was coming.

"So what are you suggesting?" Frank prodded.

"Actually, Frank, I'm not suggesting a fucking thing. I don't have all the answers right now, but I know this much; someone sent a contract killer after me within twenty-four hours of my questioning two people at FAB-MED. So you do the fucking math!"

Ross Fletcher rubbed his eyes. Kelly chuckled and Janene just sat there saying nothing at all. They all knew that if pushed too far, Keeno would shove the phone up the man's ass, whether he was Homeland Security or the Secretary of State.

"Alright," Frank Cairn started to say, realizing that he was getting riled, "obviously you're onto something. What can we do to help?"

"I got the shooter's phone. I need it analyzed fast to see if there is any way to trace this guy or who's pulling his strings."

"Give the phone to my man there," Frank said.

He shoved the phone across the table to the agent. He had already gone through the phone and emailed the essential data to Janene with instructions to see if she could trace the anonymous calls. He trusted the girls implicitly. If there was a clue, Janene and Kelly would sniff it out.

"And can you put some guys onto watching Larry Egens' home and his family? I'm sure he knew nothing about what just happened but he could easily be a target."

"We'll do that," Frank answered.

Keeno fished into his coat pocket and pulled out the shooter's gun. "See if you can trace the prints on this gun," he shoved it across the desk to the agent. "I'd suggest checking with Interpol as well. If this guy was a mercenary, then he might not even be an American."

When the conference call was done, Keeno waited a few minutes and then called Janene. He had already sent her the SMS and the photo of himself, which he had found on the shooter's cell phone. "I don't know where they got that photo from," he told her during the call, "but this operation is pretty sophisticated and they're one step ahead of us all the time."

Janene assured him she'd leave no stone unturned and as they finished the call she reminded him to be careful.

On his way to the hotel he thought to himself, why was it that people kept telling him to be careful, especially in his line of work? It seemed so redundant. Did they really think that he was romancing suicide? As if the words "be careful" would do any good in the face of an oncoming bullet or an exploding bomb?

The only philosophy that worked for Keeno, and which he had adopted since the day he had shoved the scissors into his own father's leg to protect his mother, was to ultimately trust himself, to take on life with complete reckless insouciance and laugh death in the face. To do otherwise was to allow an element of doubt into his mental equation, and as far as he was concerned, the moment he ever doubted himself, even by one percent, was the day that someone would get a fatal bullet through him.

VI

Although young for a professor of her stature, Katherine Riggs was first and foremost a competent scientist in microbiology and in the field of pathogens and viruses. She taught at the University of Toronto and was proud of her work. U of T had an excellent reputation for putting out quality graduates, who became pillars in their own fields of specialization.

Most of her students had turned in their lab reports for the week, and, as she often did, she had stayed behind to catch up on them. The 4th floor of her wing was otherwise empty as she glanced at her watch. It was 9:30 p.m. and she had just finished the last report.

She packed up her portfolio, turned off the lights in her office, and had just started to walk down the hallway towards the stairwell when she heard a sound behind her. Students were not authorized to be in this area without faculty around, so she walked back towards the labs. As she approached the glassed-in lab, she saw two men loading a canister into one of the refrigerated storage units. She didn't recognize them and they certainly weren't students under her charge.

The first thing that flashed to mind was the meeting yesterday with the two RCMP officers. Was it possible that there was a connection? Why else would two completely unknown men be inside that lab putting a canister into one of her refrigerated units? Could it be a virus as the RCMP had suggested?

She stared at them for a matter of seconds, when it suddenly occurred to her that she was alone and panic swelled inside her. She slipped off her high heel shoes and ran to the other end of the corridor, disappearing into the stairwell, just as the men stepped out of the lab. One of them glimpsed her passing through the door and they raced after her.

Katherine ran down the stairs as hard and fast as she could push herself. She slipped and fell as she came to the second landing. She heard the men as they crashed through the door above her and felt the impulse to scream. The panic inside of her was tangible and it almost caused her to literally freeze up. She'd never been in a position like this before but instinctively remembered one thing her dad had taught her when she was younger; if ever assaulted, it was best to get out into the open, get near other people.

She got to her feet and ran towards the first floor, burst through the stairwell door and headed straight for the reception desk. She quickly put on her shoes and leaned over the desk to engage in a mock conversation with the night watchman. Behind her, she heard the two men crashing through the door. She could hear their heavy breathing and it seemed like their eyes were burning a hole through the back of her head as they watched her.

She did everything she could think of to remain calm. In spite of the fact that she was breathing heavily and sweat was pouring down her face, neck and back, she tried to appear as normal as possible. She desperately wanted to look over her shoulder to see if they were approaching her but that would have been a dead give-away.

The two men stared at her, trying to determine if she had been the one they had caught a glimpse of and fortunately for her, they had literally only seen the flash of someone disappearing through the door. Finally, they turned and disappeared and she let out a deep sigh.

"You okay, ma'am?" the large bullish black security guard asked, as she leaned on the reception counter. She debated whether she should tell him what had happened but realized that it probably was best to contact the RCMP. "No thanks, I'm good."

She nervously checked over her shoulder as she walked out of the building, fumbling in her purse for the card that Keeno had given her and dialed him up.

"Keeno? she said, as he answered.

"Who is this?"

"It's Katherine Riggs at the University of Toronto."

Keeno remembered her immediately. He never forgot a good looking woman. "What's happening?" he asked, sensing the panic in her voice.

"I just saw two men in one of our labs. They were putting some kind of canister in a storage refer. They chased me but I got away."

Keeno had just stepped into his hotel room after his ordeal at the hospital, "Where are you?"

"Outside campus."

"Go to the Second Cup Coffee on Bloor, near Yonge Street and stay there. I'm sending Jake to pick you up. Don't talk to anyone and don't go anywhere – got it?"

"Okay," she said, as she hung up the line. For the first time in her life, Katherine was really afraid and she now understood the meaning of terror.

Keeno rang up Jake and told him to go get Katherine Riggs. Just as he hung up the line with Jake, his phone rang.

"You ok?" Janene asked. Even though she had just talked to him less than an hour ago at the hospital, she felt the impulse to call him again. She was worried about him and her unstated feelings were mounting like a volcano on the verge of exploding.

"A bit sore, but I'm surviving. How 'bout you?"

"Just got home," she said, but her voice was reserved. The line went silent and yet he heard a muffled sound.

"You still there?" he asked.

"Yeah," she struggled to speak. If he hadn't known better, he would have sworn Janene was crying.

"What's happening, are you upset?"

She cleared her throat. "To be honest, I'm worried about you," she said, as she wiped the tears off her cheek.

Ever since hearing that he had fought off the shooter earlier that day, she had been climbing the walls to talk to him. She wanted to tell him that she loved him, but it seemed so inane to do it at this point in time, when he was in the battlefield, with his life on the line.

Yet, with Keeno, there never seemed to be a good time for romance or true feelings. He was always running or flying off to another life and death scenario and, in the mix, their true feelings about one another remained tacit and unspoken.

When she arrived home, she decided she wasn't going to wait any longer to tell him how she felt. She had asked herself repeatedly, *why am I waiting? What if he comes back in a body bag, then what have I accomplished?*

"You're worried about me – why?"

"Duhh, contract killer, car chases, bullets, hello?"

Keeno chuckled, "That's my life, you know that better than anyone!"

"I know and I live your life every day, remember?"

"So what's up then?" he probed.

She sighed, "I was kinda hoping you'd be alive long enough for us to talk."

"About?"

"You know, sometimes you're a bit thick in the head. Are my signals that friggin' messed up?"

Keeno leaned back on his bed, taking the weight off his leg. He was tired, in fact, exhausted. He let out a long breath as he rubbed his eyes, "Nah, I'm not that thick, I'm just not as honest about this subject as you are."

"I think we should stop the cat and mouse game."

"Meaning?"

"Meaning, as stupid as it is to fall in love with an RCMP anti-terrorist fighter, not to mention violating every

RCMP rule about intra-office affairs, I can't help myself because you're the only guy that seems to interest me in this goddamn country."

He laughed.

"I spill my guts to you and you laugh?"

"Take it easy, I'm better at dodging bullets than I am at dealing with women."

"So what's your take on this?"

"Sounds like investigative talk to me."

"Frankly, I feel I need to put it in terms that you can understand."

Keeno looked out the window of his hotel room and thought long and hard for a moment. "I think it's pretty obvious the feelings are mutual. My problem is that I don't want to disappoint you."

"Why would you?"

"As much as I have no plans on dying, in my line of work, death is an implicit element and possibility. You get tangled with me and you could end up as an early widow."

"I'll take my chances."

"Well, that's good to hear, since I haven't found anyone else with legs as sexy as yours."

"Asshole," but Janene finally felt a sense of calm come over her. They had finally opened up to one another and admitted how they felt. It made her feel closer to him now, more than ever.

"I think I'll sleep better tonight."

"Good," Keeno said, "and please, don't tell me to be careful anymore."

"That's supposed to mean what?"

"It means what it means. I'm gonna find the rats nest and kick their asses and I don't want to be told to be careful!"

"That's reassuring! Anyhow, I did some more checking on the Board of Directors of FAB-MED. McDonald spends most of his time in Hong Kong. He's also a major partner in a company called CJN Holdings, a Chinese based pharmaceutical company. The major stockholder, of course, is the Chinese Government, the PRC, who apparently own 51% of the stocks. But I would bet that they own more than that."

"That figures. The PRC owns most of the big companies in China. They're the true communist-capitalists of the world. What makes McDonald so special?" he asked, as he popped a painkiller.

"Well, first of all, CJN Holdings produces certain chemical compounds, medical drugs, vaccines and more. They're sort of the new kid on the block and the Chinese contender for getting China to corner a portion of the world pharmaceutical market. They have a massive installation in Shanghai. If the Chinese government is investing this much time and money into CJN, then they plan to move it out into the international arena," she said.

"Hmm… so you think there might be a connection with the attack in Toronto?"

"It's hypothetical at this point, but if you put the pieces together, they might connect. You've got a sudden virus attack in Toronto, a dead guy connected to FAB-MED, you investigate FAB-MED and suddenly someone's trying to knock you off, and then you've got Malcolm McDonald who's on the Board of Directors and a major holder in a Chinese drug company. Seems to me like the dots might connect somehow," she said.

"I agree with the logic."

"And one other thing, remember Harold James, the NDP representative in Ottawa that I told you about?"

"Yeah?"

"All of a sudden, his face is in the media and he's the one proposing a new emergency health bill for Canada. Oddly, his timing is perfect, just when we have this virus epidemic raising its head here in Toronto."

"Interesting..."

"I got hold of the proposed legislation and studied it. There is no friggin' way that Harold James put that bill together. He's not smart enough. His whole history in politics has been to latch onto controversial issues and get on the bandwagon for anything that could increase his popularity ratings. Someone is yanking that guy's chain and using him to usher in this bill. I think this whole plot is a lot more comprehensive than we realize."

"Ok"

"Here's the spooky part, there was a tiny clause at the very end of this emergency health bill which calls for federally authorized research into RFID chip implants on Canadians."

"You mean a Radio Frequency ID chip?"

"Yeah, same chips they put in credit cards, passports, cell phones and literally tons of retail products."

"That's crazy."

"No kidding. Listen to this from that bill," she read it to him.

> *A program of RFID Implants could conceivably reduce the medical costs and medical infrastructure substantially. This is based on the simple premise that if the RFID chips can detect and flag disease and illness in advance, it is possible that medical means can then abate or eliminate disease through*

> *proper treatment. This alone would reduce medical care and facilities, as the medical establishment would no longer be treating symptoms but rather, would be cutting disease off before it becomes a fact.*

"How fucking cute is that?" Keeno retorted. "Stick a chip into every person and you've got George Orwell's predictions in *1984*, with a police state and everyone monitored by big brother."

"Exactly,"

"This really changes the picture. If these dots all connect somehow, like you suggest, then we're dealing with a lot more than just a virus attack. Someone's going for the whole pie, not just a piece of it,"

"Now you understand why I'm a little concerned that you're down there alone. I think you're up against some serious hitters."

"Ok, stay on this Malcolm McDonald trail. See if you can find out who his peeps are and who he answers to. Get me a list of any underground agencies in China that provide hit-men or mercenary services. The guy that came after me today was good and you don't find mercenaries like him on every street corner."

"Ok."

"Before I forget..." he went on to brief her about Katherine Riggs and the fact that Jake was bringing her into the office in the morning. He told her to keep Katherine at the RCMP for now, to use her knowledge of viruses to help in the investigation, and that Jake shouldn't let her out of his sight until it was clear that it was safe for her to go back to U of T.

"I doubt that Jake will have any issue watching over her, based on your last description of her," she said.

Keeno smiled as he conjured up the image of Katherine - "Indeed."

"Sleep well and try not to think about me too much," she teased.

"That was a low shot."

"Yep!" she grinned and hung up.

He leaned back into his pillow and was fast asleep within minutes.

VII

The next morning, after a solid night's sleep, Keeno woke up to the sound of his mobile beeping. Janene had sent him a text message during the night:

> *PRINTS ON THE SHOOTERS GUN CONFIRMED. HIS NAME IS GUY STENSON, FORMER U.S. MARINE. DISAPPEARED OFF THE GRID YEARS AGO, SUSPECTED HIRED-GUN FOR MERCENARY AGENCIES OUT OF HONG KONG OR SHANGHAI.*

He got dressed, inhaled a fast breakfast and then headed to Starbucks for his morning coffee. By the time he pulled into the parking lot at FAB-MED it was nearly 7:30 a.m. The same brunette from the day before greeted him.

"Larry Egens, please."

She dialed a number and spoke to someone and within minutes Larry showed up with a reserved smile on his face.

"Keeno," he extended his hand in a business-like fashion, though his body language showed he was tense.

"Just a minute of your time," Keeno motioned him to the far end of the reception.

"Just so you know, I've asked Homeland Security to keep an eye over you and your family."

"Why, am I in trouble?"

"Let's put it this way, someone tried to kill me yesterday. I think FAB-MED is involved."

Larry's eyes went wide.

"I don't have time to prove everything to you right now, so you're gonna have to trust me on this one or suffer the consequences," his eyes locked on Larry's face. He could see that he was battling with his loyalty to the company and the stark truths of what he was telling him.

"I don't think you're involved in the shit that's going down in this place, which is why I'm even talking to you. If you see some guys trailing you or watching your house, call this number," and he handed him a paper with the number to Homeland Security. "They'll tell you if it's their guys or not. Meanwhile, I need you to plant a seed. It shouldn't put you in harm's way, at least not any more than has possibly already happened, but it could help us to get to the bottom of this."

Larry was hesitant, but he nodded as he put the paper in his pocket.

"Tom Sneider will call you to his office to find out what I talked to you about just now, I know that for sure. Tell him that I was asking questions about the board members of FAB-MED, specifically Malcolm McDonald."

"That's it?"

"Yes," he said, as he looked up at a security camera that was aimed right where he stood. He smiled and winked at it and then turned back to Larry. "Watch your back, buddy," he then turned and left the building.

Keeno got back to his car and as he slipped into it, he glanced at Sneider's office and, as predicted, Sneider was watching him. He pulled onto the 295 and headed for the Trenton airport, where he turned in the new rental and booked a flight through Kennedy airport for Hong Kong.

VIII

Katherine Riggs was studying the computer at Keeno's desk. In his absence, Kelly had set her up there where she could assist in the investigation. Her education in microbiology and the viral field quickly proved to be invaluable.

She was monitoring the media and local hospitals. The sickness from the rampant new flu had now escalated by another 12,000 cases in just the last 24 hours. It was becoming a city-wide epidemic at this point. By their estimates, the number of infected people was close to 30,000. The Canadian Health Department had issued an official mandate that the situation was on the cusp of disastrous proportions and advisory notices were flying with warnings and precautionary advice to the general public in order to reduce potential infection.

In her field, she had studied comparative statistics for epidemics in recent years. The H1N1 "epidemic" in America had tallied upwards of 44,640 infections in one year, with just over 10,000 deaths nationwide. The fact that Toronto was already nearing 30,000 infections in less than a week was tantamount to the "China Syndrome" – a nuclear fission of infectious permeation. If they didn't get to the bottom of this fast, the impact on the national level would be catastrophic.

The media was ablaze with the news, not only in Canada, but across the border in America as well. The threat of a pandemic was now becoming an actual reality, as the American government made press releases about their intentions to step up locating a vaccine. Cases of the flu had already surfaced in Detroit, Erie and Buffalo, which were closest to Toronto.

The problem was that there was no specific vaccine available for this virus. It was a new breed and vaccines were not developed overnight, and certainly not released for general use without months of testing.

Meanwhile, knowing that Katherine was safe at the RCMP, Jake had gone to the lab at the University of Toronto with two other RCMP officers. The canister that Katherine had seen placed into the refrigeration unit was no longer there, and no evidence could be found of unauthorized personnel in the lab itself. They searched for fingerprints or any other telltale signs, but none had been left behind.

The obvious question that he was asking himself was how did two unauthorized guys get into a lab without being seen by the security cameras posted on each floor? That question led them to the security office, where he asked to see the video playback for the night before. The videos showed no men, in fact, no activity at all – just an empty hallway on the fourth floor.

"How is that possible?" he stared at the two security guards, who looked back at him with empty faces. "Show me the wiring panel for these cameras." They followed one of the security guards to a small room in the basement where he unlocked a panel which revealed the wiring and coding for all the campus security cameras. Everything seemed in order.

Jake turned to one of the other RCMP officers, while pointing to the ceiling, "Can you get up there and see if those wires have been tampered with." The RCMP officer pulled a ladder over, climbed up and inspected the wires, tracing each one with his fingers, when he saw several of them disappear behind a pipe. He reached back and found a plastic box, snapped it loose, and tossed it down to Jake. Inside was a device, the size of a USB, into which the wires had been rerun.

Jake turned to the security guard, "Someone re-wired those cameras. You've probably been watching a video loop."

The guard looked shocked.

The operation was sophisticated, that much was becoming very clear to him, and these people had connections.

Jake decided that there wasn't anything more to learn there, so headed back to his car, when he suddenly stopped and stared down one wing of the University of Toronto. His mind struggled for a moment to decipher what he was looking at, and then it struck him; a piece of the puzzle suddenly congealed. He dialed Keeno.

"What's up?" Keeno said, as he relaxed with a glass of Bailey's in the flight lounge, waiting to board the plane to Hong Kong.

"Just leaving U of T campus. We didn't find the canister that Katherine saw being put into the lab last night, but we did find that someone erased all the security-camera footage."

"You think maybe it's the security guards?" Keeno asked.

"Who knows," Jake answered, "besides, they did such a good job of covering up their tracks that I think I'd be wasting my time looking there. The real reason I called is because I realized where that picture came from, the one that you found on the shooter's phone in Trenton."

"Where?"

"U of T, the same wing where Ralph Ketchler's classroom is located. Someone must have taken a frame from the security-cam and sent it to the shooter sometime after we saw Ralph."

"Probably should get Kelly to check out those security people at U of T."

"Ok, and where are you?" Jake asked.

"On my way to Hong Kong, to visit Malcolm McDonald, a board member for FAB-MED and co-owner of a drug company in China. Just a hunch."

"Long flight to follow a hunch."

Keeno didn't reply.

"Hong Kong is a bit outside your comfort zone. Are you sure you don't need some help?"

"Not yet, but if I get into any trouble, I'll give you a ring."

Jake laughed derisively. "Dude, when it comes to trouble there's no *if* with you – it's a question of *when*."

"I'll call you later," Keeno hung up the line and settled back in the lounge chair. He amused himself thinking about the name the Iroquois had given him when he was born; *Storm Bringer*. He'd never paid it much attention, but maybe there was some truth to it, especially since people kept reminding him that he tended to stir up trouble wherever he went.

As he sat there sipping on his drink, he remembered something that Uncle Lou used to tell him when they'd be out hunting, "If ya wanna kill a bear, ya gotta be willing to step in its shit sometimes. It ain't always nice but it leads ya to the beast."

That story seemed to define his life.

IX

Word that the mercenary had failed to kill the RCMP agent, Keeno McCole, reached Malcolm McDonald's desk within an hour. He fumed over it for a few minutes, until his phone rang.

"Yes," he answered somberly and then listened to the short admonishment from the old man.

"I just heard about it. Trust me, I will take care of it," and he hung up.

Their conversations were rarely longer than a minute or two for security reasons, as they didn't want to compromise themselves. The old man at the other end of the line was categorically one of the most powerful men in the world, and failure at this point was simply not an option. Malcolm McDonald knew that either he succeeded and won his prize or he lost his life in the process. Having no interest in dying, he had to get rid of this McCole character fast.

He had started out in the chemical and pharmaceutical industry in Philadelphia, when he was twenty-two years old. At the time, he had worked for a small company that provided chemical constituents for pharmaceutical companies, mostly in the south. By the time he was twenty-seven, he had not only become their strongest sales representative, but he had firmly networked and entrenched himself within influential circles in the industry. In his early days, it had become clear to him that the pharmaceutical field was destined to become one of the most lucrative money making industries in the world, next to wars and banking.

One of the men that McDonald befriended at that time was the sole owner of a chemical company in Atlanta, Georgia. This magnate had a young daughter by the name of Amy, an attractive little lady of twenty-five years. Malcolm McDonald personally could not have cared less about her looks. In fact, he wasn't attracted to her in the slightest, and to accomplish his ends he would have courted and married her if she was as big as a cow, with facial hair and double jowls to boot. He needed Amy to wedge his way into a family that held tremendous sway and power in the pharmaceutical field. She was his ticket to the inner circle.

A year later, they walked down the matrimonial aisle. He had become the son-in-law of the man who owned the third largest pharmaceutical supply company in the United States. Over the following years, he endeared himself to her father, seemingly treating his daughter as a princess, while secretly despising every moment he spent with her. He did not love Amy and he cared less about sex with her, since he secretly filled his sexual fantasies by using the services of wanton women and prostitutes.

Malcolm McDonald had one ambition in life – POWER.

By the age of thirty-five, he had worked his way up the hierarchy of his father-in-law's company, and had been appointed VP of Sales. Through that position, he made many contacts and negotiations with both American and foreign owned companies in the field.

When he passed his fiftieth birthday, he had accumulated enough money to partner with two other companies, one being the corporate entity that became FAB-MED, and the other being a firm that was being launched by the Chinese government. It seemed that the Communist enclave of the PRC was quite aware of the importance and profits to be made by feeding drugs into America and the rest of the western world, and they could produce the same drugs at a fraction of the cost that other pharmaceuticals were charging. Malcolm McDonald saw the venture as a long term and very profitable relationship.

When Amy's father died, they inherited a massive fortune. Needless to say, he avoided spending it on trifles, such as new homes and other luxuries that Amy so fondly desired. She had also wanted to give millions away to humanitarian foundations to help the poor and, of course, McDonald had to convince her otherwise. In fact, he made her agree to wait for a full year before using any of the inheritance, until the profits had significantly increased on the basis of the interest rates alone.

Near the end of that year, Amy met an untimely death, when her car swerved off the road during a rainstorm. Investigations quickly cleared him of any suspicion in her death, which was summed up as an accident due to road and weather conditions. No one knew that he had engaged someone who was adept at sabotaging braking systems without a trace, so that they would fail at a critical moment during her trip back from the Appalachians.

Today, Malcolm McDonald sat comfortably with millions in accounts spread throughout American, Swiss and Asian banks. Because of his wealth, he was listed as one of the 500 richest men in the world, a stature which eventually caught the attention of some international bankers who had invited him to functions both in the States and overseas.

He had happily engaged in these gatherings, not knowing at the time that they had their own agenda and were secretly checking out his suitability for their own plans. After several such meetings, none of which spared on ample and available women to satiate his sexual desires, McDonald was eventually introduced to the "inner circle," wherein he was asked if he would like to commit to a "higher agenda."

This served his mindset precisely, the very idea of mounting and executing global power-plays that would push him and others onto a higher platform. He dove in, head over heels, first into smaller operations, then eventually arriving at the one he was now navigating from his office in Hong Kong.

Most people would question why men of power would engage in a viral attack that would kill thousands and ultimately result in deluding people into giving up their freedom. The reason can only be revealed by understanding the mindset of people like Malcolm McDonald and those who pulled his strings. He was a man who had more money in his possession than countless thousands of people combined, and yet he could not rest until he had achieved countless millions more. Greed was not the *only* impulse that drove people like him; it was power, for reasons that only a criminal mind could conceive.

The plan, so far, had come off perfectly. The virus, which had been developed right there in China, was spreading throughout Toronto. The media was playing its cards as predicted. The drafted legislation, which he had hired a special team of attorneys to prepare months before, was now in the hands of Canadian parliament. It was just a matter of time before the public outcry for vaccines would hit such a fever pitch that the Prime Minister of Canada and his office would be forced to pass the bill. With that, his company would be on the forefront, providing the most inexpensive vaccines available anywhere. It would take other agencies months before they could come up with a safe vaccine, so there was no competition in this particular arena.

The beauty of the plan, he mused, was that Canada, being a nation of only thirty million people, was far easier to leverage than America, which had over ten times that figure. But in view of Canada's proximity to America, it was also just a matter of time before they too would bend to the public pressure.

The other aspect of the strategy was the RFID chips. Although he had not been involved in the initial research steps involving RFID technology, he ultimately bought into the program when he found out what it would mean both financially and in the sense of real ultimate power.

When McDonald had been shown the scope of the RFID research by the "old man" himself, and what could be accomplished by the God Chip, his innate sense of power-hunger and desire for wealth had convinced him.

He was absolutely impassioned with the idea that the God Chip could be implanted in several locations in a human bcdy, a process that took less than twenty minutes to do in most cases. Not only did the chip provide accurate biological and physiological feedback, it also provided clear-cut audio allowing an operator to monitor any conversations in their vicinity.

But the most unique trait, which truly made it the "Supreme Being" of all chips, was that an operator could amplify a frequency in the chips causing it to resonate into the body. Such a frequency, passing between chips strategically placed in a body, could induce seizures, heart palpitations, intense pain and even hemorrhaging. It would mean that for all intents and purposes, they would control the physical state of every human being so implanted.

While others would toot the medical wonders of RFID chipping, he saw it entirely in terms of dollar signs and *control.* It was like bar-coding every human being – you owned them.

As he looked out over the Hong Kong harbor, he mentally worked over a new plan to take care of this RCMP agent, McCole. He already knew from his sources that McCole had jumped a plane to Hong Kong. He would have to accomplish two things: kill McCole and deflect any attention from his operation here in Hong Kong so that the RCMP, Homeland Security and others, would lose his scent.

He had not achieved his power and wealth without using an iron fist, and removing obstacles to his success was something he was good at doing.

X

"Anything new?" Jake asked, as he entered the office.

Janene and Kelly were in conversation with each other, while Katherine Riggs was sitting at Keeno's desk poring over some papers. She looked up with yet another perfect smile from her seemingly perfect face.

He slipped into the chair across from her, his knees weakening at the joints all of a sudden, quite inexplicably. He had steeled himself over the years to having bullets shot at him, into him, through him and around him. He had innumerable cuts and scars from knife wounds. Doctors had pulled pieces of shrapnel from his body in countless places. He'd chased terrorists at death defying speeds in cars, parachuted out of planes in the dead of night in the hopes that he wouldn't be found the next day dangling from a tree or smashed to a pulp in the side of some structure. The number of life and death incidents he had engaged was too long to even bother with – none of which had concerned him in the least.

Yet, here he was, confronted by a stunningly beautiful woman, and his legs turned to jelly. *It just doesn't seem fair*, he thought to himself.

"You talk to Keeno lately?" Kelly asked Jake, while still looking at her computer.

"Yeah, about twenty minutes ago. You know he's headed for Hong Kong – right?"

Janene shook her head, "Yeah… we know," she seemed aggravated. But then again, with Janene you just never knew which side of her was talking. Was it the professional RCMP side or the "I love Keeno and I can't stand that he's doing something to put his life on the line again" side? It was no secret to Kelly or Jake how Janene felt towards Keeno. In fact, their tacit relationship was no secret at all – except possibly to Keeno himself who seemed to think that it was best not to get involved with Janene, and while Jake could understand his logic, it still never made any sense to him.

"You doing ok?" Jake asked, as he turned back to Katherine.

"Yes, I'm analyzing these reports from the various hospitals on the people admitted with the flu symptoms," she said without looking up, although he sensed that she was somehow teasing him by not making eye contact.

"Need any help?" he casually offered.

"No, but I just got this new bag," and she pulled up a sealed plastic bag that had a poison toxic symbol on it, "with samples of the virus from people with the flu. I'm on my way to your labs to analyze it now. Want to join me?"

"Thanks, I'll pass," he said, as Katherine stood up and left the room.

"I think Keeno's walking into a Roman arena and he's the only one there for the lions to eat," Janene said out loud.

Jake turned to look at Janene. "What d'ya mean?"

"I finally got a trace done on that phone from our first dead guy – Arnie Norton. It's a Trenton, New Jersey area code - that much we know. We're still trying to break the rest of it. Secondly, the anonymous number that sent that picture of Keeno to the hit-man in Trenton came from somewhere in China."

"That doesn't mean he's walking into a bear trap," Jake challenged her.

Janene stood up and sat back against her desk with her arms folded across her chest. There was a lecture coming – Jake knew the signs.

"Look, you've been with Keeno on almost every mission. When he gets a feather up his ass about something, what are the chances he's going to walk into the middle of a gunfight?"

Jake didn't answer the question. It was rhetorical.

"What do you suggest?"

Janene sighed and rubbed her eyes, "I don't know. You know him better than I do when it comes to this type of stuff. I just think he's gonna be in trouble the minute he steps off that plane, but I can't tell him that because, you know Keeno, he's gonna do it his way."

For a long moment they all sat silent trying to figure out their next step, when the door to the office opened and Katherine walked back in with a sense of urgency on her face.

"The virus that was released in Mississauga was different than the one that came up in Oakville. This latest wave in the east end, that's another strain which confirms that they're layering the city."

"Which means we're fucked – right?" Kelly said as she lit up a smoke.

"If we don't get to the bottom of this soon, you're talking thousands and thousands of deaths, and at this rate, upwards of 60 or 70,000 infected, which for a city of Toronto's size will result in critical mass fission," Katherine said.

"The obvious question then is who is making money off this. Someone must be stepping up to the plate with the vaccine. Who's that gonna be?" Janene posed.

"Doesn't matter who steps up at this point," Katherine said. "I think they're just waiting until this epidemic hits catastrophic proportions and when they show up with the vaccine they'll be the real heroes and the general public won't care if Osama bin Laden or Charles Manson delivers it."

"In fact," Katherine continued, "I can tell you from my university studies of this subject, there is a certain flashpoint we've noticed in similar epidemics. If it threatens the economy and the infrastructure of a country, you can bet that the public demand and the pressure from the medical community will force the government and its health department to step in with mandatory inoculations, country-wide. An epidemic of this proportion could set

Canada back economically by years. It simply won't be tolerated."

"That sucks!" Jake said as he fiddled with a pen.

"Which explains why these guys are releasing the virus in very specific areas," Kelly said.

"Right, if they can intensify the number of sick and the deaths from it, they'll force the issue. Probably, at this rate, we will see legislation passed in a matter of a day or so, and you can count on the fact that the government will be looking for the best bidder to get a vaccine for every strain of that flu, so they can start nationwide inoculations," Katherine continued.

"Great," Janene said as she rubbed her eyes. "That means that the stupid bill from Harold James will pass and they'll also sanction the RFID chip research."

"The what?" Jake asked.

"RFID chip implants," she said nonplused.

"That means," Kelly started to say, "no more porno shops for you Jake. Everywhere you go, big brother will be monitoring your actions with an implanted chip."

"Screw that, anyone tries to chip me and they'll be eating it," he said, as he jumped out of his chair and left the office, slamming the door behind him.

The girls watched him as he left. It wasn't usual for him to get so riled, but what they didn't know was that he was actually worried about Keeno. His sixth sense was telling him that Keeno was in big trouble and for the first time he was nowhere near to back him up.

Chapter 4

I

René Norman, a staunch Conservative, had come into power as the Prime Minister of Canada just nine months before. In his eighteen years in the political arena, he had seen many things in Canada. It was a nation where the proverbial boat was simply not rocked very easily. Canadians were traditionally "middle-of–the-road," and didn't sway to extremes. Of course, there was hockey fever, which seemed to be a genetic alteration at birth, morphing Canadians from calm, rational people, into raving, beer-drinking, banner-waving lunatics when hockey season rolled around each year.

His first months in power as head of the Conservative Party had been stressful, but he had not had to deal with any major catastrophes as of yet. The recession in the States had already begun when he took office, and it was predictable that Canada would feel the effects of it as well. But, being a nation with considerable resources, sustainable means of production and a population one-tenth of its southern neighbor, it could and would hold its own. He had been confident that the Canadian ship would stay off the rocks economically.

All of that had been true until today. The emergency session of Parliament had been forced by reason of the circumstances in Toronto. He glanced over the report. The number of people coming down with viral infections in

Greater Toronto was alarming, with over 30,000 cases reported. There could easily be thousands more who simply hadn't checked in at hospitals and were quietly battling the infection at home. The death toll was now over 1500, mostly comprised of older people or those with weakened immune systems or other physical disabilities.

The alarm panels from across the nation were lit up and sounding in his office. Provincial representatives from British Columbia to Newfoundland were being inundated by calls, letters and emails from their electoral zones, demanding that the government avert a nationwide epidemic. Extremist groups were popping up all over the grid, threatening that if René Norman's party could not effectively act on these circumstances, then he should be removed from office as Prime Minister.

Doomsday groups were, predictably, hitting the airwaves, forecasting this as the beginning of the end. There had even been a few rumblings out of Quebec – old allies of the FLQ movement – who were feeding off the disaster and fanning the flames of dissention.

René Norman felt an inordinate amount of pressure on his shoulders today. It seemed that his entire career was now in jeopardy over this one issue, and the flashpoint was coming up fast.

He picked up another fax that had just come in from the RCMP HQ in Toronto. It was a memo from Ross Fletcher asking the PM to please consider calling him.

René pressed the intercom to his secretary, "Lilly please cancel all my calls for the next half hour and get me Ross Fletcher of the RCMP Toronto office." A moment later his intercom flashed, and he put it on speaker phone.

"Ross."

"Yes, Sir."

"Call me René, I hate formalities. What do you have for me?"

"We're still piecing it together but the short version is this – someone is orchestrating the systematic release of the flu virus into Toronto, using different strains of the flu so that we can't tackle it effectively without the right vaccines. Clearly, they are escalating this up to the point where your office is forced to sign that bill, which is in your hands. With that, the lowest bidder steps forward and offers the Canadian government a price for vaccines for all strains of the flu, a deal that you couldn't possibly refuse ."

"Ok."

"We're pretty sure that this is their plan, at least all the dots seem to connect that way right now. Obviously, if we don't respond in the way they want, they'll probably continue until the sheer force of public outcry forces the issue. Either way, they win, and as you know, an epidemic of this nature could cripple Canada within a couple weeks."

"And the lowest bidder for the vaccines – wouldn't that lead us to the source of all of this?"

"Theoretically yes, but they'll cover their tracks, and most importantly, the hero in this arena will be the man who resolves the life and death issue – that's the reality of it right now," Ross said matter-of-factly.

"So either we ferret them out before the bill goes into play, or it's a pointless exercise," The Prime Minister said.

"Basically – yes."

"Any idea who's behind this?"

"No, but it doesn´t follow the normal terrorist modus operandi, so we're looking outside the box right now.

René drew in a long breath.

"Anything else?"

"Yes, that bill has a built in clause at the end. Our intelligence so far indicates that this is part of their objective, maybe even covertly their main objective."

"You mean the RFID chip implants research?"

"Yes, of course you realize the long-term ramifications of such a program, if it was instituted in Canada?"

The Prime Minister swiveled in his chair and stared out over the large square in front of the Canadian Parliamentary buildings. Facing him in the distance was the bronze statue of Sir Cartier – one of the men who had fathered Canada into a nation and who had helped establish it as the country it was today.

He thought about the ordeals that this man had endured in his time. Exiled because he disagreed with the government, the man had never given up on his goals for a civil-ordered Canada, and he had eventually brought a sense of greater unity to the fledgling nation. *How did Cartier's challenges of that time compare to what he was facing today*, he wondered?

"Yes, I do. But you do realize that this bill is now in the hands of every member of the legislature, and they are under the same pressure that I am, and don't forget, they have friends and families who are liable to catch the flu. Everyone is in a quiet state of panic about this," the Prime Minister answered.

"If the bill gets passed, how long do we have before it becomes law?" Ross asked.

"Usually a week, following all protocols, but in this case, it will probably go through the system like shit through a goose, and the normal bureaucratic delays will be expedited so that we can authorize federal funding, purchase the vaccines and start the inoculations before this gets entirely out of hand – if it isn't already."

"If I were to get tangible evidence that this was a planned attack on Canada, could you navigate getting the bill stopped before it becomes law?"

"If you show me that this is an act of terrorism, I will put my career on the line and burn that piece of legislation. But you don't have much time, Ross. I'm pretty sure, with the national panic level escalating, that every member of that parliamentary body is going to vote it in. I'll try to throw some roadblocks in the way to buy you some time, but as I said, there will be a point where even I can't prevent it from happening."

"Ok, I will let you know," Ross said.

Ross Fletcher hung up the line and looked across the table at Janene and Kelly, who had listened to the entire call. In fact, it had been the two of them who had suggested that he contact the PM directly.

"We need to nail this fast." Ross said as he rubbed his eyes. "If they pass that bill and start chipping people, I may have to resign, because I´ll be damned if I´ll support a government that turns Canada into a de facto police state."

II

Dubbed the "Golden Pond," by local engineers and technicians, it was 1.3 kilometers in length, fifty meters wide, twenty meters at its deepest end and slowly rising up to ten meters in depth at its far end where it was fed by an underground source. The water was channeled along man-made conduits from hundreds of miles away, home to several large lakes to the north.

Once the water arrived at the entrance to the pond, it flowed down the large collection runway through a series of filtration systems enclosed in the plant, and eventually came out the other end as safe drinking water. The pond served nearly 200,000 households and businesses as far north as the cities of Vaughan and Richmond Hill, and westward into Markham and eastward into Brampton.

It was dusk and the sunlight was fading fast. There were a few wisps of clouds hanging on the horizon, reflecting the last traces of sunlight in hues of pink and orange before the mantle of darkness would once again engulf the land.

The black pickup came to a stop under some trees in a distant field. The men parked it where it wouldn't be seen in the ensuing blackness of night. They jumped a small picket fence and waded through several fields of tall corn stalks that came up to the top of their heads. Besides the occasional movement of a stalk here or there, no sign could be seen of their stealthy approach to the edge of facility. With the pond in sight, they crouched down in the forest of corn stalks and patiently waited until darkness would finally chase the remnants of light from the sky.

A tall fence, four meters in height, surrounded the entire facility. It contained enough voltage to kill a man in seconds. Huge lights shone down on the whole perimeter, including the pond itself. In fact, it was so well lit up that it could have passed as a football stadium had it not been for the fact that it was simply a huge basin of water. Motion detectors were set up every three meters to detect anything that might come within range of the pond, which were monitored by a security booth and security team that patrolled the perimeter every hour. No one was going to get close to this pond without being detected, which is why these men had come prepared.

Their faces were greased with black anti-reflective matter. They were wearing black matt outfits and black wool caps. They had rehearsed the procedure to the point where there was no need for any verbalization between them at all. When the sky was pitch black and the security patrol had passed by on its usual rounds, they pulled out a small, remote-controlled plane from their backpack. It was a third of a meter in length, painted black so as to be invisible against the night sky, and was battery operated, allowing it to fly silently. Attached to its undercarriage were two pods containing the virus.

One man checked the device to ensure that everything was intact, and then he held it up carefully on the palm of his hand so that it cleared the tops of the corn stalks. The other man held the remote control with the joystick. The miniature plane started, then lifted quietly from the man's hand, and flew up into the air, well above the fence and beyond the range of the motion sensors.

They watched it on a small laptop, following its movement on the screen. The plane showed up as a yellow figure moving through a three-dimensional graphics program which illustrated the plane's exact height and its relative position to the pond. The man carefully navigated it over the water, and when the plane was flying on a parallel course to the reservoir, he flicked a switch and the two pouches dropped silently into the waiting maws of the pond below. They directed the plane back to the cornfield where it quietly landed amidst the stalks of corn. In silence, the men retrieved it and then disappeared into the night.

III

Keeno landed in Hong Kong the next morning. He hailed a cab, which he took from the airport to the nearest electronics store, where he bought a small transmitter.

When he got to his hotel room, he called Janene.

"Hey, I'm here, anything new?"

"Shit's really hitting the fan. Nearly 35,000 reported flu cases and deaths are around 2000. Parliament met today and passed the Emergency Health Bill. The PM says that unless we can show him concrete evidence that this is all an act of terrorism, he won't be able to stop that bill from becoming law."

"How much time do we have?"

"Three days max.

"What's Jake up to?"

"He said he was going out to check on some stuff – but that was early this morning and I haven't seen him since."

"Ok."

"We also found out that they're dropping different strains of the virus around Toronto to maximize the collateral damage. There's already talk about the WHO calling for a quarantine on Canada to prevent a pandemic."

Keeno was fiddling with the transmitter as he talked. "Did you find anything else on Malcolm McDonald before I pay him a visit?"

"He's got a sordid past. He married into a big pharmaceutical family some decades ago. Got a huge inheritance when his wife's old man died, and then a year later his wife had an 'unfortunate' car accident."

"Convenient."

"He took sole ownership of her father's company after her death. I'm still tracing his companies overseas. We know he's a main stockholder at FAB-MED and from what I can tell so far, he has other corporations in Asia and China, not to mention his piece of the pie at CJN. The corporate umbrella over CJN Holdings is not transparent, as the Chinese government doesn't like to tip its hand to the world, revealing how much they are involved in running and profiting from such companies.

"I get the picture," Keeno said as he thought over what Janene was telling him. In his books, communism and criminality went hand-in-hand, and as far as he was concerned there had never been a communist state on earth that had been anything but corrupt, and historical precedence seemed to support his interpretation on the matter. Not to mention the fact that every communist regime had eventually failed, and in its wake was a procession of dead bodies and skeletons enough to sicken anyone with a sense of ethics. While Keeno held the Chinese culture and its people in high regard, he viewed the PRC's government as nothing more than vipers in a pit, snaking their way into the international community, proffering cheap labor to the whole world, while filling their coffers with the money they need to finance other plans.

"One other thing, you asked me to see if we could find anything about agencies that hire out mercenaries in Hong Kong. First of all, you can practically find one on every other corner. They're as common as fast food restaurants. The question is – which one? Until I crack the code on that cell phone you took from the dead shooter, I can't give you much more."

"That gives me something to go on," Keeno said.

"Just watch your back, I don't like that you're over there by yourself."

"I'll be fine."

Keeno smiled as he hung up the line. There was that redundant warning again.

He finished activating the transmitter, then sent a text message to Kelly with the transmitter code and frequency in case he needed backup.

After a quick shower, he got dressed and secured his knife in his hip pocket. The knife had saved his life in Trenton, New Jersey, and he had no doubt that it would serve him again.

When he stepped out onto the street from his hotel, he was momentarily struck by a storm of humanity. Hong Kong was the diametrical opposite of Toronto. Everywhere, there were people vying for a small piece of the road. It was wall-to-wall bodies, mopeds, cars, push carts, bicycles and every other imaginable form of transportation. On the one hand, Hong Kong had some of the most artistic and high-tech looking skyscrapers anywhere in the world. Adjacent to those were wooden kiosks and shanties lined up by the dozens, selling everything from dead chickens, gutted pigs, hand-made crafts and, of course, black-market goods.

Using what little Chinese he knew, he found a cabbie willing to take him through the winding streets into an area of Hong Kong where tourists simply didn't venture, and finally stopped in front of a shabby looking place that had some meats and chickens hanging in the window.

"Wait here," he said, handing him some money as he did. He went into the shop and was greeted by an old Chinese lady who nodded with a slight bow. She was tiny, hunched over from age, with a sea of wrinkles on her face.

She smiled at him, revealing missing teeth, and said something in Chinese, to which he responded with a moderate smile and the word – "Guns?"

The old lady said nothing but she obviously understood what the word meant. She meandered through some beaded curtains and a moment later a man emerged. He studied Keeno with some suspicion, sizing him up, before saying, "What you want?" which he uttered with a heavy Chinese dialect and a dose of antagonism in his voice.

"Guns."

"No do guns here – go away!"

Keeno pulled out a roll of bills and flashed them in the man's face. "You still want me to go?" he smiled.

The man looked around the shop to make sure no one else was there, "Come."

Twenty minutes later, he left the shop with two handguns: a Browning special strapped to a holster around his chest, and a Walther P99 semi-automatic, which was slipped into a Velcro-sheath inside his coat pocket, not to mention extra clips of ammunition for both.

After successfully navigating the Hong Kong streets, a feat that seemed on a par with flying to the moon and back, the cabbie dropped him off at the base of the Bank of China Tower. Keeno walked into the building, flashed his RCMP badge, and informed the security guard that he was here on official business for the government of Canada. The guard hesitated as he eyed the credentials and finally waved him through.

When he arrived at the offices on the 43rd floor, he found a young Chinese receptionist smiling at him. "My name is Keeno McCole, I'm here to see Malcolm McDonald."

She smiled and asked him to be seated while she disappeared down a long hallway. She reappeared a moment later, "Please follow me."

He was ushered into a large office that was structured so that it was centered on the angle of two huge bay windows, with a magnificent view of downtown Hong Kong. The windows extruded outwards like the prow of a ship. Situated in front of them was a large desk with a polished steel-like finish.

Standing facing the windows was a large man who turned to look at him. He had a cigar perched in his mouth with a cloud of smoke billowing up above him. He had a balding head, a fat, wide face with fleshy jowls to match, and a large portly belly. He appeared to be well into his sixties.

"Mr. McCole, it seems that this meeting was destined. Please have a seat."

Keeno looked around the office and then sat down across from the large metal desk. McDonald also sat down.

"You were expecting me it seems," Keeno said, his eyes subtly, yet rapidly, scanning the room. His radar was suddenly on high alert.

"Considering that you managed to evade getting killed in Trenton, I did take an interest in you."

"You're well informed."

"I have my sources, and Trenton is not a place where high-speed car chases occur very often, especially with a bullet-ridden car that was seen flying across the highway. Local news stations did report on it, so it was no secret."

"Would I be surprised to find out that you were involved somehow?"

"Now, now Mr. McCole, let's not jump to conclusions. Besides, this is our first meeting and I think cordiality would be in order," McDonald said with mock finesse.

"Sorry to disappoint you, but that's not my style. Tell me, what are you gaining from this virus attack? Is CJN Holdings going to step forward with the anti-virus? "

"Your lack of formal protocol is somewhat annoying."

"I've been told that before, thanks."

"Well, for the record, CJN Holdings is nothing more, nothing less, than the Chinese version of any other pharmaceutical company."

"That may be true, but you're on the Board of Directors of FAB-MED, and you have a stake in CJN, so that tells me something."

"Which is what?"

"Rats collect in packs," Keeno said, purposely needling the man, seeing if he could throw him off his game.

McDonald's demeanor remained unchanged.

"Let me be more direct; I happen to know that the guy carrying a lethal virus was a former employee of FAB-MED. He screwed up, got nailed by a car during his delivery, but then somehow, you guys had an inside man, who got into a very secure location, recovered the virus and then started releasing it in Toronto."

"Very good theory, but still I fail to see how you can possibly conclude any of this has anything to do with myself."

Keeno watched McDonald, assessing the man, looking him in the eyes as he did. McDonald was a consummate actor, and better still, an arrogant liar, a man who enjoyed twisting facts, playing mind games designed to delude others into believing the words coming out of his mouth. If he was going to learn anything from McDonald, he would have to aggrandize his ego, inflate his head and play on his arrogance.

"Theoretically speaking," Keeno started to say as he leaned back in his chair, "if you *were* involved in this plot, what would be your assessment of this whole scenario, I mean, professionally speaking that is."

McDonald eyed him like a wolf might eye a lone sheep; his suspicious mind weighed up the pros and cons of saying too much, but at the same time, he had plans for Keeno, and there was nothing he could say that would ever make it out of this room.

"Naturally, I have been following the news, and it appears that nearly 38,000 people in Toronto alone have been infected with the virus, and the death toll is somewhere up around 2300. Hypothetically speaking, if I were involved, I would consider this operation to be moving along quite well in fact."

Keeno continued to play McDonald, much the same as a fisherman might reel in his catch, playing it in and out.

"What about all these innocent people who are being killed by this virus?"

McDonald waved a hand dismissively, tipping it a little more, and revealing his personal lack of compassion. "Kill - such a brutal word. Killing is the stuff of the Mafia or the acts of soldiers shooting at one another in the battlefield. I would say that the people behind this particular operation are much more sophisticated than a bunch of cheap terrorists."

"Sophisticated or not, murdering people is criminal," Keeno shot back.

Keeno's senses were tuned to every noise and possible movement in the room. McDonald was too confident. He chuckled as he stood up and walked over to the massive window looking out over Hong Kong. "We live in a different world today Mr. McCole. You of all people should know this to be true, since you head-up anti-terrorism for the RCMP." McDonald pointed his cigar at Keeno. "You say killing innocent people, like it is a terrible thing, but I say that this virus attack in Toronto is quite possibly part of a broader plan."

"Meaning?" he prodded him on.

"History tells us that the events that shape our world are not a matter of chance, they are largely a matter of causation. Take a classic example; America didn't get involved in World War II until nearly two years after Germany had severely bombed the British, invaded Europe and were heading into Russia, why was that?"

"You're the history teacher, you tell me." Keeno smiled.

"Causation. America had no reason to get involved in that war, no motive, that is, not until the military community came up with the plan to let the Japanese bomb Pearl Harbor. To maximize the collateral damage they also made sure that most of the naval personnel were on shore leave that day, leaving the ships unguarded, and that most fighter planes were nosed in, instead of being in combat formation for rapid deployment. All of these factors combined gave America good cause to declare war against Japan and Germany, with unanimous support from most Americans."

"And your point?"

McDonald smiled, he was enjoying the lecture.

"Let's take a more recent incident; 9-11, the twin towers in New York City, another planned moment in history. What would give the US government and the military establishment the motive it required to invade Afghanistan and eventually Iraq – in fact, to establish a military presence in these countries unlike before? Of course, hit America where it hurt the most – the Big Apple. President Bush declares war against "terrorism" and launches an invasion, with unilateral support. Meanwhile, caught up in the horror of the deaths of some 3000 people at ground zero, American's lose sight of the fact that it was a literal impossibility for three buildings to collapse, as they did, unless of course they were rigged with demolition style explosives designed to bring down those structures with perfect orchestration."

He smiled as he sucked on his cigar. "Causation. This is the way of the world today. The whole aspect of America changed after 9-11; the Patriot Act, surveillance, heightened immigration laws, intrusive scans and so much more – all because two towers were taken down."

McDonald walked over to his chair and leaned his bulky frame on it. "You call it killing, but I think you overly dramatize the matter Mr. McCole – the world has changed, events are planned and executed to accomplish strategic ends."

"What's your motive McDonald?"

McDonald stood up straight and stepped back by the window. "I am a man of wealth and I intend to remain one of the wealthiest men in the world. But that is no crime, is it?"

Keeno had waited for this moment, the precise second when he had McDonald off-guard and overly-confident. He launched his next question while looking him in the eyes.

"So then implanting RFID chips in people must be your next big move, eh McDonald?"

McDonald's aspect suddenly wavered, ever so slightly, and the relaxed smile faded from his face. Keeno knew at that point that he had pressed the right button. McDonald's body language had confirmed it. He grinned, a wolfish leer, and stepped over to his desk to douse his cigar. His intercom rang at that instant.

"Yes?" he answered.

"Your next appointment is here," the receptionist answered.

"I'll be right there."

McDonald looked up at Keeno. "Give me a moment please, so that I may say hello to my guests, and then we can resume our talk."

McDonald stepped from the room, closing the door behind him as he did. The alarms went off inside Keeno's head – something was wrong. He never tried to explain to himself why he felt the danger signal, or what sense he was operating on – he simply trusted himself in this regard and that trust had kept him alive. He started to reach for his gun when he caught the glint, the subtle, yet definitive gleam of light from a window directly across from the building he was in. Keeno dove to the right just as a series of high-caliber bullets smashed through the plate-glass window, cutting the air where his head had been, just seconds before.

He rolled to his knees and quickly moved to the wall, then peered through the window to the building adjacent to his own. There was no sign of the shooter.

He grabbed the Walther P99 from his pocket, slipped off the safety and quickly moved to the door, and then out into the hallway. There was a deathly silence that filled the air. No voices, no sign of McDonald, nothing.

As he approached the reception area, he saw the receptionist lying dead on the floor, in a pool of blood. Keeno didn't see it coming, but the first shot came from the elevator lobby, grazing him in the left shoulder.

"Shit!" He dove to the ground and rolled through an open door into a smaller office. The windows of the office shattered around him, imploding glass everywhere. The wall nearest to the hallway was suddenly being chewed up, sending a cloud of drywall dust and pieces flying into the air around him. An otherwise calm and peaceful office setting had suddenly turned into a war zone, with him as its one and only target.

IV

Katherine was staring at a grid showing locations of every hospital in the GTA, Greater Toronto Area. She had highlighted the ones that reported significant number of virus cases. Clearly, the epidemic had spread from west to east for the most part. The rapidity and pattern of contagion pretty much corroborated that it was being spread by water, and some tests conducted on the tap water in the infected areas confirmed that conclusion. She stared at the grid and wondered to herself, *where would they hit next?*

Kelly looked over Katherine's shoulder at the map. "You know, if we take a completely mathematical approach to this, I'd say the odds are in favor of north Toronto being the next target," she said.

"Why?"

Kelly leaned over the map and traced the pattern of the infection with her pen. "With the exception of the hit at Rogers Center, which caused a sort of unilateral infection throughout the city, they seem to have been concentrating on moving west to east," she pointed. "The west end, especially by the airport, is a huge business and manufacturing district, causing a lot of collateral damage in itself. If I wanted to get the biggest bang for my buck as a terrorist, or whatever these fucks call themselves, I'd hit north Toronto next because that's going to hurt the city more than the east end. The 400 highway runs up through York, Markham, Vaughan and right on up to Barrie. A lot of people, very wealthy people, live in that corridor."

Janene came over and laid another sheet on the table. She'd been listening to their conversation.

"I agree with Kelly's theory. This," she pointed, "is a very large water treatment plant just west of the City of Vaughan. They call it "The Golden Pond," and it feeds water into this whole region," she circled with a finger. "It makes sense that if they're going to layer the city they'd want to hit this area next. It's the most logical target."

"How would we ever know if they dropped the virus into that? I mean, it's practically the size of a small lake," Katherine said as she looked at the map.

"Let's assume the worst. Let's say that they're gonna make a drop there, maybe even tonight. What we should do is get the Water Works Department to shut off the water to that whole region and examine The Pond to see if it tests positive," Kelly said.

"Wouldn't that just push another panic button, or maybe even alert the perps that we're onto them?" Janene asked.

"It could, unless we play a fake hand,"

"Yes, but the media. If these people don't see the rise in sickness, the media flashpoints, etc., they'll know something went wrong," Katherine said.

Kelly looked at her watch. "It's 8.15 p.m. If we move fast, we can get the Water Works Department to put out a notice to their customers in that area that service will be down temporarily for technical reasons, and meanwhile, we get them to check the pond tonight. If it tests positive, they drain it and restore business tomorrow. Meanwhile, get the major hospitals up there briefed and playing ball with us. They can leak some fake figures to the press about a sudden influx of flu cases, and the press of course will fan the flames and make the terrorist dick-heads happy that their next hit was a success," she smiled and took a long drag on her cigarette. Both Janene and Katherine were looking at her, each weighing the pros and cons in their heads.

Janene nodded, "Could work".

Moments later, they had Ross Fletcher down to their office and were briefing him on the plan. Ross was tired of running behind the train and cleaning up the wreckage. If this could put them ahead of the perps, then it was worth a try.

Ross set the wheels in motion right away. The Department of Water Works put a team on The Pond, and by midnight they had indeed detected a strong dose of the virus in the water supply. Ross had his team contact hospitals throughout north Toronto to brief their directors and key staff on the plan so that they would play along with it. Meanwhile, he had his media department prepare the press releases. By morning, the media would be reporting a new wave of sickness in north Toronto.

The Department of Water Works began a massive all-night project to send automated messages to their customers about the temporary cut in service, while teams of engineers worked throughout the night and well into the next day to flush the pond of the contaminated water.
For the first time since the attack had hit Toronto, the RCMP had an ace card in the game.

V

Richard Jacobs had taken over as the Director of Homeland Security at more or less the same time as the new Presidential administration had come into office, two years before. He had never personally agreed with the former presidential administration, which spouted propaganda that there were terrorists "on every street corner in America" and had attempted to create a state of panic in America just because someone managed to take down the twin towers.

He had been trained too well in the area of anti-terrorism to gloss over the flaw in the "official" story that Islamic extremists had succeeded in orchestrating the perfect destruction of two of the tallest structures in America.

Nonetheless, he had to keep his mouth shut. As much as America was the land of the free, it didn't gain someone working within the intelligence community any brownie points by spouting off one's personal views, especially when those views countered his own government.

He had waited, performed well at his job, and had gained the trust needed to be promoted to his current Director position. As such, it was his intention to ensure that Homeland Security did not become an abusive, intrusive hand of the government, violating people's rights in the name of "national security."

He had just finished reading the latest report prepared for him on the Canadian virus attack in Toronto. The new virus was spreading quickly, and the Canadian parliament had just passed a bill to initiate nationwide mandatory inoculations.

He hadn't gotten to this position by being just a good agency man and following orders; Richard Jacobs was a strategist and had a sharp mind for predictive forecasting. He balanced all the factors and decided on his approach to the matter. While he could sit back and wait to see what the RCMP did to handle this attack, it seemed that it was better to take an aggressive approach and help the Canadians to nail those behind this operation.

He picked up the phone, dialing directly to Ross Fletcher at the RCMP HQ in Toronto.

"Ross, this is Richard Jacobs, what the hell's going on up there? I've been reading the reports and I can tell that you're not saying everything you know or don't know."

"How much do you think you know?" Ross hedged, not wanting to tip his hand until he had a better grip on the situation.

"Well, it's not every day that I get calls from the President's office, but today I attended a meeting with him. He's being hit with a lot of crap right now because of the spreading epidemic along the US/Canada border. He wants to know the real dope so that he can figure out his tactic to deal with this."

"I haven't even told my own PM everything yet."

"I understand, sometimes silence is the better side of discretion."

Ross briefed Richard Jacobs on the salient points.

"So basically, this viral attack in Toronto is a precursor to what we can expect here in the States."

"Yeah, we think so."

"What's Keeno up to?"

"He's in Hong Kong checking into McDonald."

"From what I know of Keeno, wherever he pokes his nose he tends to flush out rats."

"That's putting it mildly," Ross said.

"Since Malcolm McDonald is an American citizen, I'll have some of my guys at the American embassy in Hong Kong check up on Keeno. He may need some help."

"Thanks."

"Keep me posted, Ross. I know you're knee-deep in shit right now, but it's starting to spread to my office now too."

VI

When the shooting momentarily abated, the wall and the door to the office where Keeno was huddled, were entirely shredded. Keeno hadn't fired a single shot yet, as he didn't want to give himself away. If he was outnumbered, which he suspected was the case, deception was his best strategy.

He waited as shards of glass and broken drywall clinked and thudded to the floor around him. He strained his ears for any sign of movement, but there was none. Using a piece of drywall he made a path through the fragmented glass, then crawled to the door and peered through a hole where he caught the subtle movement of someone coming nearer. The man was wearing black from head to toe, eliminating any distinguishing physical features.

Keeno prepared himself mentally and physically. He slowed his breathing while tensing his body, readying it to spring with lethal force. Seconds later, as the man eased his head through the shattered door, Keeno flashed his hand upward, grabbed him by the back of his neck, and drove his knife into his throat. It took only seconds for the man's body to go limp and lifeless, at which point Keeno dragged it into the office.

Keeno slipped through the door and darted across the hall into an adjacent room, just seconds before another figure appeared from the other end of the hallway.

He hid behind the office door, which was partially open, and pressed against the wall, waiting until he saw the figure stop in the middle of the hallway between the two offices. The man hovered like a shark, preparing to strike, and as he did, he glanced into the other office, where he caught sight of his dead comrade. The shooter then turned and looked straight into the office where Keeno was hidden. In the space of a second, the two men locked eyes before Keeno shot at him through the small crack in the door. The bullet slammed into the man's thigh.

Keeno used that precious second to dive out from behind the door before the shooter filled it with lead. As he rolled up onto his feet, he slipped his throwing knife out of his back pocket and let it fly. The knife sliced deep into the man's chest, cutting a mortal wound in his heart. For a moment, the shooter hovered, teetering on his feet as he looked down at the hilt of the knife and the blood seeping out from his wound. Then he mustered up what life was still in him, and raised his gun hand.

The cacophony of two guns going off in the small space was ear-shattering. Keeno's bullet slammed into the man and knocked him back into the wall, but not before the man got off a shot which cut into his side, ripping the skin and barely missing a rib.

As if this wasn't enough excitement for one day, he saw two more men running into the reception area to his right, pointing their guns at him. He dove for the wall as the room turned into a shooting gallery. He worked feverishly to snap another clip into his gun, but the blood on his hands from his wound was making it difficult. Just then, the glass above his head exploded, and a man torpedoed through the partition into the room, pointing a gun straight at Keeno's head as he did.

He wondered if this was it – *had his time come*? He waited for the bullet, but it never struck. Instead, he heard the report of another gun, and watched as the man's chest exploded, cascading blood against the far wall as his lifeless form hit the opposite wall with a dull thud.

Keeno just sat there for a moment holding his bleeding arm, until he recognized the familiar figure standing in the doorway.

"Jake, what the fuck!"

Jake stepped into the room, quickly reloading his gun as he did. "You ok?" he asked as he looked up and down the hallway.

"A little sore."

Jake came over to help him to his feet, "Do me a favor, if you're gonna have a gun fight, invite me too."

Keeno inspected his latest wound. "Thanks."

Jake was happy to see Keeno alive and not in a body bag. He motioned his head through the shattered office window towards the reception area, where two men in civilian clothes were checking out the bodies of the mercenaries, "Thank them too – Homeland Security. I met them in the lobby on my way up."

Keeno dabbed a piece of his shirt over the bullet wound to stem the blood loss. "How'd you know I was here and what the hell are you doing in Hong Kong anyhow?"

"I figured you might need some help, so I jumped a plane."

"Ross knows you're here?"

"By now he probably does. I grabbed the fastest flight to HK. I called Kelly when I landed and she told me where to find you. She had the coordinates from the transmitter frequency you sent her."

Keeno had forgotten all about the transmitter in his pocket. He reached in and pulled it out. It was still blinking. "Amazing this thing didn't get crushed in all the action," he said.

Keeno approached the two other agents, "I'm Keeno, thanks for the help."

"No problem, we got a call from our boss in DC, said you might need some back up. I'm Neil Hamilton and this is Jed Nichols."

"Any idea who these peeps are?" Neil asked as he pointed to the pile of dead men. "They had nothing on them to ID them."

"Mercenaries, low grade," Keeno joked, as he turned to see the body of the young Chinese receptionist, not more than nineteen or twenty years of age, steeped in her own blood.

Keeno leaned against the reception desk and pressed his hand against his skin wound. "Sometimes I think I hate this fucking job," he said to Jake, as he stared at the dead girl.

"What about McDonald?" Neil Hamilton asked, shaking Keeno's attention from the dead girl.

"He had a sniper set up to take me out, and these goons as back-up," Keeno pointed to the dead bodies nearby.

"We need to get you out of here," Neil Hamilton said, just as the elevators opened and a team of local police poured into the lobby. "I'll handle this," Neil said, as he turned to speak to the police.

They left the building moments later. "We'll go to the American embassy and call in to the RCMP," Neil said. "It's better if we let the Hong Kong Police clean up this mess. They'll figure out a shore story once they realize that the four dead guys are mercenaries. Even the cops here don't like to cross paths with the underground."

VII

Keeno sat at the conference table, popping painkillers as he waited for the call to begin. Fortunately, the American embassy kept a resident doctor on-hand, who had quickly stitched up the skin wound in his shoulder and side. For Keeno, it meant another couple of scars to add to his already ample collection – but he could live with that.

The large HD screen in front of him suddenly flashed to life, and he saw the faces of Ross Fletcher, CC – his Operations officer, Janene and Kelly sitting at a conference table in the RCMP CIC. On an adjacent screen, he caught his first glimpse of Richard Jacobs, head of American Homeland Security, who was with a few of his staff.

"Bring us up to speed, Keeno," Ross said.

Keeno told them everything that had occurred just before Jake and the American agents had arrived to save his bacon.

"Unfortunately, my conversation with McDonald didn't provide anything really useful, just a hunch." Keeno said.

"Which is?" Ross prodded him.

"When I confronted him about the RFID chipping that's when the mood of the conversation changed, so that tells me that McDonald is connected to this plot."

"What do you think needs to be done now?" Richard Jacobs asked Keeno.

Keeno let out a deep sigh. "They have the better hand, so we need to see what they do next, but I think we should be watching FAB-MED like a hawk, maybe even CJN at this point."

"Hmm. But this is China and we can't have Canadian and American agents nosing around that facility without a good reason – that would really set off explosions if the PRC got hold of that," Richards said.

"I agree," Ross concurred. "You two better get back here. If we find something substantial on CJN then we can take it from there. Besides, the Prime Minister told me that if we could provide proof that this whole virus outbreak was conclusively terrorist in nature that he would throw roadblocks in front of that emergency health bill. I think the recent events in Hong Kong will be enough to prove to him that we're stepping on the snake's tail."

Keeno was quiet as he listened to Ross. He wanted to stay in Hong Kong and find that bastard McDonald, yet at the same time he saw the logic of heading back to Toronto until they had something substantial, and with the number of people getting sick and dying from the virus, time was not on their side.

"Ok – we'll talk when you get back here," Ross said.

"Damn, I was just starting to enjoy China," Jake murmured loud enough for everyone to hear.

VIII

It was a large facility on the 53rd floor of the Bank of Montreal building in Toronto. Precautions had been taken to set up devices to scramble their voices through encoding equipment of the highest technical excellence. Anything said in the room would be distorted beyond recognition, which is why the "old man" liked to call it his "talking room" – a place where he could converse about anything, and with anyone, with infallible security.

Eight people gathered around a large conference table. One entire wall was a huge pane of glass that looked out over Lake Ontario.

Heading the meeting was a man who was a venerable icon of the banking institution. Although eighty-six years of age, with bleached white hair, he still carried himself with a strut that signaled he was in control.

When he entered a room, his somber attitude squelched any conversation, and people were quick to look up, waiting for him to speak. He had a reputation for biting, and few were interested in crossing paths with him.

His name was Harold J. Rosenfeld, but most people who were close enough to him referred to him as HJR or the "old man." He was the second wealthiest person in Canada, and headed up a banking empire that embraced not only the Canadian domain but also put him in league with some of the most powerful international bankers in the world.

He had financial subsidiaries and other commercial investments that spanned the globe. If the Canadian people actually knew where their banking money was invested, and what corrupt means he used to aggrandize his wealth, they might be less inclined to use his banking and financial services. He had major investments in the growth and manufacturing of chocolate in the Ivory Coast of Africa, where child slavery was a well-known fact. He had provided millions to sustain the development of oil resources in Sudan, not the least of which included funding for local factions to keep the "religious war" piqued between the Muslims of the north and the Christians of the south. Canadians, rightly so, would be shocked to know that this "pillar" of righteousness was, in fact, a snake in their midst. Nevertheless, his PR department kept up a good public face for the magnate.

He had long ago given up on any sense of remorse, humanity or other human feelings that he regarded as weaknesses. In his estimation, men of wealth, of his stature and league, had no time for fruitless concerns, so he thought. His world was fueled by an aggressive and relentless drive to do what "had to be done". He had long since passed the point where money was of any concern. In the worst of times, he would remain at the top of the list of wealthiest men in the world for generations. The banking institution, regardless of economic hiccups, was structured so that all roads eventually led back to refueling the very institution that was causing the major economic issues.

"Ladies and gentlemen," his voice began with a slight quiver in its tone, "by all indications our operation seems to be moving ahead as planned. I don't need to elaborate on all the details, as each of you possesses a brief in your hands," he paused. "In approximately seventy-two hours, so our sources inform me, the Canadian emergency health bill will go into effect as law. With that accomplished, we will see pressure mounting in the United States as the public outcry demands the same level of initiative from its own government. We will give them a matter of days to act, and if we don't see the expected response, then we will take an aggressive stand across the border to the south."

All eight faces stared solemnly at him. Each of the men and women in the room represented a constituent or a vested interest from major banking and financial institutions from across the globe.

Everyone who knew of HJR's scheme was, of course, interested in seeing him succeed, but no one wanted to tip their hand too much or to compromise their identity. If, in fact, the "old man" accomplished his goals to set the initiatives into motion, then everyone in that arena would benefit from the ultimate outcomes. If he failed, they could cut their mooring lines and sail out to sea with hardly a notice.

"I have prepared a short video presentation to bring you up to speed on the technological advancements being made on our chip implanting process, which we call, the *God Chip*. Enjoy the presentation."

The room was darkened as a blind descended over the large window and the lights were dimmed. A panel on the opposite wall retracted, revealing a massive screen on which the video began.

IX

Before boarding the flight from Hong Kong to Toronto, Keeno had called Janene, telling her not to send anyone for him, that he was taking a cab from the airport, and that she should meet him at their favorite coffee shop in downtown Toronto.

Ever since they had opened up to each other about their true feelings, Keeno felt closer to her. In a way, he didn't feel so alone in his world, she was there to talk to, to buffer his concerns, and mostly, he was happy that he could do something else with his life than just chasing down the criminal element. Yet, as much as he loved her, he could not help thinking that he might be setting her up for a huge disappointment. In the last two days alone he had been nearly killed two times. *What woman could possibly want to latch her rope onto a man with a death expectancy as high as his own*, he thought?

Nevertheless, as the cab came to a stop and he saw her standing there smiling at him, all his concerns seemed to melt away. As he stepped from the cab, Janene launched at him and planted her lips squarely on his; their first kiss - ever. He didn't even have time to breath as she pressed herself into him. Although he could feel his shoulder wound suddenly throbbing, the pain was numbed by the sheer pleasure of her soft lips against his.

She pulled back and looked him in the eyes. A vagrant tear rolled down her cheek. "If you ever get that close to being killed again, I'll do you myself," she said.

"Promise?" he joked.

"Don't push me," she said with a deadly eye and then she wrapped her arm around his. "You have no idea how happy I am to see you."

Keeno smiled, yet inside he was struggling with how to deal with the sudden overwhelming affinity from her. He had never experienced anything quite like it in his life. There was the special bond between himself and his mother, but that was love on a different order. Janene was like warm honey pouring through his veins.

He said nothing as they walked into the coffee shop, ordered coffees and sat for a time in relative silence. He suddenly realized a whole new side of Janene, one which he had not seen before, probably because he had been too busy avoiding telling her how he really felt about her. As they sat there staring at the street and sipping coffee, he saw a kindred soul, someone who enjoyed the same simple things as he did.

One of the greatest qualities of life on the farm with Uncle Lou had been the solitude and premium time he had for himself. Time and people did not interfere with the simple beauty and serenity of that life. Since moving to the city years ago, he had found it hard to find any time for himself. People and friends demanded attention, which is why he had finally opted for buying the small plot of land north of Toronto where he had a cabin, one horse, and enough space to wander about without hitting someone's fence line.

Janene seemed to understand the importance of silence, and did not take it as an insult that he wasn't talking or paying attention to her. It was a relief to know that if they decided to spend their lives together, he wouldn't have to expend all of his free time trying to entertain her, as he had experienced with other women who demanded this – as if they owned him.

When they arrived at the RCMP HQ, Ross Fletcher was sitting across from Keeno's desk listening to Katherine. Ross stood up and smiled, noticing as he did, that Janene had just released Keeno's hand. He couldn't help but smile inside.

"Welcome back."

"Thanks," Keeno said. He looked over at Katherine and could tell that she had been losing a lot of sleep since he last saw her. Her face was showing the strain of long hours and she was lacking the usual make-up and stylish hair. Nonetheless, she was still strikingly beautiful in any sense of the word.

"You look good there," Keeno said to her, as he walked over to the small conference table and dropped into a chair.

"I think you should hear what she has to say," Ross said.

Katherine turned to face everyone as they took up seats around the office. "I was just telling Ross that I think we're chasing a red herring on this virus attack."

She paused, but no one said a word, so she launched into her theory.

"Logically, if they're pressing to get legislation passed to usher in chip implants, then they must be way ahead in the research. They probably just need the green light to get going with official sanctions."

"I would tend to agree with her, especially after that whole conversation you had with Malcolm McDonald in Hong Kong," Ross said to Keeno.

"What do we know about RFID chip implants?" Keeno asked.

Katherine continued, "The subject of RFID chips being implanted in humans is actually not as controversial as you may think. RFID chips can be made so small that they can be implanted in less than twenty minutes, with only a small injection of anesthesia applied. The Japanese are already doing it with school children so that their parents can track them – like a GPS. Millions of pets around the world have RFID implants that allow owners to find them easily."

"How big is a chip?" Kelly asked.

Katherine took a sheet of paper and made a line one millimeter long and a dot next to it. "They can be this small – the size of a dot or a small line. Larger ones have batteries in them. Smaller ones, which are most typically used, are not battery operated but are activated or awakened when they receive a radio frequency tuned to their particular code."

"So right now, chips are mostly used for tracking and location purposes – right?" Jake asked.

"Yes. That aspect of the technology has existed for years. Most passports, driver's licenses and other documents you carry have RFID chips in them. When you swipe or scan your credit card to buy something – the RFID chip is the mind of that transaction. Some companies are now putting RFID chips into consumer products like blue jeans and car tires. In the good old days if you didn't want to be tracked you could use real money, but RFID chips are being imbedded in money these days, making every transaction traceable.

"Big brother," Keeno said.

"Precisely. At the University of Toronto, they've had a discussion group going about RFID chip research as it applies to humans. It was not my department but they often consulted with me because of hypothetical issues where a body might reject an electronic chip implant. So we used to collaborate on information between my department and the RFID research group."

"Were they actually implanting chips in people at U of T?" Keeno probed.

"No – that simply is outlawed in Canada."

"I had no idea U of T was involved."

"They're mostly looking at it from the perspective of the medical perks, but there's also been a lot of discussion about the downside of chip implants. I've sat in on student and faculty forums at U of T where heated discussions were engaged about the moral and ethical aspects of implanting human beings. It's a divided arena right now. There are those that see *huge* dollar signs on the horizon with RFID implants. Scientifically speaking, it's just a matter of time before the technology escalates to the point where they can develop a chip that diagnoses a body's physiological condition. What that means, is that the medical field could make a phone call to you and inform you that your red cell count is high and you should come in for a checkup and maybe even treatment. Or they can tell you that your heart rate or blood pressure is off and recommend the pills to resolve this. It all sounds good, until you realize that you're no longer in the driver's seat – someone else is monitoring you and telling you what to do with your body and your life."

"Sucks!" Jake said out loud to the room, but no one paid attention.

"We're looking at twenty-four hour surveillance. It's really no different than bar-coding everything that walks out of a store, except in this case they're bar-coding people." Katherine ended.

Keeno let out a deep sigh. His coffee cup was almost empty and the jet lag was starting to set in.

"Well… on that happy note, where do we go from here?" Jake asked.

Kelly lit up a smoke and handed one to Janene.

"You said that there is an RFID research group at U of T, who heads that up?" Keeno asked Katherine.

"It's actually a panel of people, composed of three senior faculty members who have selected a team of students to review papers and research information. It only started in this past year," Katherine answered.

Keeno's curiosity was stirred. "Who are they?"

Katherine said the names and for a long moment Keeno sat there, his face becoming more solemn as he did. Suddenly, he clenched his jaw and walked out of the room without a comment.

Jake watched as Keeno went through the door like a charging bull. It was then that it dawned on him what had set Keeno off, and he had a bad feeling that the shit was about to hit the fan – again!

X

Keeno parked his jeep in the faculty parking lot at U of T, jumped out, and whisked up the large concrete stairs that lead into the ornate central administrative building. Jake followed. They went down a familiar wing and as they did, Keeno spotted him and called out his name.

"Ralph!"

Ralph Ketchler had just packed up for the day and was heading home. He was about to take the back stairs to the parking lot when he heard a familiar voice, turned, and saw Keeno McCole bearing down on him like a train.

Keeno came right up to him, uncomfortably close. "We need to talk!"

Ralph felt cornered. He could already tell by the look on his face that he had found out about the one secret that he had tried to hide from his friend. There seemed no way of avoiding a confrontation at this point, so he turned around and led them back into his classroom.

"Why didn't you tell me that you are heading up RFID research at U of T?" Keeno yelled. His face was red and his eyes were intense as they bore a hole into the back of Ralph Ketchler's head. Ralph continued to stare blankly at his desk – finding it hard to face up to his old friend.

"Didn't it occur to you that this might be relevant to my on-going investigation? Considering the fact that Parliament just passed an emergency bill that authorizes opening the door to human RFID implanting – it didn't occur to you that maybe you should share some information?" Keeno glared.

Ralph stared at his feet. He had been a professor at U of T for twenty-one years. He had been admitted into the venerable league of senior faculty members some years back, and with that position had come not only increased wages, but other perks which allowed him to "float" into other departments. In his new position as senior faculty, he could teach his classes, but he could also choose to engage in other studies or forums that aligned with his particular zone of proficiency. Since he had specialized in microbiology and viral studies, the whole field of RFID chip implants had appealed to him so much that when they had first approached him about heading up the research team – his interest had been piqued instantly.

He slowly turned and looked Keeno in the eyes.

"I..." Ralph started to speak.

"In the last week, about seven different people have tried to kill me, not to mention the over 2000 people who have died from this virus. Have you been tracking this latest emergency health bill?"

Ralph nodded, feeling abashed.

"Then you know that this fucking bill has a clause in it to initiate research to corroborate RFID implants?"

Ralph said nothing but his eyes conceded.

"We're pretty sure that the people causing this virus attack in Toronto are the same ones pushing this bill, and now I find that *you* are heading the research team. So you tell me – what the hell is your connection to this?"

"It's much deeper than you can possibly realize my friend. The people behind this are men of great power and influence."

"I'm all ears," he stepped closer. Keeno looked into the saddened eyes of his friend and suddenly felt a tremendous sense of pain for Ralph – something was very wrong with his friend. The very fact that Ralph had purposely withheld this information from him immediately screamed that he was in some kind of trouble.

"I'm just the messenger Keeno, I'm bringing their research into the public forum, tacking on some credentials to it – that's all."

"What's in it for you?"

Ralph shuffled his feet nervously, "You realize that if I say anything, and probably I've already said too much, that I'll be a dead man. I don't care about myself – I just don't want those bastards to touch my wife," he said with pleading eyes.

"Ralph, people are dying by the hour because of this virus."

"Ok," he paused, "I was approached just over a year ago by a private group to oversee an RFID research program and to "evaluate" the value of RFID implants in humans. There was no research involved because they assured me that they had already developed the technology to the point where they had tested chipping humans very successfully. They didn't need corroborative evidence from me, or from the U of T. They just wanted our name to undersign their results and documentation. They needed me to set up a study group, entertain forums with select aspects of their material, and then undersign it with the University of Toronto stamp of approval." He shook his head, "I was just a salesman for the new and improved vacuum cleaner, that's all."

"What did they offer you?"

"Exclusive rights to publish future papers on their research findings in my name," Ralph paused and looked at him with pleading eyes. "It was a chance of a lifetime. Put yourself in my shoes. If they had in fact developed RFID technology to the point where it could be used diagnostically in the medical field, it would become the new wave of the future. It seemed, at least at the time, that it was an opportunity I couldn't pass up."

Keeno didn't know what to say, he just stared at Ralph, "How advanced is their research?"

"Very. They have a facility somewhere and they've been testing chip implants on people for at least a couple of years. I saw their results in a video presentation. It was shocking to see what they could do with those chips."

"You said that if you told me too much your life would be in danger, why?"

Ralph looked down at his feet and said nothing for a time. "When I saw the last video and what they could do with those chip implants, I realized that it was beyond anything I considered morally acceptable. When I originally agreed to undertake their project, I was doing it for medical reasons. That's how they presented it to me. As time went on, I realized that they had another entirely different agenda and I tried to back out. That's when I got an anonymous letter reminding me to stay on track and not reveal anything to anyone or there would be serious repercussions to myself and to my wife."

"How are you keeping this research under wraps if you're using students at the U of T?"

"Nondisclosure bonds; the participating students are being fed bits and pieces, nothing that reveals the true extent of the real research already done."

Keeno rubbed his eyes, "What can they do with these chips that made you go sour on their program?"

Ralph took in a deep breath and let it out slowly as he looked down at his feet again. He was shaking his head as he spoke, "I don't think they showed me everything, but the first video I saw, showed conclusively how the chip implants were providing infallible diagnostic reports on the physiological status of the test cases. It was amazing. They were getting reports back within seconds on the state of kidneys, heart conditions, low blood cell counts and even viral infections.

It was when I saw the second video that I realized the true nature of their RFID program."

"Meaning?"

"They have developed chips with the potential of resonating a frequency into a human body and synthesizing physiological conditions," Ralph sighed. "Their frequency resonation technology can cause untold damage, even fatal results in a human body."

"Like what?"

"Hemorrhaging, heart attacks, and more."

"What could be more than that?"

"The new chips they developed can actually pick up audio frequencies in the vicinity of the subject," Ralph said.

"What do you mean?"

"They can listen in on conversations, these chips are that sensitive. It's like having a built-in microphone in a human body."

Keeno shook his head, it sounded so incredulous. "Why didn't you tell me about this?"

"And what, have you chasing after people that disappeared into thin air? Have the RCMP snooping around just after they warned me and threatened my wife?" Ralph shook his head, "No, Keeno, as much as I trust you, I got myself into this mess and I was determined to get myself out without putting Betty in harm's way any more than I had already done."

Keeno understood Ralph's mentality and he probably would have done the same thing in his position.

"Any idea where their facility is?"

"No, I just know the code name for their program."

"What is it?"

Ralph took a deep breath and was about to open his mouth when the window behind his head shattered inward, spewing glass across the room. The high caliber bullet smashed into Ralph's left shoulder blade, cutting a wide hole that went through his chest and exploded outwards sending blood splashing onto Keeno.

Ralph's body pitched forward. Keeno reflexively caught him and lowered him to the floor.

Jake ran to the wall, pulling out his gun as he did and glanced through the shattered glass. He saw someone running away and tore out of the room after him.

Ralph's face was ashen white as the blood drained from his extremities in a last ditch effort to save itself. Keeno held his head off the floor as he began choking up blood and struggled desperately to say something. His body began to convulse in the final throes of death, yet, before his head slumped over, Ralph frantically grabbed for his portfolio and his eyes looked into Keeno's with desperation as if telling him something. Seconds later, Ralph Ketchler was dead.

For the first time in many years, Keeno felt grief. But there was no time for tears. He was madder than all hell and the rage exploded in him like a bomb going off. He grabbed Ralph's brief case, bolted out the door and caught sight of Jake running across the campus lawn in the distance. Keeno hurdled a railing, slid over the hood of a car and charged after them. He pulled out his cell phone as he ran and called Ross at RCMP.

"Shooter at U of T; we're in pursuit, heading for Bloor Street," he yelled into the phone.

He watched as the man in the distance ran across University Ave and then jumped inside a waiting car. Keeno's mind was focused on only one thing, nailing the bastard that murdered his friend. He finally caught up with Jake who was standing on the sidewalk watching the car speed away.

Keeno saw a woman stepping out of her Audi nearby. He flashed his badge, "RCMP ma'am," and then jumped into the car. Jake followed suit and slipped into the passenger side as Keeno shoved the gear stick into first and fish tailed the Audi across University Avenue, sending up a plume of burning rubber and smoke as it screeched away.

Keeno's cell phone rang, "I've got a chopper on its way – should be there any second," Ross said.

"The shooter's in a silver SAAB. Didn't get a license but they headed up University towards Bloor," he said back to Ross, and then tossed his cell phone to Jake. He floored the Audi and raced past other cars as if they were standing still and speared through a red light at Bloor Street barely missing several cars as he did.

Keeno was outraged. His mind had stopped working on any plane of logic. He wasn't measuring his actions against the risks. He wasn't seeing anything, in fact, except the vision of slamming into the shooter's car and venting the sheer rage that flamed inside of him.

Jake had seen him do this before – casting off the safety nets and charging the ramparts against all odds. These were times when you had to believe that you had nine, ten or twenty extra lives, because you were going to need them all.

Jake was listening to Ross Fletcher, who was still talking to them on Keeno's cell. "Chopper pilot says they turned left on Dupont Ave," Jake yelled out over the whine of the engine. No sooner had the words passed his lips when Keeno veered the Audi on a sharp left onto Davenport Road. The car skidded sideways as it fought to stay upright – yet against all odds, it didn't tip over and continued to charge down the street.

Jake knew exactly what Keeno was attempting. Both Dupont and Davenport converged up ahead. He was going to ram the shooters car. Jake watched as the intersection of Davenport and Dupont approached. He glanced at the speedometer as it edged upwards and held his breath, bracing himself for the impact that seemed inevitable. Just as they entered the intersection, the silver SAAB streaked in front of them like a torpedo and as it did Keeno twisted the steering wheel to the left, slamming the Audi into the back end of the SAAB just before it passed by.

Although happy that they hadn't collided full-on, Jake's momentary elation quickly came to an end as their

Audi began to spin out of control. He felt his entire world going tits up. The Audi screeched and screamed as it tore down the street, burning rubber and sending up a cloud of thick black smoke. It twisted uncontrollably and finally crashed into a parked car, coming to a bone-jarring stop. Jake lurched forward, his head slamming into the dashboard as he did.

At the same time, the impact to the rear end of the shooter's SAAB caused the car to fishtail out of control, then tilt onto its right wheels and flip over onto the hood, in which position it continued to screech down the road. It shot sparks twenty feet into the air as metal and concrete gnashed and screamed like two colossal giants thrashing at one another in a life and death battle. Finally, the car speared through a huge pane glass window and smashed into the inside wall of a building. This final collision blew out several more windows of nearby buildings, driving on-lookers to the ground.

Keeno pulled himself from the Audi and looked over at Jake who was squirming to get out through the passenger window. He ran around and helped him out of the car, "You ok?"

"Oh yeah, great ride. Can we do it again?" Jake said but his head had a deep cut in it and clearly he was still disoriented as he fought the urge to throw up.

"Stay here," he said, as he began running down the street, pulling the gun from the side holster as he did.

People had already gathered around the wreck, watching as a thick pall of black smoke started pouring out of the front of the SAAB, which seemed to still groan from the impact into the building.

As he approached, he saw two men trying to get out of the smashed car. The driver was covered in blood and seemed to be pinned against the steering wheel. The shooter was squirming to get through the passenger door, which was partially open but crushed to half its size.

Keeno's first instinct was to put a bullet into the man who had murdered his friend, but at that exact instant the shooter looked at him, almost pleading with his eyes for help.

"Shit!' Keeno said to himself. Sometimes he wondered why he was in the RCMP fighting terrorists at all when he had some inner well of compassion for people. As much as he tried to steel himself against moments like these, he couldn't just stand by and watch men die helplessly. He started running for the car to get them out. When he got within several feet of the vehicle, it exploded, sending a blast wave that knocked him to the ground like a sumo wrestler hitting him at a dead run.

Keeno's head hit the pavement causing his world to spin, and his ears ached from the concussion. After a moment or two, he looked up, the car and both bodies were engulfed in flames.

He just sat there watching, with no way of saving the two men he had wanted to kill just moments ago.

Jake teetered up behind him – still fighting the feeling that the whole world was turning the wrong way. His face was cut in several places and blood was oozing from the laceration on one side of his head. He looked at Keeno's face and saw the trauma in his eyes, "Sorry about Ralph, man."

Keeno let out a deep sigh as the flames danced and taunted him, reminding him that not only was he no closer to solving the case, but one of his best friends was now dead.

XI

By the time Keeno got back to the office, it was nearly 9 p.m. He slumped into his chair, still feeling the weight of recent events. Besides some bruises and a couple minor cuts, he had miraculously survived the car crash. Jake, on the other hand, was getting his head stitched up by the RCMP in-house doctor.

Keeno had gone straight from the car wreck to see Betty, Ralph's wife, to break the news to her that her husband had been murdered. He had spent the last two hours watching as the threads of her world came apart. After receiving the news, Betty sat down on her couch and stared at the floor without a word for what seemed a very long time. Indeed, no words were said between them until she finally raised her head and looked at him, tears rolling down her cheeks. "Married thirty-four years to the man and it never occurred to me that he would be gone from my life in this way. One assumes, or maybe we take it for granted, that our soul mate will be there to our last dying breath, but life has a way of crushing our illusions," she smiled weakly but the tears pooled and flowed even more.

Now, alone in his office, the vision of Betty sitting across from him, her eyes red and swollen from hours of crying, still haunted him. "Ralph always talked about you as a man of honor," she had said, as her lips quivered. "I hope his death was not in vain." Her words continued to echo in his mind.

The door suddenly opened, shaking Keeno from his reverie. Janene walked into the office with a large bag of Chinese food and sat down across from him.

"You ok?" she sensed his sadness.

Keeno let out a sigh, “Not really,” he subtly turned his head. The grief was choking his throat and he didn’t want to show it.

There was a long silence that ensued as he fought back the emotions inside. Finally, he let out a deep breath and turned to face her.

“He was a good man, one of the few people that I really loved.”

She had never seen Keeno so upset before.

“I got you some Chinese food,” she said softly, to help break his attention, “and a Molson’s – figured you needed a good beer about now.”

He forced a smile, but he still felt the crushing weight on him, the onus of having failed Ralph, of having put the man in a position where these bastards had taken him out.

She gingerly slid a plate of Chinese food toward him. “You’ll get them Keeno, you always do.”

He nodded, “I know, but it doesn´t change the fact that Ralph is dead.”

“It never will. But I think that Ralph would agree, you just need to do what you do best. That’s all he’d expect from you.”

Keeno stared at her for a long moment, realizing how much he loved her and yet, at the same time, he sensed the pain of Ralph’s death even more. If he lost Janene, it would just about push him over the edge, he thought to himself. And that’s exactly why he didn’t want anyone close to him; it hurt too goddamned much to lose people that he loved.

XII

Larry Egens, Operations Manager at FAB-MED, had watched his life morph dramatically in the past week. Up until recently, things seemed so predictable, so "normal." Now, it seemed that all his illusions of living an average life, following the American dream – working, raising a family, watching football on Sunday and all the other perks – had suddenly been overturned by the realization that all was not well in the world around him. It had opened his eyes to the fact that the fabric of society, as he once saw it, had been torn.

For the past several days since Keeno had warned him to be on his guard, he had been looking over his shoulder constantly. When he went home, there was always a black Lexus following him. When he woke up in the morning, the same or a similar car was parked not far from his house. Larry had taken Keeno's advice and called Frank Cairn at the Homeland Security's Philadelphia office, who confirmed that the vehicles were his agents watching out for him and his family.

Tonight, he had to finish some paperwork. He had a quarterly report to prepare, which had to be ready by the morning. His wife had needed the car today, so he had taken a cab to work – which accounted for the fact that the FAB-MED parking lot was devoid of any vehicles. When the eleventh hour rolled around, he rubbed his eyes and decided that it was a good time to get another cup of shitty vending machine coffee.

As he passed by the U-shaped loading dock, he saw something that shouldn't have been there – an eighteen-wheeler being loaded with pallets. He didn't recall having signed off on a late night shipment. He watched it for a moment longer when it struck him that something was very wrong about this picture. Larry raced back to his office, found the number in his coat pocket and dialed it up while dimming the office lights. As he waited, he had this sudden sense of fear surge through him like electricity – followed by the realization that he was alone in the building with no safety net under him. The image of Arnie Norton's battered and bloody body flashed into his mind once again.

XIII

In her six years of investigative work with the RCMP, Kelly had never failed to get to the bottom of any puzzle presented to her.

She had been the one who had cracked the "Montreal Bomber" case earlier that year, when no one else had. The man, calling himself by that title, had managed to set-off bombs in eight different towns and cities, injuring, but not killing, anyone. He had also managed to evade authorities for months because "he had no apparent pattern," which is what had been noted in the reports.

She had finally outsmarted him using what she liked to call "stupid-logic", which really amounted to "think-like-the-criminal". In the course of her forensic training, and her experience within the RCMP, she came to learn that if she could assume the perspective of the criminal it sometimes had the virtue of revealing things not seen through normal eyes.

The Montreal Bomber, who, as it turns out, was nothing more than a twenty-four year old computer geek with a perverse obsession for exploding bombs, was, in spite of earlier conclusions made by other investigative personnel, most definitely following a pattern. To understand the pattern, Kelly took his perspective, studied his modus operandi, tried to see the world through his eyes, which is when it hit her; he was following a geometric pattern across the grid, in tandem with the astrological clock. The geometry was a simple algebraic equation which Kelly's mathematical astuteness finally broke open; each targeted bombing was exactly proportional, in distance, to the *Golden Ratio*, Phi, which is 1.62. With that, she was able to precisely map-out where he would go next, which was to be Markham, in North Toronto.

She then took the particular dates when the bomber had hit previous centers, then Googled everything she could find and that's when it came to her; his bombings matched Zodiac predictions, each of which resonated the same basic message: *today you will leave your mark in the world.*

The bomber was symbolically-impulsive, push-button, waiting for Zodiac signs to catalyze him into performing his next attack – as if he was playing out his predetermined destiny. It didn't take her long to find the next daily horoscope where the same message was repeated, and alerting RCMP personnel, they were able to mobilize an undercover operation in the main business zone in Markham. Within hours they had identified a 1994 Nissan, parked for longer than any other car. The team moved in, discovered a trunk-full of explosives, and by checking footage from a video camera outside an adjacent bank building, they were able to catch the Montreal Bomber, who was about to board a bus at a nearby bus-depot.

She was tired, having lost a lot of sleep over this virus attack, and was starting in on her second pack of cigarettes. Yet, she fully intended to break the back of this new mystery before giving herself the luxury of sleep.

She stared at her timeline, showing the various incidents that had occurred over the past week since the first dead guy had shown up in downtown Toronto. *I'm missing something obvious*, she thought to herself.

The latest piece of the puzzle was the recent call from Larry Egens, informing Keeno about the illegal semi-truck being loaded up at FAB-MED. Keeno had assured Larry that they'd take care of it, and had immediately contacted Richard Jacobs at Homeland Security, who dispatched vehicles to follow the truck, while also ensuring that Larry got home safely.

Something about the Egens' phone call had stirred a question in the back of Kelly's mind. *If a semi was being loaded at FAB-MED, without Larry Egens' approval, then where the hell was their security*?

Yet, another piece of the puzzle suddenly floated into view – *if their security protocols were so stringent at FAB-MED, then how did Arnie Norton get in and out of their plant wearing civilian clothes?* That anomaly led her to the next obvious dot in the matrix, the fact that the security cameras at the University of Toronto had been compromised. Security, security and more security – *somethin' really stinks here*, she thought.

She called up her contact at Homeland Security in Philly and within minutes he was able to provide her with the profile and information of people employed in FAB-MED's security team. She ran the names through a data-base to see if any of them matched known IDs in Canada, but nothing came up. Then something occurred to her; it was one of those, "you gotta be kidding" epiphanies that she had missed as too obvious. She called up the night watchman's desk at the University of Toronto.

"My name is Kelly, I work with the RCMP," she said.

"Yeah, and I'm Charlie Brown," the night-watchman said with a cynical tone.

"Listen asshole, if you prefer I can send down a couple of RCMP officers and you can repeat that verbal diarrhea to them - your call."

"Ok, calm down! I get prank calls all the time at this time of night," he quickly back-peddled in his defense.

"Do you have a computer in front of you?"

"Of course," the man said.

"Give me your email address, I'm sending you a few photos. I need to know if you recognize any of these guys." A moment later he came back to the phone.

"Yeah, I know one of them. New guy, by the name Jim – I think."

"Jim Vaughn?"

"No, Jim Ellison, but the picture you sent is a definite match."

"When did you last see him?"

"When I started my shift at 5:30, he was investigating the shooting of Professor Ralph Ketchler."

Kelly smiled to herself. *I bet he was investigating it*, she thought.

"Thanks."

Now she had her finger on the pulse. Jim Vaughn was a real link. He worked for security at FAB MED and had infiltrated the security at the U of T under false ID.

The next question, she thought to herself, *why kill off Ralph Ketchler, right in front of two RCMP officers? He must have known something that was critical to them, making his murder an immediate necessity.*

Ralph Ketchler's briefcase was still sitting by Keeno's desk, where he had dropped it after returning from seeing his friend murdered. Kelly grabbed the briefcase, started leafing through its contents until she found a paper with a written notation at the top of the page; RIIP.

This looks a good place to start, she said out loud.

She lit up a smoke and started reading.

Chapter 5

I

Carol Bielaska worked the graveyard shift in the forensics unit at the OPP in Toronto. She had been doing it for three years now with Lacie Martin as her mentor during that entire time. Lacie had been the veteran at forensic analysis, and she had taken Carol over the hurdles and through the hoops of criminal investigation. Carol had learned to dissect the remains of bodies, the burned or disfigured pieces of what used to be a human being, or the smallest piece of DNA in order to solve murders and all manner of crimes. She usually approached her work with a tacit excitement, even though it could sometimes be unequivocally gory, repulsive and even sickening.

Today however, she was nervous and still shaken by the death of her friend and mentor, Lacie Martin, who had been murdered not three meters from where Carol was standing. She found it hard to accept the fact that her partner had been stabbed to death by someone who had managed to make it through three security access doors into the inner sanctum of the Ontario Provincial Police Toronto HQ.

She stole another look at the spot on the lab floor where she had found Lacie lying in a pool of blood.

No one had found any clues about the killer, as if he knew exactly how to navigate his way in. The whole affair had resulted in a major shake-down within the OPP. Security measures had been stringently tightened up, with a battery of new background checks on every OPP personnel. In effect, everyone was watching their back and watching everyone else in some macabre nightmare of "who killed Lacie?"

Carol went into the database and opened up the file that Lacie had been working on just before she was murdered. She played back the narrative and watched the video as the microscope zoomed in on the virus. When the video ended, she clicked on another small video segment, only 67 seconds in length. Days ago, when she had clicked on that segment of video, it was so blurred that she had relegated it as useless, probably just an error in a recording process; but this time she decided to watch it through to the end before archiving the documents.

Close to forty seconds into the footage it was still just a blur, when suddenly, an image started taking shape. Carol leaned closer to the computer as the picture began to morph into a face. At sixty seven seconds into the recording, the footage stopped with the microscope clearly focused on a face staring right at the lens.

"Oh my God," she covered her mouth. Her throat suddenly constricted and she felt nauseous at the sight of him. She stared at that face, her eyes watering up as she did. It took her several minutes to calm herself. Then she watched the video again and then copied it onto a flash drive. She left the building, walked up the street and hailed a cab – looking over her shoulder as she did.

II

Janene had insisted that Keeno sleep over at her place that night. In fact, she wouldn't even take a "NO" from him and drove him straight to her apartment. She fed him, gave him coffee and then fixed up her couch for him.

Keeno smiled but otherwise was relatively silent most of the time, still upset over Ralph's death. He remembered lying down on her couch, falling asleep, and that's pretty much all he remembered. When he woke up in the morning, she had breakfast and coffee ready. Somehow, during the night, he had shaken himself out of his mourning.

"Sleep ok?" she asked.

"Felt more like being unconscious. I must have been really out of it."

"You're looking better."

Keeno smiled, "Thanks."

"Next time, maybe you don't need to sleep on the couch," she leered.

"Sounds good to me," but even as he said the words, Keeno's mind was already racing ahead to something else.

When they got to the office Kelly was interviewing a lady. "Hey guys, this is Carol from OPP Forensics. You need to see this," she clicked excitedly to the video footage on her computer as Keeno and Janene looked over her shoulder.

"Who is that?" Keeno asked.

"His name is Molijnet Cryzki. He's an OPP officer," Kelly answered.

"Shit! I knew it had to be someone inside," Keeno exclaimed. "You can't just walk through OPP HQ straight to their lab unless you've got some kind of pass."

"Exactly," Kelly said. "Look at his right hand."

Janene leaned closer to the computer. "He's holding a knife."

"Right!" Kelly said. "He's the guy that did the lab technician," she said as he nodded at Carol who sat next to her.

"Why didn't we see this clip before?" Keeno asked.

"Oversight," Carol answered. "No one expected anything of value on the video footage which was recording microscopic entities. Who would have thought that there was a short segment showing the killer?"

"But how would a microscope of that magnitude suddenly be trained on him?" Janene probed.

"When Lacie's body was autopsied they found a lump on the back of her head and traces of her scalp on the joystick that operates the microscope on the control panel. When he jabbed the knife into her midsection, Lacie probably fell backwards, hitting the joystick with the back of her head which shifted the scope to him. These machines are designed to focus on anything they are aimed at, until they get a clear resolution. That's why it took nearly a minute for the microscope to produce the picture of him. The chances are one in ten thousand that this could have happened."

"Where is this guy?" Keeno asked.

"Conveniently, he's on vacation and not due back to OPP for another two weeks," Kelly said. "We've made a few calls and no one knows where he's vacationing either."

"Ok – at least we know who took the virus, and who might be spreading it, if it's the same guy," Keeno said.

"Let me take Carol up to our debriefing area so they can get all of this on record, and then I'll tell you some more juicy stuff," Kelly said. Moments later she returned and lit up a cigarette. She told them everything she had found out about Jim Vaughn, the security guy from FAB-MED. As Keeno listened, he no longer felt sad about Ralph's death – he was pissed.

"That's not all. I went through Ralphs' briefcase and I found a file in there called RIIP."

"Which is?"

"All his notes about RFID chip implants."

"I wonder what RIIP stands for?" Janene posed.

"That is the question which might lead us to the real assholes behind this," Kelly said, as she inhaled on her smoke.

III

Jake had taken Katherine home, shortly after Keeno walked out the door with Janene. He wasn't distraught about Ralph Ketchler's death, not in the way that Keeno was, but he was certainly concerned about Keeno.

Katherine invited him up to her apartment for a drink. She poured a glass of wine for both of them.

"Thanks," he sipped on the wine.

"Keeno was pretty beat up about his friend's death."

"He doesn't usually get this way. To be honest, in all the years I've known him, this has only happened one other time."

Katherine sipped her wine and just watched Jake.

"When he was eleven, he lost his uncle; he was quiet for a week after that. I mean, this is a guy that you can't kick down, but man, was he down. I saw that same lifeless look in his face last night after the car chase. He looked beaten," Jake sighed.

"What about you, what gets you down?"

Jake smiled. "Women."

She tilted her head playfully. "Women, indeed! You don't seem like a guy that would have women-issues."

"I'm not. I'm just disappointed that I haven't found a woman who can keep up with my lifestyle."

"Oh, you mean chasing criminals, terrorists and dodging bullets – as if that wouldn't be a downside for a successful and lasting relationship?" she teased.

"And so you understand my dilemma, unhappily single."

Katherine smiled, but inside she was sizing him up. She was fascinated by him. His utter transparency and complete frankness made him so diametrically opposed to anyone she had ever met before.

"Why do you guys do this? You're always putting your lives on the line?"

Jake got a faraway look in his eyes, "Why do I do it – to protect God and country, of course?"

"Somehow I doubt that. You don't strike me as the patriotic type."

"When I was twelve, we were walking home one day from school when I saw these kids beating up on this girl. She probably wasn't more than ten or eleven, and these three older boys were pushing her around. They knocked her to the ground and all three of them started kicking her. I got so pissed that I ran across the street, tackled two of them, and pretty much grounded their faces into the pavement before Keeno dragged me off of them. There was blood everywhere and of course I got a lot of shit for it from my parents. The school wanted to suspend me for violence and insisted my parents send me to a behavioral counselor, but I told them all to shove it. It was a rough time because I got the cold shoulder from everyone. The only person that stood by me was Keeno.

"And the girl?"

Jake smiled. "She was my first girlfriend, of course! Anyhow, it was after that I decided to go into law enforcement. I figured the best way to use all these muscles and my bullheaded "fuck you" attitude was to channel it into nailing assholes," he smiled.

They spoke for an hour more, getting to know one another and ambling their way through the evening. Close to midnight, Katherine got up to get some more wine, and when she came back she found Jake slumped over on her couch, fast asleep.

IV

Molijnet Cryzki had just arrived in New York City on his second week of his presumed "vacation" and checked into the Marriott near Times Square, a room that cost a "mere" $650 a night. Expenses were of no concern, *and why would they be?* he thought, since he was executing their plan flawlessly. He had successfully spread the viruses in several locations in Toronto and was now awaiting his orders to do the same in the Big Apple. Tomorrow, he would go to Rockefeller center, pick up the package and await his next instructions.

Molijnet felt a certain sense of exhilaration about being in New York City, knowing that he could be the one to hit them with a real terrorist attack.

When this job was done, he would go back and resume his normal life at the OPP. In due time, he'd fade into the woodwork, leave the OPP and move to the Caribbean or somewhere where he could enjoy his millions.

While most people would consider his actions monstrous and murderous, his perspective was quite different; he had one life and he intended to live it to the fullest. He had been raised in the west end of Toronto with a family of five brothers and sisters. His father and mother had emigrated from Russia. He had attended high school and then enrolled with the OPP just over six years ago.

Although he had done well within the OPP and had moved up several ranks, he had never achieved anything more than a sufficient level of income. As the years progressed, Molijnet's familiarity with the workings of syndicated criminal networks and the underworld gave him the idea that there was a lot more money to be had in crime than in stopping it.

Some cops had gone sour, engaged in drug dealing with the very dealers they were supposed to bust, or had become party to illegal syndicates, making huge kickbacks by protecting them instead of busting them. Molijnet watched, looking for the proverbial hole in the fence, a way to milk the dark side without exposing himself.

His "dream" came true one day when he met Camilla, a stunningly beautiful woman with a mixture of French and Turkish background. They had met one night by "chance" at a club and the relationship quickly progressed. Camilla exploited his sexuality, giving him more than he thought possible, and increasing his palate for sex exponentially. She engaged him in fine dining and expensive clubs, all of it designed to whet his appetite for the more expensive things in life – things he could never afford on an OPP salary. Unknown to him, Camilla was testing him and luring him deeper into the rabbit hole. She had led him down the golden path, the river of wine and honey, the traditional and yet delusional road where men were turned into assassins, molded into killers with hopes of an idyllic afterlife. He basked in the sensual world of sex, food and entertainment, all of which Camilla had opened up to him.

When he was firmly entrenched, she opened the next door to him, wherein he received a text message from Camilla telling him to meet her at a warehouse on the outskirts of Toronto. Drawn by her magic, he arrived at the location and was ushered into a room by a stranger before he had a chance to decide otherwise. He was asked to sit down in front of a small table with a microphone on it. There was no sign of Camilla to be seen anywhere. In fact, he never saw her again.

"Thank you for coming," a voice said from a speaker in the ceiling. "We need to know what your level of commitment will be."

"That depends on what you're offering and what you need," he answered matter-of-factly.

"Complete dedication – a willingness to do anything we ask you to do – and in return, your personal accounts will accrue substantial funds."

"How substantial?"

"Beyond your dreams - enough to retire and live a life of luxury."

He paused to consider the options, but he didn't have to think long or hard. In truth, he was in – hook, line and sinker – having become obsessed with the lifestyle that Camilla had revealed to him. He craved luxury, to be basking in money, sex and women. He simply could not envision himself returning to the salary of an OPP officer and living his life chasing after criminals.

"So you want someone killed?"

There was a long pause that ensued, until the door opened and three men walked in, two of them had masks on. The man in the middle, wearing little else than a torn and ratty t-shirt and a pair of pants, was made to sit on a chair in the corner. The masked men stood on each side of him.

"Open the drawer," the voice said through the speaker.

He did so and found a gun with a fully loaded clip.

"Shoot the man in the chair," the voice said.

Molijnet picked up the gun, wondering to himself as he did, *what had the man done to deserve to die? Was he just another person, like himself, who had failed these people and now was nothing more than a target for their newest recruit? Or did it matter at all what or who he was? They were testing him to see if he could kill without provocation.*

For a split second he did hesitate. He had taken his oath as an OPP officer and dedicated himself to protect and to serve. But now he was being invited to engage in the worst crime of all – murdering another human being. If he refused and walked away he would never get another chance. Maybe they would put a bullet in his head before he left this very room.

He felt the sweat trickling down his neck while staring at the man sitting on the chair in front of him. The man stared back, his face ashen white, his lips tight and his eyes revealing stark terror in anticipation of what was about to happen.

It was like a dream, some drug induced nightmare, and yet, he raised the gun, aimed and fired two rounds into the man's body, splattering blood against the wall behind him. The man's limp form toppled to the floor.

There was a moment of exhilaration as the adrenaline rushed through his system. There was no sense of guilt or remorse about having just murdered a man whom he knew nothing about. What followed was purely impulsive and unplanned, and surely showed the depth of Molijnet's cruel and corrupt nature. He aimed the gun at one of the two men still standing, and fired a shot into his head. Then he did the same to the other man before he could move. Both bodies crashed to the floor, leaving three men dead in a heap.

There was a long silence during which the only sound he could hear was that of his own heavy breathing. The moment seemed almost orgasmic for him. He had just murdered three men, and it felt as good as anything he could remember having done.

"Very good," the voice boomed from the speaker above. "We will be in touch."

When he left the warehouse, he knew for certain that he had categorically convinced these people that he was the man for the job. The next day, he received notification of a bank account opened in his name in the Cayman Islands, into which had been deposited $200,000, over double his normal annual salary.

Six weeks later, he was called to a private location north of Toronto, where he was briefed and prepared for his mission. That had been four weeks ago.

V

The Prime Minister of Canada entered the conference room with a solemn look on his face. The room, located adjacent to his main office, was the one place in Canada where its leaders could talk about anything without the slightest fear of it ending up in the wrong hands.

Five men and one woman sat around the conference facility, each one a senior member of the Conservative party.

"Gentlemen, and Maggie," he nodded to her, "we've got a serious situation on our hands. You've read the brief from Ross Fletcher, head of RCMP Ontario. The epidemic in Toronto is unquestionably terrorist-related, although I use that word very loosely, since this attack does not carry the usual markings of a foreign terrorist cell. It is far too organized, and typically speaking, terrorists prefer more dramatic results which they can instantly lay claim to. This entire episode, to date, has been unclaimed by anyone.

"The RFID chipping, as shown in the last part of this report, appears to be the final objective of these people.

"I am no authority on RFID chips, but I certainly have done my share of study on the subject in the last several days, and clearly, this is not something we want to legislate into Canada. The report speaks for itself," Norman paused to group his thought process. He was addressing his closest allies in his cabinet – it was time to skip the rhetoric and protocol.

"Honestly, guys, we have to step off our political platform and take an honest look at the future. What we decide here and now about this emergency health bill can have disastrous effects on our country, on our world. What are we looking at? Our kids getting implanted with GPS chips, monitored 24-7, their conversations echoed through a microchip in their arms so that some technician somewhere can spy on them and report them if they're smoking or hanging out late? Or worse, people being watched by some “big brother” to make sure they are toeing the line, not subversives, or what? What are we committing our future generations to if we endorse this bill or let it go through?”

René Norman stood there staring at the table for a moment, and then looked up at the solemn faces that watched him. He rubbed his eyes. He hadn’t slept for two days now, and the stress was wearing him a bit thin. “I want you to know which way I’m going with this. I warn you, if you stand by me, you could go down with the ship.”

No one moved. No one said a thing.

“I’m going back into the Legislature tomorrow to veto that emergency bill and I’m going to make a real stink about it too, in the hopes that maybe I can sway some of those people to join the ranks of us who want no part of that clause. I will stand up for emergency inoculation of our citizens to protect them from this virus, but I won’t endorse any part of that bill, and I am willing to put my career on the line in taking that stand.”

He smiled at them, “I know in Politics 101 it’s tantamount to political suicide, but right now, if I don’t do something to stop this, we’ll have a far bigger mess to clean up later, if it can ever be cleaned up.”

“What about the virus?” Maggie spoke up.

“We propose our emergency handling, which I had drafted up today, to authorize federal purchase of two million doses of anti-virus from any company that can come to the table with a workable antidote.”

“That’s going to be a tough pitch, considering the NDP and every other camp are vying for your position and fanning the flames to discredit you and the party." Maggie said.

"Yep, like I said, our ship's taking in water right now. Question is, are you going to stay on-board or bail? I leave that up to you, but tomorrow I am dropping the gauntlet. I'll be damned if, on my watch, some pricks somewhere end up getting the green light to change this country into some Orwellian state.

VI

Richard Jacobs, Director of Homeland Security, had been on the phone with Ross Fletcher at RCMP off and on for hours.

Jacobs had his predictive team working all night, projecting every possible scenario based on the information received from the RCMP. After eleven hours of back and forth, the results had come through to his office. Their extrapolations showed a 58% chance that the next attack would surface in New York City. The whole subject of predictive intelligence was a tricky arena at best. While there wasn't a single bit of hard evidence to show that the people behind the Canadian attack were even vaguely considering hitting the Big Apple – the conjectural formulas still pointed to that possibility, on the simple premise that if you wanted to hurt America and leverage its government, New York City was still the tender spot.

It was the ultimate nightmare for him as the Director of Homeland Security. His agency had been conceived in the wake of the 9/11 attack, and now the Canadian RCMP were telling him that their intelligence also pointed towards a conceivable attack in the "city that never sleeps."

Richard rubbed his eyes, and like his counterpart at the RCMP Toronto office, he was feeling the strain. Lack of sleep was one thing, but the more tangible stress was the anticipation, like tying a 100-pound weight to a string above your head and waiting for it to eventually drop.

His cell phone rang. It was Ross Fletcher.

"Hi Ross."

"Looks like we may have found who's been spreading the virus," Ross downloaded the details about Molijnet Cryzki to Richard.

"Based on the fact that Molijnet has disappeared off the grid, it seems that you would be well advised to step-up security measures in NYC. Additionally, we haven't had any more reports in the last 48 hours of escalating flu cases in other parts of Toronto, which makes me think that they accomplished what they wanted here and now they might be headed your way."

"Ok – send me all the stuff you have on Molijnet. Let Keeno know that the eighteen-wheeler out of FAB-MED just arrived in Timmins, Ontario. I had my guys follow it there."

"We'll get satellite surveillance onto it and track it from there, thanks!" Ross said.

VII

The unassuming-looking oriental man, wearing a black tie, white shirt and outdated black suit, flew in from Shanghai, landing in Chicago where he then connected with a flight to Toronto. He had only one carry-on; a customized black-case containing a built-in coolant system and several small sealed canisters of vaccines.

His arrival had already been cleared in advance by Canadian immigration and border authorities, who ushered him to the waiting car. He was driven to a hospital facility near Toronto Pearson International Airport, where a team of medical personnel and specialists were standing by.

Canadian Ministry of Health officials and the medical establishment in Toronto were working on borrowed time now, and they knew it. Hospitals were overflowing and the death-count was already well over any previous mortality rate for a recorded epidemic in recent history.

The CJN representative turned and faced the other nine medical people in the room.

"Thank you for having me here," he said, with polished English and a faint undertone of his mother tongue. "My name is Paul Chang and my client company, CJN Holdings, as you well know, has offered a very reasonable price tag on the quantity of vaccines that you require on an immediate basis. I have brought samples of each vaccine, which you can test to ascertain the efficacy of the vaccine, at which point, if all is satisfactory, we can finalize the paperwork and engage our services. We can have the vaccines on their way to you within twenty-four hours of finalizing our contractual terms," he smiled in a business-like fashion.

The lead-man of the Canadian team took the case of vaccines and handed it off to his people, who promptly took off to their stations to start the tests. The lab had been prepared with samples from every hospital where flu infections had surfaced in the last week. They would match the vaccine to the respective pathogen, then observe and document the results. If effective, he was authorized to negotiate payment for enough vaccines for two million people.

VIII

Tom Sneider had just come back from doing a short walk-through of the processing plant at FAB-MED, putting on a good show for his employees, inspecting their work and chatting them up as he went along, but his main purpose was to ensure that everything appeared as normal as possible.

With the RCMP snooping around, and the fact that Keeno McCole had evaded death two times in the past week, he knew that the possibility of his plant coming under more scrutiny was all too real.

His cell phone rang as he entered his office and he answered abruptly, “You took a chance by sending your security man up to Toronto the last time. Although it worked, we cannot underestimate their law enforcement agencies anymore. Remember, any compromises and the matter will be dealt with most summarily,” the authoritative voice said with a thread of threat.

“I understand. I sent him off this morning to make sure RIIP gets closed down. When he’s done there, I’ll make sure he disappears off the grid for a while. Anyhow, no one is going to find him in the middle of the Canadian Shield.”

“You better be right about that,” the voice said, and then the line went dead.

Tom stood unmoving, staring out the window at the expansive parking lot that bordered three sides of FAB-MED like a huge moat surrounding a castle. He had known that he was stretching the envelope by sending Jim Vaughn, his own employee, to Toronto to enlist as a security officer at the University of Toronto. But, it was a necessary move in order to open all the doors for them to temporarily house the virus there and to act as insurance that all went as planned. Vaughn was on his payroll, answered to him only, and had been loyal. Possibly, the right word wasn't so much loyal, but dependable. He was, after all, just a mercenary who was being paid the right price, but the right price evoked the right level of commitment and loyalty from men such as Vaughn.

He knew Jim Vaughn had two vices – money and women. With that, he made sure that he had plenty of both, just like the sugar-daddy that keeps his prostitutes on a short leash by providing for their drug-addictions.

He'd come across Vaughn when he had dropped in at a local strip-joint late one night in nearby Trenton. Vaughn was sitting alone at a table watching the strippers, so he struck up a conversation with him and several beers later, he had learned enough to know that he was a potential asset to him.

Vaughn had been put through the hoops as Special Forces. He'd been trained in every form of combat known. He was a walking lethal weapon – trained and tested by Uncle Sam himself. Tom had been looking for someone that he could put on his payroll under the guise of one of the company security people, someone he could use for special services and who would have the perfect cover.

In view of his new association with the "old man" and McDonald, Tom needed someone in his own camp to do his bidding.

His intercom lit up, breaking his train of thought. "Sir, there are two men here asking about Jim Vaughn," his secretary announced.

"I'll be right down."

Tom arrived in FAB-MED's football field-size reception area to find himself facing two muscle-bound men with tattoos on each arm, short cropped hair, and ex-military written all over them.

"I'm Tom Sneider, VP of Operations here at FAB-MED."

"Hey man, I'm Tony Pinachi and this is Phil Allens. We're old buds of Jim Vaughn. We were on detail together in Iraq. We heard he was working up here and since we were driving through Trenton from New York, we figured we'd stop in on him," he smiled.

"Unfortunately, Jim just left this morning. He's off on a project and won't be back for a while."

"Ahh shit, too bad. We haven't seen him in a while."

"I can take a message," Tom said.

"Yeah sure, tell him to give us a call. Here's my cell phone number," he handed him his card.

"Do my best," he shook their hands and watched them leave. When he got back to his office, Tom dialed Vaughn. He needed to know if these guys were legitimate, or if they were just posing as Jim's friends. He couldn't afford any more people snooping around the operation.

"Yeah," Vaughn answered.

"Two guys just came by to visit you, a Tony Pinachi and Phil Allen. They said they were with you in Iraq and were passing through town on their way from New York. Are they for real?"

"Yeah, they're legit. I think I mentioned to Tony that I was working at FAB-MED, maybe in an email or something."

Tom felt more relieved about the matter, "Ok – how's it going up there?"

"Good, I landed in Toronto two hours ago and jumped a flight to Sudbury where I am now. I'll catch up with the truck soon. Everything is on schedule."

"Call me when you're there."

"Sure."

Tom looked at the business card that Tony Pinachi had given to him. *What the hell kind of name is Pinachi,* he thought to himself, as he dropped the card on his desk.

Two miles down the road, in a parked car, the same two men who had posed as Vaughn's friends were recording the conversation that Tom Sneider had just finished with Jim Vaughn. They sent the recording to Homeland Security.

Posing as former military friends of Jim Vaughn, they had done their best acting job in years. Surveillance on FAB-MED, very early that morning, had shown that Vaughn had taken a flight to Toronto. Homeland Security checked up on his background and quickly put together a plan to flush the rat. The two agents were rapidly selected, briefed on the profiles of Tony Pinachi and Phil Allen, actual friends of Vaughn, and used the ruse to get to Tom Sneider.

The entire purpose of the operation was to get the business card into Tom's hands. They knew full well that if Tom Sneider was involved, he would immediately call someone, if not Jim Vaughn, to determine if they were in fact legitimate friends. The tactic had worked and the small transmitter chip imbedded in the business card had picked up and relayed the entire conversation with perfect clarity.

IX

He watched Janene as she walked toward him, through the lobby of the RCMP building. For a woman who had not slept more than a few hours each night for the past week, she still looked remarkably beautiful – certainly from his perspective at least. Clearly, she was choreographing her walk in such a way that all her physical attributes contributed to the effect. She had that down to an art of subtle sophistication, a combination of understated elegance and sex appeal, all crafted into one package, which she managed with effortless finesse.

Some women from his past had called him a sexist for his views about the gender, but in Keeno's mind, if you were a woman, then you should simply act like one. He didn't objectify them as sexual objects – but he certainly expected them to exemplify the beauty of mankind. Some women appreciated his views, while others resented it, feeling marginalized and judged by him.

She wrapped her arm around his and they walked down the street for lunch.

An hour later, when they returned to the office, Jake looked up at them. "Uhh, hello!"

Keeno smiled, "What's up?"

"Well, I talked to customs and they checked the manifest on that semi when it passed through late last night."

"And…"

"It's filled with chemicals compounds produced at FAB-MED – nothing else special."

"Where was the truck headed?"

"To a company in Sudbury that uses the chemicals for medical drugs that are distributed into the Northwest Territories."

"Could be a cover for something else."

Calvin Cole stuck his head into the office at that point, "Ross wants you guys to come up to CIC right away."

"We're on our way."

Ross was sitting at the conference table with a remote control in his hand, clicking it at a screen with a map projection of Canada.

"Got some good news, guys," he said with a sparkle in his eye. "I just got a call from Richard Jacobs at Homeland Security. They pulled off a nice little ruse at FAB-MED a few hours ago. Found out that Jim Vaughn, your security boy who slipped in and out of University of Toronto, is on his way to Sudbury to connect up with that truck shipment from FAB-MED. Turns out he's former Special Ops, and he did a tour of duty in Iraq until he got discharged from the US military."

"Certainly not honorably?" Jake asked.

"Definitely not, this guy was dirty as hell. He was found making drug deals over there. When the MPs found out about it, he got a court martial and was sent off with his walking papers. Less than eight months later, he connected up with Tom Sneider at FAB-MED, and was hired on as part of their security detail."

"Apparently, Vaughn has a weak spot for strippers, so Homeland Security interviewed some of the strippers at one of the clubs he attends, and found one that he was with just last night. They encouraged her to spill the beans on Vaughn, and apparently, in a drunken stupor last night, he let on that he was making a special trip to the Canadian northland."

Ross flashed a laser pen on the map in front of them. "That is where he is headed right now."

"You're kidding me," Keeno said, as he squinted to see the name on the map, "Rankin Inlet!"

"That's what the stripper told them and they checked it with her a number of times."

"That's practically the North Pole," Jake said.

"What the hell is in Rankin Inlet?" Keeno mused out loud.

Katherine Riggs suddenly spoke up, "Maybe the word RIIP refers to Rankin Inlet."

"Whatever it means, if Jim Vaughn is on his way there, then it means it's connected with this operation, and we need to get there before he does to catch him in the act," Keeno said.

"It would almost make sense to have their research facility up there," Katherine Riggs continued.

"Why?" Ross asked.

"Because, from what I know of that Inuit territory, the economy is limited, and I bet they probably offered those people a large sum of money to be part of a research group. Secondly, it's so off the beaten path that they probably could get away with doing RFID implant research without high-profiling themselves."

"Maybe even buy off the local cops or authorities to keep their mouths shut," Jake suggested.

"We need to crash that party," Keeno said, as he looked over at Jake with a smile on his face.

"Don't even think about it!" Jake pointed at Keeno with mock threat in his eyes, "I'm not jumping out of a friggin military jet doing 500 miles an hour over the Canadian tundra."

Keeno smiled at Jake, "If we're going to beat Vaughn, we need a way to get to Rankin Inlet in a matter of hours," he said, as he studied the map – trying to negotiate the logistics of traversing some 2000 kilometers as the crow flies. A broad smile formed on his face. "I think it's time to call in our favor with the British."

"How so?" Ross asked.

"Remember we bailed them out last year. They owe us for averting that international flap and saving their royal asses.

"And?" Ross probed.

"They've got three Harrier jets parked at Downsview Airport, on lay over from Chicago, where they performed at an air show yesterday."

"No shit!" Jake said, relieved that he wasn't going to have risk his life doing something crazy.

"And you know this how?" Ross challenged.

"I read it in the in-flight magazine on my way back from Hong Kong. I happen to know the team leader," he smiled. "Besides, Toronto represents major investments for the British Empire – they'll be equally interested in making sure that Canada doesn't experience a financial melt-down over this whole virus attack."

"It's already happening anyhow," Kelly added.

Ross was nodding his head as the idea filtered in, "Ok – I'll make a call to the Brits. You guys get ready to leave."

Keeno turned to Katherine Riggs, "And you're coming with us."

"What!" she yelled. "Are you out of your mind?"

"We're going to bust into that facility up there, find all the evidence of what they've been doing with illegal chip implants, and I need someone like you who knows what to look for. Besides, this is your area of expertise, right?" Keeno tilted his head with a challenging look.

"My area of specialty is viral and bacterial studies, not flying in Harrier jets to the friggin' North Pole or fighting off bad guys." She looked over at Ross, then Janene and Kelly, for moral support, but they sat there with poker faces. They knew it was pointless to argue with Keeno. Whether she liked it or not, she was getting an A-ticket ride to the Great White North.

X

Molijnet arrived at Rockefeller Center just minutes before the scheduled pick-up. He walked up to Mezzanine 1 and slipped into a janitorial closet, just out of sight of the nearest security camera. A moment later, he emerged with a canister of toxic viruses hidden in his backpack. Twenty minutes later, back in his hotel room, he made the call.

"You have the package?"

"Yes."

"Good. The text message is arriving to you now. Report back when it is done."

Seconds later his cell phone buzzed and he clicked on the text message. It was innocuous enough, just a series of numbers, until one realized they were coordinates for his next target.

Molijnet felt the adrenaline rushing through his system, giving him a heady-feeling, a sort of high just from the anticipation of what he was going to do to the Big Apple.

The very idea that he was going to change the course of history imbued him with a god-like feeling. It was like a drug, the exaltation of being more than just Molijnet Cryzki, more than just another OPP cop on the treadmill of endless crime prevention. This was true power!

XI

When they arrived at the Toronto-Downsview Airport, a facility located on the west end of the city, three British Harriers stood on the runway like giant birds of prey, being topped up with fuel in readiness for their flight to Rankin Inlet. Their jet engines quietly hummed, hinting at the power they would soon emit as they flew sub-sonic to the Canadian Shield.

The unique design of the Harrier, or VSTOL (Vertical-Short-Take-Off-Landing) gave them the capability of vertical take-off and landing on a plot of land the size of a small house. This accorded the jets tremendous military superiority; not only did they not require a runway, they could also hover, like a tiger, wait for their targets to come in sight, then strike a lethal kill with accuracy.

Jake walked Katherine across the tarmac to a waiting Harrier Jet, just as one of the pilots stepped down from his cockpit. “I’m Mac,” he introduced himself with an Aussi accent.

“I thought you pilots were all Brits,” Jake said.

“The Aussi government bought a few of these Shirleys and sent me up to train under the Limey’s. But no worries mate, flying this baby is as easy as hunting down a “roo” – just aim and fire.”

“Fair enough,” Jake said. “This is Katherine Riggs. She’ll be flying with you.”

The pilot smiled at her, but he could see that she was in a quiet state of panic, as her eyes flitted nervously at the jet. “It’s ok, I’ll get ya there before you need to take a pee,” he joked.

Katherine rolled her eyes and resigned herself to what seemed clearly an act of insanity on her part.

Meanwhile, Keeno approached the hangar where he found Lt. Major Phillip Maroon speaking with the other two Harrier pilots. Maroon nodded at him. "Gentlemen," he turned and smiled, "this is Keeno McCole from the RCMP. He's heading the operation at Rankin Inlet," he said, with a heavy dose of his Wales dialect thrown in. Keeno brought them up to speed on what was going on and why time was a critical factor. When he was done, the pilots stepped away to their aircraft.

"Phil, I appreciate this," Keeno said.

"You're lucky, my friend, because had your boss not called the RAF HQ when he did, we would have been on our way home to England by now. I'm missing my son's final soccer match in Wales, so you realize the sacrifice," he smiled somewhat graciously. "Then again, the RAF owes you Canuks a return favor for saving our asses last year over that stupid boating incident."

Keeno smiled, "Indeed, the French government would have loved to stick that one up your butts."

The situation that Maroon referred to was an attempted terrorist attack a year earlier, by a small French terrorist-cell, who wanted to stir the soup of dissension. They had hijacked a French whaler and were planning to ram it into an approaching British vessel, arriving from England with 900 civilians aboard. The collision was about to take place on the St. Lawrence River, opposite the shores of Quebec City; chosen by the terrorist cell because of the historic symbolism of this location, where the British had defeated the French in battle for the ownership rights of Canada, some two-hundred and fifty years earlier. Phillip Maroon, heading up a team of RAF fighter jets, arrived on the scene just in time to see the gap between the two boats closing at a rapid rate. He ordered a lethal attack on the whaler, killing the men at the helm, and disabling the ship before it could ram into the huge liner.

Keeno and Jake had been called in to help with the incident and had witnessed the British planes taking out the terrorists. In the flurry of tracers, explosions and flames spewing out of the dying whaler, Keeno had seen one of the terrorists dive overboard, so he took off in pursuit of the man. The chase reached critical mass when Keeno cornered him, in a cul-de-sac, down a narrow alley, wherein the man turned and displayed the trigger mechanism in his hand. Unknown to Keeno, he had a bomb in his backpack, powerful enough to level one entire city block. Considering that they were standing in Quebec's "old-town" with thousands of tourists and locals enjoying the night life, the situation looked pretty grim. The man screamed some obscenities in French and was about to press the detonator when his forehead exploded, shredding nearly half of his head in the process. Keeno looked over his shoulder at the source of the report, just as Jake stepped out from the nearby shadows with a smile on his face.

Before the French government in Paris had a chance to retaliate against the British for taking "unwarranted acts of violence on the French whaler," an assault they were about to level at the Brits, the RCMP had presented evidence that clearly showed that if the British had not acted as they did, hundreds of civilians could have died. The French government backed down and the British were saved from a nasty PR battle.

"How much leeway do I have with your boys?" Keeno asked.

"None," Phillip smiled. They shook hands and promised to meet up for beer the next time Maroon was in town.

Moments later, Phillip Maroon watched as the three Harriers taxied to their launch point. The planes faced their noses into the wind, then, in almost perfect choreography, they rose vertically into the air, hovered for a moment, then shot across the runway and swooped up on a 45-degree vector.

As he watched the planes disappear into the clouds, he had the distinct feeling that the idyllic simplicity of the mission, which Keeno had described to him, was a delusion. He knew enough about Keeno McCole to know that if this man walked into an ice-cream shop, something could happen. So it was best to assume that the proverbial shit was about to hit the fan in Rankin Inlet.

XII

Dr. William Ackerson, or Willie, as he was mostly called, was sitting at his computer reviewing the latest case reports. In the last twenty-four hours, they had examined twenty-five of the local indigenous test cases, verifying that the chips were resonating the correct information on their physiological status. Essentially, they had to do a full physical on every test case in order to compare those results to the information coming from the RFID chips implanted in numerous locations in their bodies. The comparative reports showed that the chips were infallible and that no further testing was needed. Ackerman was proud of the results.

In this remote patch of earth, Dr. Ackerson and his team had been executing RIIP, **R**ankin **I**nlet **I**mplantation

Program, for three years under the funding of a rich philanthropist – so they were told. They had recruited the test cases by offering an appealing sum of money to mostly local indigenous peoples to be, essentially, medical guinea pigs.

They selected a variety of people, including those with acute illnesses, moderate physical conditions, and those who were completely healthy, and used them to implant the chips. Test cases were studied and monitored closely, with results summarized and sent electronically to their supervisor at a remote, unstated location.

Over the three year period, modified renditions of the chips were evolved and sent to Ackerman and his team to test. The process eventually led to the finalization of the most advanced chip to date, dubbed the God Chip – or GC. A proactive chip that not only passively reported on the physiological status of a body's organs and internal systems, but also, and equally importantly, could be used to synthesize physiological conditions by resonating certain frequencies between the chips located in different spots in the body. He jokingly referred to it as "making popcorn," since the intensified frequencies acted much the same as a microwave oven, causing stress to organs or blood vessels, even to the point of inducing hemorrhaging, causing heart palpitations or worse – irreversible damage resulting in death.

In the name of science, Willie Ackerman had advanced the testing to a level that was irrefutable. GC would revolutionize the field of medicine, providing the medical community with the means of detecting and fighting disease on a predictive basis, as opposed to waiting for symptomatic signs, which often heralded advanced stages, which made treatment difficult or even impossible.

GC opened new doors to science, and as much as Ackerman had wrestled with the proverbial "ethics or morality" of his research, he always fell back on a safe cushion, and the only safety net that made research of this nature justifiable: "the greater good." The fact that some of his test subjects had died in the process of achieving this technology and knowledge, was an acceptable margin of loss in the field of science – a mantra he constantly repeated to himself in an attempt to obscure what little remained of his moral scruples and sense of humanity. The death of a handful of people compared to the benefits that would morph society for generations to come was not comparable.

It scared Willie at times to think what could be accomplished with GC in the wrong hands, but he trusted, idyllically so, that GC would be used responsibly and not to the detriment of mankind. *Besides*, he often thought to himself, *any knowledge can be abused,* his ultimate justification to buffer himself against any accusations otherwise.

He had just finished reading the comprehensive summary of their research on the God Chip. Its merits were beyond imagination – none the least of which included the fact that GC was powerful enough to record audible sounds in the vicinity of the subject. Conversations were transmitted with clarity and permitted the operator to "listen in."

What this would do for the law enforcement community, in tracking criminals or terrorist elements, was revolutionary. Criminal types could be chipped, tracked and monitored to make sure they were toeing the line. Predictive measures could be engaged to prevent crime, resulting in a much safer, criminal free society.

Unfortunately, Willie Ackerman was unable to see the Frankenstein's monster he had helped to create. He did not see the seeds of destruction associated with chipping human beings, nor what it would do to reduce their freedom, potentially reducing society to a George Orwellian police-state – and all in the name of science, greater safety and the wonders of medical advancement.

Like a man blinded by a love-lust, Ackerman could not see past the set of breasts staring him in the face. He was obsessed with his project, convinced that his employers would hold good to their promise to use the research for scientific and medical advancement only.

He clicked the send button and forwarded the final document to the anonymous email address. His job at Rankin Inlet was done. They would start breaking down the facility in a matter of days, and he would move on with his life, living off the very large account that had accrued in his name over the last three years.

Blinded by his ambitions and his ultimate betrayal of his fellow man, Willie was about to drive over a cliff into a very deep, dark chasm.

XIII

Jim Vaughn landed in Sudbury just as the final shreds of sunlight had been engulfed in the cold darkness of the Canadian northland. If he thought that Jersey was cold, the impact of the north wind that smacked him in the face as he stepped onto the tarmac, made Trenton feel like a Caribbean vacation in comparison.

He quickly located the private pilot, paid him the sum for his services, and moments later boarded a single engine Cessna headed for Cochrane, a town deep into the

Canadian hinterland, where he would rendezvous with his next ride, on his way to what he silently referred to as "some piece of shit town in the middle of nowhere."

As they flew northward, Jim found it difficult to make any distinction in the darkness surrounding them. With the exception of an occasional vehicle snaking along a road, its headlights lighting up the terrain, or the sporadic residence, this was a land devoid of the usual signs of humanity. It was a rugged, unforgiving landscape – and while mining camps and other ventures threaded their way through this vast land, it was nonetheless a little unnerving to him to ponder over what would happen if the plane went down or crashed in this desolation.

He shifted his attention onto the rewards he was soon going to bask in when he finished this final mission at Rankin Inlet. He conjured up images of the beaches in the Caribbean, the warm sun, the endless supply of alcohol, drugs and women that he was going to drown himself in.

In less than a year with FAB-MED, he had pulled off a number of critical jobs for Tom Sneider, none the least of which included running interception in Toronto, making sure the virus was properly maintained at the University lab, controlling the security monitors and even taking out that loose-mouthed professor who was about to open up to the RCMP.

The only disappointment was that he never got a shot at taking out Keeno McCole. Unknown to Keeno and Jake, during their second visit to Ralph Ketchler, was that Jim had been hovering nearby, monitoring their conversation through a mike installed in Ketchler's classroom, just as insurance to make sure the man wasn't overstepping his bounds. When it was clear that Ketchler had been cornered by McCole and was about to say more than he needed to, Vaughn had his hired gun take him out.

If Tom Sneider hadn't ordered him back on the next plane to Trenton, Vaughn would have happily stayed behind to finish the job with McCole.

He prided himself on his special skills; he was a trained hit-man, assassin and killer – courtesy of Uncle Sam. He had no remorse about the people he terminated, another perk from his mental conditioning. Trained shooters like himself were stripped of their conscience, replaced instead with a push-button response to their handlers. The Marine Corps had trained him to kill the "enemy," which was defined by bureaucrats in Washington DC, who dictated where the battles should be fought and in which direction the bullets should fly. Yesterday it was Afghanistan and the Taliban, today it was Iraqi extremists, tomorrow – Iran, North Korea or China?

Vaughn's loyalties, already weak at best when he joined the ranks of the Marines, were thoroughly washed away after his short term in Iraq and his dishonorable discharge. When he returned to the US, he was loyal to only one person – *himself*, and he reckoned that if the US government and its many agencies could fabricate reasons for killing off thousands of people, then he could certainly justify making a living at it. *Besides*, he chuckled to himself as he watched the black mantle slide beneath the plane, *we certainly don't want all those tax dollars that were invested into my training, going to waste.*

He flipped open his cell phone and made a call.

"Yeah?" a man answered.

"Everyone there?"

"Yeah."

"I'll be there early tomorrow morning," he hung up the line.

Everything was going as planned. He had five ex-Marines waiting for him at Rankin Inlet. They'd get the research materials, computers and equipment loaded up on the ship, making sure that everyone at the facility was sent on their way, and then they'd shut down the operation. If anything went wrong, his orders were to handle it as smoothly and tactfully as possible, but to leave no loose ends.

Vaughn smiled as he recalled Tom Sneider's admonishment of the day before, *"No loose ends"* – a euphemism that people in suits and ties used so that they didn't have the words, "Kill them," on their conscience. *What the fuck,* he thought, *for the right price, he'd hose down anyone's shit.*

XIV

It was well after 1 a.m. and Ross Fletcher was still sitting at the CIC conference table, staring at the map on the wall. He was projecting what could happen up at Rankin Inlet. *What would Keeno find there, and more importantly – what would he do?* he thought to himself.

He knew the relative futility of trying to second-guess Keeno. The fact of the matter was that Keeno was his best ace against terrorism.

Keeno had an ability to think outside the box – not to mention that he had a keen sense for sniffing out the criminal mind. There was no fooling McCole; in a face-to-face, he could see through a ruse or a lie in seconds.

Ross had stopped trying to analyze how he did it or why, and instead, focused on how to manage Keeno and his team without ever letting on that he was doing anything of that nature.

It was times like this, when Ross simply could not sleep. To go home to his wife and kids would just be bringing his baggage through the front door and disturbing his home life. His wife knew him too well and could read the stress lines on his face like a fortune teller could read the palm of someone's hand. She would try to get him talking, and Ross would resist giving her the bad news about the state of affairs, so instead, he called his wife and told her he'd be staying late tonight.

To make matters worse, he'd just gotten off the phone with the Prime Minister, who informed him that with the escalating sickness, death toll and the consequent financial fall-out caused by the virus, the political arena in Ottawa was turning into a Roman Circus and out of his control now as the media poured gas on the existing fire that raged on Parliament Hill.

The NDP leader, Carrie Levine, had just gone public through the media portals, announcing that Canada's leadership was in question and that he was proposing an emergency electoral vote to the Canadian people, based on the billions lost in revenue because of the epidemic-ridden Toronto – the largest and wealthiest financial anchor in the nation.

Unfortunately, despite the fact that Levine was kicking an injured bull, his platform was solid. Canadians would not stand by much longer and watch the economy tip over. Everyone knew that if Toronto crashed, Canada would follow. The media had profiled the extrapolated financial losses, which were already astronomical. Canadians, understandably, would not passively stand by and watch their jobs, their investments and their lives disappear.

The Prime Minister was doing everything he could to delay the bill from becoming law, but time was not on his side. Carrie Levine was fanning the flames of dissention and the camps were lining up for battle.

Ross finally shook himself out of his reverie and walked downstairs where he found Janene and Kelly still hunkered over their computers. Their faces were drawn and stressed. Fatigue was taking its toll, as shown by the bags under their eyes.

"How's it going, ladies?"

"Oh just peachy," Kelly said, stretching her legs and craning her neck as she lit up a smoke. Ross pulled up a chair and smiled reassuringly.

"I'm still going through security cam footage from Grand Central station in New York. I figure that if Molijnet is going to the Big Apple, he will do it by train." Janene said.

"Makes sense – easier to stay off the radar," Ross agreed.

Kelly tilted her head to the right and rested it on the palm of her right hand. The tattoo of the orange and green parrot on her neck was suddenly animated, seemingly craning its neck to look Ross straight in the eyes. Its coal-black orbs appeared to have a life of their own.

"What's the latest on your end?" Kelly asked.

Ross shook himself from the mesmerizing effect of the parrot. "Spoke to the PM just now. The political gladiators are coming into the arena, with Carrie Levine swinging the biggest sword. He's calling for an emergency electoral vote to take the Conservative Party out of office.

The PM says we have about 48 hours before Ottawa goes into full-scale meltdown, politically speaking."

"If the PM vetoes that bill before we get to the bottom of this case, it could really screw us over, right?" Janene asked.

"We have to get there first otherwise these people will still hold the aces and could retaliate if they see that he's trying to stop the bill from going through."

"The media is tearing the PM to pieces." Kelly continued, "They just announced 51,000 people infected in Toronto alone, and over 3,000 deaths. Schools are closed and about 28% of Toronto's work force is either sick, stranded at home watching kids, or can't get to work as the TTC has cut way back on service. The financial loss is off the charts. People naturally need someone to point a finger at, and he's getting the brunt of it because he's at the helm."

"I know, and the PM knows it too," he rubbed his eyes.

"You look tired – you should get some sleep," Kelly said.

Ross smiled, "When we get a breakthrough, I'll sleep. Until then, I'm doing coffee intravenously like you guys," and he walked out of the office.

Janene shook the tiredness from her head and resumed going through the security videos. Trying to find one man passing through Grand Central Station suddenly gave the saying, "looking for a needle in a haystack," a whole new meaning.

After hours and hours of watching faces pass by multiple security cameras, she was no closer to finding him than when she had started. She slumped back in her chair.

The sense of mental exhaustion was creeping in. *There had to be a better way of doing it,* she thought.

She thought back to what she had studied about Molijnet from his OPP file. He had a totally clean profile, not a single crime or misdemeanor on his record. He had nothing but positive remarks and performance reviews in his six year run with the OPP. He was a complex paradox in terms of someone that would murder other people and who might be spreading a virus. The only thing that made sense to her was that he must have been duped or recruited into some organization, one that had found a weakness of his and used it to grip him. Many terrorist or criminal types were known to be sexually messed up, obsessed with women, kids, or whatever. Or they were druggies or alcoholics or had other phobias or manic conditions. Molijnet had none of these – at least nothing was noted in any of his OPP psychological reviews.

She pulled out his file and studied it again. One of his trainers had remarked that Molijnet was a chain smoker and that he smoked upwards of two packs of Marlboros every day.

On a whim, she calculated the length of time between stations on the Toronto to New York train lines. How long would a chain-smoker last, and what was the likelihood that his first stop at Grand Central Station would be at a store or kiosk to buy cigarettes?

It was a long shot, more or less on the order of jumping the Grand Canyon, but at least it was the Grand Canyon and not entirely a needle in a haystack.

She located three security cameras in Grand Central which were aimed at kiosks. She started scanning through footage, concentrating on the arrival times for trains coming from Toronto or upstate New York.

Three hours later, when her eyes were about to fall out of their sockets, she saw something that caught her attention.

She ran back the footage and watched it over again. The man, standing with his back to the camera was buying a bag full of Marlboros. His hair was cut short and tight, just like Molijnet's. His build was similar too. Suddenly he turned, lit up a cigarette and as he did the camera caught his profile.

"Oh my fucking God! It's him!"

XV

The three Harrier jets flashed out across the western shores of Hudson Bay. From an altitude of 6.3 miles above the earth, Hudson Bay looked like an ocean, and essentially it was, considering that it was one of the largest inland bays on the planet. To the left, the northern terrain was growing progressively whiter as the cold Canadian winter started its systematic march southward.

Flying at a maximum speed of 662 miles per hour, with a climb rate of thousands of feet per minute, the Harriers had pinned their passengers to the back of their seats with their G-force alone. However, once they had hit cruising mode, they were like Cadillacs to fly in.

"Hey!" Keeno said into his headset. "You there, Katherine?"

"Yes,"

Keeno detected the resentment in her voice.

"You ok?"

"Oh, you mean besides the fact that I peed my pants after take-off and then nearly chucked up my last meal during acceleration, I'm good. Thanks for asking."

He chuckled and then settled in for the flight.

"Got a plan?" Jake whispered through the headset to Keeno.

"Nope."

"How can you not have a plan?" Katherine suddenly piped in.

"Simple. I have no idea what we're going to run into. Improvisation – makes life more exciting," Keeno replied.

Katherine let out a deep breath of frustration. "Maybe for you, but I have this idea that prediction is better than surprise."

"Boring!" Keeno chimed back at her as he closed his eyes to take a nap.

One hundred and fifty two minutes after leaving Toronto, the first Harrier swooped in from the north, landing at the far end of a small runway on the outskirts of Rankin Inlet. Keeno had a short conversation with the lead pilot and then jumped out of his plane. The frigid air hit him as he landed on the ground, as if someone had just slapped him in the face with a sheet of ice, or a sumo wrestler had just landed on him without warning. The effect was the same – it knocked the wind out of him. He quickly slipped on his gloves and flipped the hood of his parka over his head.

Moments later, the second Harrier began its descent. It was an impressive sight to watch thirty million dollars of technology hanging fifty feet above the runway, lowering itself gracefully to the ground like a bird. Even though the cross winds buffeted and rocked it horizontally, the pilot smoothly countered it by tipping the windward wing just enough. As it hit the ground, Jake jumped down from the cockpit. "Oh my God, that's friggin cold," he shouted, as he quickly donned his gear.

The third Harrier lowered down not thirty feet away, and both men went over to help Katherine. Keeno waved at the pilots and all three planes rose up into the air, leaving the three lone figures standing on the snow covered terrain.

They lowered their heads and started walking as the wind screeched and howled at them for having come uninvited to its domain.

XVI

Cain Daley, or "Cannon" as his associates called him, was standing outside the small bar having a smoke. He had been dubbed Cannon by the other guys in his unit during their military term in Iraq, during an offensive where he had stood up with an RPG on his shoulder and a cigar in his mouth, and had taken out three entire ground-level buildings by himself. When the dust had settled, they found the remains of twenty-eight Iraqi's in the rubble. The fact that some of them had been civilian didn't particularly ruffle Cannon's feathers – *war was war and the collateral damage was not his responsibility,* as he saw things.

After returning from Iraq, as with many other veterans, he found that his life was now marginalized. While the military tooted the perks of joining Uncle Sam's "winning" team, they omitted to tell you that four years of separation from society and your friends would put a large chasm in your life. When he got back to his hometown in Green Bay WI, he was shocked to find out how distanced all his old comrades were from him. Most had finished university, started careers, or had families, and as much as they were happy to see him, they shared very little in common anymore, and they weren't particularly interested in being a part of his life.

In some ways, he felt like a marked man. He had killed people, but unlike others, he had enjoyed it. Where other soldiers did it for "country and honor", or "to protect democracy", whichever mantra made them feel good about invading another country, Cannon simply enjoyed the buzz that came with the "legal kill". He enjoyed aiming a gun at the "enemy" and taking them down; with about the same level of compassion he had when shooting deer during hunting sprees.

Coming back state-side, and walking the streets of America, he felt like a fish out of water. He soon came to realize that the only thing that really suited him was the threat of violence, the adrenaline rush that came from holding a weapon, and yes, killing the "enemy."

When Jim Vaughn had contacted him to recruit some vets for this job up in this hellhole, he was more than happy to dump the shit-job he had and dive in. *Besides*, he mused, as he stood outside the bar in the blistering wind with just a t-shirt over his bulging muscles, *the price was right.*

The wind pounded into the small wooden bar behind him. Like a savage monster, it slashed at him, trying to take him down, but his sheer 250 pound bulk resisted its onslaught.

It was then that he heard the sound, one that almost any military man who had spent time in a battle zone would recognize in a split second. It was the undeniable roar of a military jet engine. Cain looked towards the sound, watching as three jets streaking away in the distance.

British RAF! What the fuck are they doing in Rankin Inlet? he wondered suspiciously.

Cain flipped open his cell phone and called Jim Vaughn. Something didn't smell right to him.

XVII

Dr. Willie Ackerman picked up a coffee on his way into the facility, as he did every morning. He arrived at the compound just before 8 a.m. The research station, called RIIP, was nothing more than four large modules connected by a series of short expandable tunnels, which lead from one to the other in a snake-like fashion. Contained within the modules was the cutting-edge medical equipment used to facilitate their research. In one module, they maintained records for all their test subjects, covering the three years of RIIP. This included samples of every chip ever tested, along with comprehensive notes on each. Naturally, everything was electronically backed up and had been sent to their supervisor, someone that Ackerman had neither met nor talked to in his entire time heading up the facility. The nameless, anonymous "supervisor," for all he knew, could be a team of technicians sitting in Miami, Chicago or in some other continent.

Ackerman enjoyed the fact that here, he was king. He oversaw the facility, helped with the research and compilation of results, and sent his reports in a timely manner. Beyond that, he received his instructions along with new chips to test, and he executed his job without questions.

He unlocked the door to the main unit, stepped inside, and became immediately aware that something was wrong. He turned to see a man sitting at his desk.

"Who are you?"

"My name is Keeno. I'm with the RCMP."

Willie felt a sudden tightening in his stomach.

"You look like you just saw ghost, Willie," Keeno said. "Sit down, let's talk."

Willie lowered himself into a chair. "What do you want? Am I in trouble?"

"You tell me," Keeno said, while fixing his glare straight into the man's eyes. Willie Ackerman was in terror and Keeno could see it.

"This is a private research facili…" he started to say but Keeno cut him off.

"Yeah, yeah, let's cut the bullshit! We know you're doing RFID implants on the local Inuit."

"We're not breaking the law," he said as a feeble defense.

"I'm not so sure about that, Willie. I think the authorities might be interested in some of your case files. Let's see…" he pulled up a document that they had found in their research files. "There was the fifty-five year old man who suffered cardiac arrest eight weeks ago, when you turned up the juice on his chip," Keeno tipped his head. "And then there was the forty-two year old mother, who suffered paralysis in her left side after you implanted her." He continued looking at Willie, who was nervously wiping his forehead. "Or what about the man who was found half eaten by a polar bear? The autopsy showed that he had a brain aneurism, but of course you guys covered up the fact that he had chips on each side of his neck, and the fact that the frequency amplification you pumped into him through those chips caused an arterial constriction which cut off the blood flow to his brain." Keeno's eyes bore a hole into

Willie's forehead as he watched him. "How many people have you killed in the name of science?"

"That's experimental research information and is proprietary domain," Willie said.

"Yeah, I know, and I'm fucking Mickey Mouse."

By now, sweat was pouring off Willie.

"What I want to know is who's pulling your strings?"

Willie shook his head, "I don't know."

The back door of Willie's office opened and in walked Katherine and Jake.

"Got everything?" Keeno asked.

"I've got the bio samples and copies of all of their diagnostic reports," Katherine said. "It's all on this flash drive."

Jake held out his hand and in it was a small plastic bag, "I grabbed samples of all the RFID chips," he jiggled the bag purposely, so Willie would see it.

"What is this? Are you raiding us?" Willie implored.

"You don't get it, do you? Your employers are criminals and they are involved in a terrorist plot that you're either knowingly involved with, or you're just a stupid pawn in their game plan."

Willie was shaking his head in denial. He was digging in his heels and refusing to accept any of this. "No, this is a medical research facility, nothing more, nothing less. What others do with the information is a matter that is outside my jurisdiction as a scientist."

"Bullshit!" Keeno stood up and waved a hand around the facility, "You're messing with the future of this country and probably other nations too. Get a fucking clue, man!" Willie flinched at Keeno's sudden angst.

"Research and science, by all means, but what you're doing up here is not being done in the best interests of people. Do you even have a concept of what they're planning to do with this God Chip?"

Willie looked at him with guilty eyes, "All science can be abused. If scientists stopped researching just because of the possibility of misuse of knowledge, then we'd be nowhere today."

"I want names? Who's your boss and where do I find this bastard?"

"I don't know. I send my reports to someone every month. I have never met him."

"How do you contact that person?"

Keeno leaned down on the desk in front of him. "There are over 3000 dead people in Toronto. More people are going to die if we don't stop them."

Willie's eyes flicked nervously.

Keeno continued, "And they've killed off everyone that has been connected to this plot so far. So you do the math, Willie, how long do you figure it will be before you end up as Polar Bear meat?"

Willie wiped his forehead and then reached over to the computer and clicked open his email. "That's the email address I use to send the reports."

Keeno wrote down the information.

"That's all I have. That's all I've ever had," Willie said with a tone of despair, feeling his whole world coming apart at the seams.

As Keeno turned to look at Willie, he caught a subtle movement through a window. Instinctively, he dove to the floor, grabbing at Willie as he did. The bullet exploded through the same window, striking Willie in the left temple, and killing him instantly.

"Fuck!" Keeno yelled, as he pulled his gun from his holster and shot back.

Jake had already grabbed Katherine and was running through the short tunnel connecting the modules. Keeno continued shooting as he ran after them. Bullets were smashing into the wall behind him as he dove into the next module.

"How'd they know we were here?" Jake asked, as he reloaded his gun.

"No idea," Keeno said, snapping a new clip into his gun." Then, without hesitation, Keeno grabbed a chair and ran straight for the nearest window. The chair smashed through the glass and he followed behind it, sailing through the shredded opening and landing on a snow-covered embankment. Jake had already hefted Katherine off her feet and was shoving her out the window to Keeno when the door imploded from the impact of high caliber bullets. Jake dove out the window headfirst as a storm of bullets shredded the small room.

Chapter 6

I

Madison Square Garden was packed, as New Yorkers came out en masse for the concert. Molijnet Cryzki had gotten himself a seat where he could easily slip out unnoticed. In his overcoat were five sealed pouches, enough to start the meltdown in the Big Apple.

Waiting until the rock concert was going, he then slipped out the back exit, to the men's room at the far end of the mezzanine, took out the first pouch, punctured the seal and dropped it under the sink in a corner, where it melted in with a pile of paper towels.

He casually made his way down the stairs to the main level, found the next bathroom and repeated the same process.

From there, he went to the main concourse, bought a hotdog and Coke and blended in with the ebb and flow of people. He was in no hurry as he'd been inoculated against every virus he was spreading. When he finished eating, he slipped another pouch from his pocket, broke the outer seal and dropped it into a waste bin in the middle of the concourse.

This was just a teaser, he thought to himself, just enough to set off the panic alarms. The big one was coming tomorrow, when he would infiltrate their water system and infect thousands of New Yorkers, possibly even more than in Toronto.

For a brief moment, watching people pouring through the concourse, he sensed a slight quiver of remorse. It was the faintest touch of humanity pricking at his conscience, like a ghost knocking on his door, reminding him that he was human. As he looked at the faces of those that milled around him, he saw the images of his own brothers and sisters, his mother and father, and even others that he had known. His only defense was to force the memories from his mind, close them behind steel doors, and in so doing, he became someone else. Ever since the day when he had shot three men dead in that warehouse, to prove his credibility to men that he never even knew, he had morphed into a different person. He had to bury the real Molijnet, assume another mental outlook, in fact, don a synthetic personality; someone who did not feel compassion or remorse – two qualities that could destroy him faster than anything else.

II

Jake yanked on the wooden door of the dilapidated shack, nearly tearing it off its hinges. Before going inside, Keeno looked back to see five men gathering, and he recognized one of them right away. The image of Ralph Ketchler's dead body suddenly flashed in mind.

Jim Vaughn locked eyes with Keeno, and realizing whom he was up against, a smile formed on his lips. *Now he would have his chance to get rid of McCole and no one could say a goddamn thing*, he thought.

One of the men dropped a large duffel bag to the ground, unzipped it and pulled out two RPGs, or Rocket Propelled Grenades. Two of them hefted the RPGs to their shoulders.

"Shit!" Keeno shouted to Jake, "Get her out of here."

Jake looked around for another way out, and seeing no options, he simply turned and ran towards the back wall of the shed, and impelled the weight of his body against the wooden slats. The building shuddered from the impact.

Jack backed up and rammed it again and felt the crack of several boards breaking. He kicked a hole through the slats and shoved Katherine out, and then followed her.

They found an abandoned tractor in a field behind the shack. "Stay here," he said. She nodded and slipped behind the rusted relic. Jake handed his gun to her, "Use it if you have to."

"You need it more than me," she insisted.

"I'll make do, but if one of those guys comes for you, put a bullet in his head."

She nervously took the gun, "You better come back alive, mister," she said.

"Sounds promising," he leered, as he slipped his knife from his belt and started running back to help Keeno. It sounded like a war zone as gun shots filled the air.

Keeno shot at the first man holding an RPG. The bullet grazed his arm, forcing him to drop the weapon. He then tried getting off a shot at the second guy, but he did not have enough time before the guy triggered the other RPG.

Keeno threw himself to one side of the shack and covered his head, just as the grenade slammed into the back wall of the shack. The explosion rocked the tiny wooden structure, sending pieces of wood flying everywhere, creating a clamor that hammered his body to the floor and sent intense pain screaming into his eardrums.

Outside, Jim Vaughn and Cain unloaded a hailstorm of lead into the building, pinning Keeno to the floor, while another man negotiated the second RPG and took aim on the shack.

At that instant, Jake came around the corner of the building, saw what was about to happen and let his knife fly. It sliced the air with deathly silence, impaling the guy through the cheek. He toppled over, dropping the RPG as he did.

Jim Vaughn and Cain diverted their fire power at Jake, who took his cue and dove over a small mound of snow as the ground around him was turned into craters.

He crawled deeper into the nearby brush, looking for something to defend himself with, but all he found was cold frozen ground covered in a layer of snow.

"Get that asshole," Vaughn told Cain.

The other two men on Vaughn's team moved forward, picked up the RPGs and pointed them at the small wooden building, which by now was starting to cant to one side from the onslaught.

Keeno peered through a crack in the wall and saw what was about to happen, "Oh shit!" he said aloud. "Not again."

Just when it looked like the curtains were about to drop on Keeno, the ground around Vaughn and his men trembled and dirt, ice and snow suddenly pitched upward. The high-pitched twang of bullets filled the air, followed by a deep thrumming sound. They looked up to see two Harrier jets dropping down towards them, like hawks coming in for the kill.

The two men holding the RPGs turned to fire on the jets, but the sophisticated weaponry of the Harriers already had them in the cross hairs. Vaughn dove to the side to avoid the killing shots that pummeled the two men into the dirt. When the dust had finally settled, they lay dead in a heap. Vaughn knew at that point that his chances of success, or even coming out of this mission alive, were next to none, but one thing was for sure; he was going to kill Keeno McCole if it was the last thing he ever did. He jumped to his feet and ran straight for the shack, crashing through the door before the pilots could get a shot at him.

He rolled in one smooth motion, landed on his feet, and aimed his gun at Keeno. "We meet again, asshole," he said as he pulled the trigger.

Whether attributable to Keeno's good fortune or to Vaughn's impulsiveness, no bullets came out of the gun – the clip was empty. Vaughn smiled, "I guess we're gonna do it the old-fashioned way," he said, as he pulled out a large hunting knife from the sheath on his side.

"You know, I was actually looking forward to meeting you again. In fact, I was disappointed when Sneider told me not to kill you when I had a chance to."

"Why'd you do it, Vaughn?"

"Oh, you mean Ralphie boy?"

"You know exactly what I mean," Keeno answered, as they began to circle one another, adjusting their knife-hands as they did. It was obvious from his stance that Vaughn was no amateur when it came to a knife-fight.

"We had what we needed from Ralph Ketchler, the study was done and endorsed. We didn't need him shooting off his mouth to the RCMP."

"You shouldn't have killed him."

"Ahh, now you're threatening me, I thought you Mounties were all good guys, you know, by the book, big smiles and friendly attitude."

Keeno shifted his weight subtly, "Sorry to disappoint you."

"I can understand that you're a tad upset about your friend, but business is business, and Ralphie boy was about to screw things up."

"You made it personal when you murdered my friend," Keeno said, as he continued the dance routine, waiting for Vaughn to attack.

"Don't be bitter, Keeno, everyone dies eventually, even you." He lunged at Keeno's face, slashing his knife as he did. Keeno smacked his knife-hand away, side stepping the attack, but just barely. Vaughn was strong and his attack had power behind it.

Vaughn spun on his heel, "You're fast, McCole." He speared in again, faking a move to the right, but Keeno saw it coming. Vaughn swung his knife at Keeno's chest, but Keeno kicked his left foot outward, hitting his stomach and momentarily knocking the wind from him.

Vaughn winced slightly while struggling to catch his breath. He had a crazed look on his face, one that subtly reminded Keeno of how his own father had looked to him during one of his many drunken, violent sprees.

"You're wasting your time McCole, you can't beat Special Forces training," Vaughn said as he regained his breath.

Keeno adjusted his footing, while watching Vaughn like a hawk. "You're arrogant Vaughn – it's gonna kill you one day," he said.

Vaughn chuckled as he switched the knife to his left hand. "Ah, speaking of arrogance, you Mounties with your lame "We always get our man", what a fucking joke!"

Vaughn charged in again, swiping his knife in a wide arc back and forth in front of Keeno's face, and as he did, he kicked Keeno in the left thigh. Keeno twisted slightly to deflect the full force of the kick, then slipped under Vaughn's reach, where he smashed the heel of his foot into Vaughn's ribs. The painfully loud sound of cracking ribs reverberated through the air. Vaughn stumbled back, gasping and grimacing, his breathing suddenly reduced to short gasps, as pain streaked through him.

Keeno watched him anguish, trying to overcome the pain. He could have attacked Vaughn at that very instant when his guard was down, but he did not. As much as Keeno wanted to avenge his friend's death, he took no joy in killing another human being unless it was a matter of kill, or be killed. Some inner code still ruled within him, that if a person was to die, there should be honor in it. He would respect that code, even with Jim Vaughn.

Vaughn adjusted his weight to the other foot, trying to lessen the waves of pain strumming his body like a guitar.

"We can call this off, Vaughn. As much as I'd have no problem killing you, I'm not a murderer," Keeno said.

Vaughn's lip curled slightly. In his eyes was a look that Keeno had seen before in men just like him. It was the look of a man who knew that there were no more doors left, that his road had just come to an end.

"Look who's being arrogant now," Vaughn said, with a maniacal aspect in his eyes, and then he charged in with reckless insanity. His knife-hand slashed straight at Keeno with a ferocity and power that could only come from a man who was throwing every last ounce of his energy into one final desperate act.

Instead of trying to block the assault, Keeno simply dropped back, feigning a retreat. Vaughn fell for the ploy and came in even harder. Keeno waited for the hole in his defenses, at which exact point he shot his right foot up with deadly accuracy. With the same force and speed of a spring-loaded crossbow, his heel smashed into Vaughn's throat – crushing his windpipe.

Vaughn stumbled backwards, gasping, trying to draw air through his shattered windpipe, but none was to be had. He reached up, frantically clawing at his throat, before coming to the realization that there was absolutely nothing he could do about it - death was inevitable.

He dropped to his knees, his eyes bulging as his body screamed for oxygen, and seconds later he toppled over face first – dead.

III

Lefty Lou was one of the best pickpockets in New York City. He considered himself on a par with some of the best thieves he had known in prison. He'd been caught in the act a few times, and Uncle Sam had provided him with free room and board for upwards of three years, none of which dissuaded Lefty from picking up on his career when he left the joint each time. Picking pockets was his best skill, and when he wasn't in prison, he made a good living from it – so why stop?

He'd just finished a nine-month stint at Hotel GoGo, the name that local inmates had dubbed the facility located on the Jersey shores. He secured a small apartment on the east side, washed some clothes and then headed off to one of his favorite spots. For a time, he just stood to one side of the main concourse at Madison Square Garden, scouting out his first mark, looking for a woman with an exposed money purse, or a man with his wallet bulging from a pocket. His technique was simple: get up beside the mark, pretend to bump into the person, and then negotiate the pick. It never failed to work – and most people never even noticed it.

As he scanned the crowed, Lefty was completely unaware that he was also being watched by two rookie cops in plain clothes. They had been assigned his case as part of their internship with the NY Police Academy. Lefty was considered by the NYPD to be a low-risk criminal, and a good case for these two rookies to observe. They had been briefed on his past history of extensive petty theft, and they knew his modus operandi.

The rookies watched as he slipped next to a man, pretended to bump into him, and deftly slipped his hand into the man's coat pocket. It all happened so fast, that had they not known about Lefty's skill, they would have missed the subtle sweep of his left hand.

Lefty slipped off to the side and opened the palm of his hand, revealing a small green translucent pouch. "What the hell is this?" he said to himself. He held it up to the light, and at that moment two agents from Homeland Security bolted at him and grabbed him by the arms.

"Where did you get that?" one of them asked, as they dragged him over to a nearby wall.

Lefty pointed down the concourse, at a man in a trench coat.

"Stay with him," said one of the Homeland Security agents to the other, as he started running after the other man. The agent bolted down the concourse and through the exit door where the man had disappeared. The alley leading to the street was empty, or seemingly so.

"Looking for me?" a voice said from behind him, and as he turned, Molijnet drove a knife into the pit of the agent's stomach, pulled it out and walked away.

Two minutes later, five more agents came crashing through the same door, only to find their man on the ground, bleeding out his life.

By that time, Molijnet had already made it to the end of the alley, crossed the street and melted in with the crowd.

IV

Katherine was still huddled behind the tractor, where Jake had left her hiding. She was shaking from a combination of the intense cold and fear of the pounding gunfire in the distance. Suddenly, she heard the sound of jet engines, followed by the thundering clamour of machine–guns, the likes of which she had never personally experienced. It sounded as if a war had erupted, and all she could think was that Jake and Keeno were outnumbered, maybe even dead.

She stared down at the gun in her lap. In all her wildest dreams, she would never have envisioned herself holding a weapon. She had grown up in upper-middle class suburbia with a gold-paved path, and had never been exposed to the criminal elements of society.

Now, she had to make a decision: sit here and wait, possibly only to find out that Jake and Keeno were dead, or come out of hiding to help them, and possibly die at the hands of the same assholes.

Something switched on inside Katherine and the congenial university teacher went through a metamorphosis in just seconds. She realized that her fate was to either become a survivor or a victim, and personally, she wasn't ready to die.

She stood up from behind the tractor, just in time to see Jake diving over a snow bank. Behind him, another man was firing rounds at Jake, spewing up puffs of snow as the bullets plowed the ground around him.

Cain Daly walked with a confident stride. He was in no hurry. He had the gun, two clips in his pocket, and the man he chased had nothing. This was target practice, like shooting a turkey on the range, and Cain was enjoying the chase.

He took another shot at the man just as he dove over the snow bank.

Cain advanced, snapping another clip into his gun as he did, and watching in the distance as the man made a feeble attempt to slip behind some bushes. Cain let off another two rounds to one side and cut him off.

He slipped over the embankment of snow, walked another few feet, and then stopped. Not ten feet away was his mark. The man was looking straight at him.

Jake realized at that point that he was out of options. He was standing in the middle of an open field with no defense and no way out. If he was going to take the bullet, then he wanted to do it his way, so he turned to face the shooter.

"Go ahead, asshole," he prodded Cain.

Cain smiled and raised his gun, tightening his finger over the trigger as he did, but then an overwhelming pain streaked through his head, consuming him from head to toe.

Cain Daly dropped to his knees, looking at the ground around him as his own blood sprinkled the snow in a stark crimson. He had never experienced this kind of pain before, neither the numbing sensation that permeated his body, nor the sense of intense coldness that followed.

He willed his finger to pull the trigger, but his motor functions did not respond – in fact, nothing responded anymore.

What a fucking place to die, he thought as he fell face forward into the snow.

Katherine was still standing to one side, with the gun pointed where Cain had just stood. Jake stepped up to her and eased the gun from her trembling hand. Tears were rolling down her cheeks and her lips quivered.

He pulled her into him and wrapped an arm around her as she sobbed. "You did good, babe, you did really good."

He looked back at the shack and then to the Harriers, still hovering over the facility. Just then, Keeno stuck his head through what remained of the back wall of the shack and gave him a thumbs up.

"You ok?" Keeno said to Jake as they approached.

"Thanks to her, yeah."

Two police cars arrived on the scene, along with a crowd of other locals. Keeno engaged the police, giving them an acceptable shore story while Jake and Katherine slipped back into the facility and recovered the evidence which they had dropped during the gunfight.

Keeno got Ross Fletcher on the line and turned the police chief over to him to handle. As usual, Ross would run damage control.

In spite of some minor cuts and bruises, Keeno hurried them back to the small landing strip outside of town, where they met up with the same three Harrier pilots, who had already received orders to pick up Keeno and his team. "How'd you guys know we needed help back there?" Keeno asked, as he approached the lead pilot.

"We got a call from the team leader, Maroon. He told us that some locals had reported gunfire at Rankin Inlet. I guess the RCMP must have been monitoring radio traffic up here. We were already across Hudson's Bay getting refueled at a military base in order to make the jump across the Atlantic. When we got back here, we picked up the gun fire with our heat signature recognition equipment, and it didn't take us long to figure out who was shooting at who, so we requested an 'ok' to engage and got the green light. That's when we dropped in on the party."

"Damn good timing. I don't think I would have survived another RPG landing on top of me." Keeno said with a smile.

"Our pleasure, and by the way, Maroon wanted me to give you a message."

Keeno waited.

"He says that the debt is paid, thank you very much."

"Tell him thanks from all of us, but we still get a ride home – right?"

The trip back to Toronto was entirely uneventful. Overtaken by exhaustion, they all fell into deep sleep within seconds of taking off.

V

Molijnet Cryzki had ducked into a coffee shop and gone out the back door into an alley. From there, he made his way to another street, grabbed a cab and headed to his hotel. He could not figure out what had gone wrong until he realized that one of the pouches was missing from his coat pocket and that someone must have spotted him.

In any case, he thought to himself, he would not let this interfere with getting the job done. Besides, there were no alternatives with his employers – either he succeeded and enjoyed the fruits of his work, or he'd end up in an alley somewhere with a bullet in his head.

Arriving at his hotel room, he pulled out a small bag from his suitcase, in which he kept a handful of disguises for contingencies such as this. He picked out a wig and a moustache and quickly secured them in place. Then he changed out of his clothes, strapped his gun harness over his shoulder, and slipped into a different colored jacket. For all intents and purposes, he looked like a completely different person now.

Standing across the street from the Marriott Hotel were the same two rookie cops who had been doing surveillance on Lefty Lou at Madison Square Garden. When the Homeland Security agents had gone chasing after Molijnet, the two rookies had decided that this looked more exciting than tracking the Jurassic Lefty Lou, so they took another exit out of the Garden, where they immediately spotted the mystery man disappearing into a coffee shop. They followed him to the Marriott, not knowing that they were actually trailing the most wanted terrorist anywhere.

Standing on the street corner, they called their training officer at the New York PD with a description of the man and what had happened. They were instructed to stand by. Within minutes, several cars pulled up, and Homeland Security agents poured out.

It only took the agents a few minutes to locate Molijnet's room, and at that moment, Richard Jacobs, head of Homeland Security, stepped into the Marriott lobby, taking control of the operation. He had his team get all the civilians out of the lobby and secure the hotel. Then they made their way up to the 11th floor, and positioned themselves outside of his room.

Inside, Molijnet had just put the finishing touches on his new face and was walking into the living room, when the door burst open. Agents flooded in, with guns cocked and aimed at him.

He smiled arrogantly, "Is there a problem?"

Richard Jacobs walked up to him, "Molijnet Cryzki – you're under arrest for acts of terrorism against two nations."

Molijnet smiled defiantly, "Says who?" He continued his act but he knew now that his time was finally up. There was no way to escape his circumstances, and even if he miraculously got past all these agents, the people hiring him would consider him too compromised and would arrange for his timely death.

"Take him," Jacobs said, as he stepped back. Molijnet's hand flashed up to his gun. It was uncanny that he would take a suicide route with a room full of agents, but Molijnet saw this as his final act, and his mentality, at that instant, dictated that he'd been robbed of his chance to hit the Big Apple, so he wasn't going down without a fight.

As he swung the gun at Richard Jacobs, every Homeland Security agent in that room opened fire, filling him with enough lead to kill five men – but he wasn't a normal man. His body had been conditioned to endure pain and suffering, and his mind was so corrupted that torment and anguish were welcomed guests. For a brief moment, as the pain filled his brain and consumed every nerve in his body, Molijnet's gun-hand wavered. Yet, in some final burst of life, some demonic impulse to kill just one more person before he died, he focused every particle of his remaining energy and pushed through the numbing sensation in his body, to press the trigger of his gun.

Richard Jacobs had seen that look before in the faces of suicide bombers, and he knew from his training the lengths to which a man or woman might go in their suicidal impulses to kill, or to be killed, in the name of some crazed and insane martyrly ideal. Jacobs instinctively swung his left hand up, barely deflecting the gun. The bullet grazed the side of his head, burning the skin as it did, and splashing a small amount of blood onto his face.

He watched Molijnet sink to the floor, his body shaking and convulsing as it fought against the inevitable death throes that consumed it. Then his head rolled to one side and he slumped over, dead.

Jacobs pulled out his cell phone as he wiped the blood from his head with the back of his hand, and called his team leader back at Madison Square Garden to confirm that they had found and secured all the viral pouches which Molijnet had released.

Although some of the virus had been leaked into the air, and some people would be affected, they had averted the real catastrophe. New York City was safe and Molijnet Cryzki was headed for the morgue.

VI

René Norman was faced with a very difficult task. He would have to announce a decision that could result in many more deaths to come. But it was a decision that had been made on the basis of the greatest good, with due regard to the future of his country.

He would not bend to terrorism – ever. To do so was to tell the lowest possible ilk of mankind that they could control the lives of decent people with their insanity. No, he would never give them even an ounce of glory – not in his country, not on his watch as the Prime Minister!

In the wake of the growing flu epidemic, the astronomical death counts, and the financial meltdown in Toronto, climbing Mount Everest seemed like an easier task than having to explain to the nation why he was vetoing the bill. Not to mention the fact that every enemy he had, would use this to fuel their attack against him and his party.

He wondered to himself just how far these terrorists would go to accomplish their ends. He had no former experience in his political career with terrorism. But he knew that *he* was an expendable element in the overall equation. He could be forced out of office, since public opinion was as moldable as clay, given enough money and enough influence.

The only solace he could find at this time, the only moor he could latch his ship to before it drifted off to sea, was the thought that when he had taken his oath as Prime Minister of Canada, he had promised that he would make Canada an even brighter and better place to live. He was not going to go back on that promise. If it meant forsaking his career to fight these bastards, he'd do it. He'd be damned if he was going to be pressured into passing legislation that would ultimately make slaves of his nation's citizens. He was not going down in the history books with that on his record.

VII

"Welcome back from the Great White North, guys," Ross said with a smile on his face, as Keeno, Jake and Katherine walked into RCMP CIC and slumped into chairs.

"I think we should get these to the lab for analysis," Jake said, handing the samples and evidence they had recovered from Rankin Inlet over to the Operations Officer. CC scooped up the bag and briskly exited the room.

Ross could see that his team was beat up, tired and in the case of Keeno and Jake, wearing bandages on their arms where they had taken some wounds in the battle.

Ross felt bad that he couldn't send them home, especially after what they had gone through up there, but the stakes were beyond high, they were at a critical mass stage. "I know you guys are probably looking forward to some sleep, but I have to bring you up to speed on something," he said, with a large dose of humility.

"Actually, I'm thinking about a Starbucks right about now," Jake said. "How 'bout you?" he said to Keeno, to help disarm Ross's obvious feeling of guilt. They knew that the pressure was still on and that it wasn't over until the fat lady sang her final tune.

Keeno forced a tired smile, "Sounds good."

At that moment, as if on cue, Kelly and Janene barged into the room with trays of coffee and dropped them on the table.

"Thanks, guys," Keeno said. Janene plopped down next to him and shoved herself hard against his right side. He leaned into her and she felt warm.

"The PM is going to make an announcement that he's vetoing the bill. There are various possible fall-outs from that, one being that the attackers will step up their operation and hit us even harder, while using that to leverage the entire nation against the PM's office. Or, they'll pack it up and disappear into the woods for a while and come back again later. Either one is not good, but I'd far prefer the first scenario. We've got them in the ring now and I want to finish this fight."

Keeno sipped on his coffee, quietly agreeing with Ross. He felt Janene squeezing his leg under the table. "Cheeky," he whispered, and she smiled.

"I guess that means that we load up on the coffee and get to work," Keeno said.

Ross smiled humbly in appreciation.

Keeno turned to Janene, "Were you able to source the anonymous email address which Willie Ackerman was sending his reports to?"

"It's an IP address in China, looks like a Shanghai designation, but they're running all sorts of firewalls and multiple security screens to protect it."

Jake looked at Keeno, "You think it's CJN?"

Keeno nodded, "Their headquarter is in Shanghai."

"What about the Chinese government? If we go after CJN, how many political toes are we stepping on and what's the potential fall-out?" Ross asked. He knew it was a rhetorical question, but one which needed to be tabled to make sure they were looking at all the consequences.

"We know that the PRC and its senior members have their hands in almost every major industry in China, and many of them are secretly board members and get major kick-backs," Janene said. "They use their 'state owned' manifesto to justify sticking their hands into any industry that is making money," she continued.

Keeno nodded in agreement, "Bottom line is, the communist regime will be slithering wherever we go in

China, and if CJN is involved in this attack, I guarantee you that the PRC has a hand in it."

Ross thought about admonishing Keeno, to not rock the boat in China, but it was a useless gesture considering that was his specialty. "What are you thinking?" he asked.

"We'll pay CJN a visit."

"Keep in mind that the Ministry of Health just purchased two million vaccines from CJN for the virus, so we don't want to screw that up in the process." the Ops Officer interjected as he stepped back into the room.

"When is the delivery supposed to happen?" Ross asked CC.

"Tomorrow at 5 p.m., the shipment arrives from China."

"Jake and I will fly over on the next flight, relax over a couple Mai Tai's until you let us know that the vaccines are received, and then we'll snoop around CJN and see what skeletons they're hiding."

"Remember, this is China, not Canada, the rules of engagement are different," Kelly spoke up.

"Yeah, and more dangerous," Janene said, as she eyed Keeno warningly.

"We'll try to minimize the damage, but if a few PRC boys get in my way, I'm making no promises," Keeno said, as he stood up and headed out the door with Janene. Before they got to their office, she pushed him into a small storage room, closed the door and lunged into him. The kiss seemed to go on forever.

She finally let him go and he took a long deep breath. She no longer concealed her love for him, beaming as she smiled. "That arm," she pointed at the bandage that had some blood seeping through, "please try not getting it shot again, I need it too."

Keeno looked down at it, "Yeah – no shit."

Two hours later Keeno and Jake were on their way to Toronto International Airport in an RCMP chopper. They had a flight to catch to Shanghai, via San Francisco. Before boarding their flight, Keeno made a phone call to Richard Jacobs at Homeland Security in DC.

"I heard you guys had a little excitement up in the Great White North!"

"You could say that, probably about as much fun as you had in the Big Apple," Keeno replied.

"Yeah, we got Molijnet and his virus, but he had nothing on him that we could trace to anyone," Jacobs said.

Keeno briefed him on his plan, if indeed flying to Shanghai and paying a surprise visit to CJN Holdings could be categorized as a plan. When he was done, he asked Jacobs if he could arrange for a package to be sent to their hotel room in Shanghai, through his Hong Kong office. Richards agreed, but only if he was allowed to join in on the operation.

When Richards hung up the phone, he called his Operations Manager and told him to prepare the team and the package. He sat back in his chair and wondered where this was all going, but there was one thing he knew for sure – as long as he stayed close to Keeno, more dead bodies would show up on the grid!

Chapter 7

I

"The operation has been compromised. You should consider holding it in abeyance until circumstances are more favorable," the deep authoritative voice sounded over the secure phone line from Switzerland.

The old man stood facing a wall-sized window looking over downtown Toronto. He listened to his counterpart across the ocean, a man of similar stature and power, but as he did, he was actually running the next steps of his plan through his mind.

It was his philosophy in business, and life, that if he started on a course to accomplish something, then he never hedged, withdrew or flinched. Sixty years later, he now headed a major banking institution with affiliates that girded the globe.

The old man had studied the Rockefellers and the Rothschilds in their ascent to global power. They were mentors to him, and if there was anything he had learned, it was that if one set out on a course of action, then one should finish it, at any cost. To do otherwise was to show weakness, a vulnerability, one which could be used to bring one down.

His plan to leverage the Canadian and American governments using the virus attacks was still winning him the major battle. A few lost skirmishes here and there were of no consequence.

As he listened to the other man admonishing him about the operation, it did not weaken his resolve to see his plans through to the end.

"I understand your concern and I appreciate your advice," he said with timed precision, according the man a sense of respect, "but I assure you that in spite of these minor setbacks, the main operation is still well intact."

"How can you be so sure?"

"I have anticipated this contingency. I have not yet played all my ace cards," he said

There was silence for a moment as the man on the other end of the line consulted with someone and then returned to the phone. "Ok, we will be watching, but do not over extend your confidence in the matter, there could be serious repercussions," the voice said as he ended the call.

The old man wasn't worried, and why should he be? He owned more property than most people in the world, his financial assets were in the billions, and he had friends in very high places – friends he could call upon if needed.

Beyond all of that, he still had his wild card to play, one that would set off the panic button in Canada and America like never before.

II

Jake and Keeno arrived at the Crowne Plaza Hotel in Shanghai after an overnight flight from Toronto. When they got to their room they found a package in the closet, the one Keeno had asked the Director of Homeland Security to arrange. He hefted it onto the bed, unclipped the locking device, and flipped open the top, revealing an assortment of handguns, ammunition clips, smoke bombs, transmitters and even some C-4.

Keeno smiled, “Leave it to the Americans to throw in a bit of C-4 just for good measure.”

Jake grabbed a gun and snapped a clip into place. “You can keep the C-4,” he said, “that shit creeps me out.”

Keeno found a note taped to the inside of the package, “We’re in room 418,” it was signed, “The Posse.”

They loaded up with their new toys and headed for their rental car. Keeno called the number for “The Posse” as they drove out of the hotel parking lot.

“That you Keeno?”

“Yeah, who’s this?

“Neil Hamilton, Homeland Security. What’s your plan?”

“We’re paying a visit to CJN Holdings. We’ll call you if we need backup.”

“No problem, amigo,” Neil said, but he already had his marching orders from his boss, Richard Jacobs, in DC. He was to stay on McCole’s butt and not wait for a call for help. If need be, he and his team were authorized to crash the party. He remembered what Richard Jacobs had told him in their last phone call, “Listen, McCole is a maverick. He’s got a reputation for getting stuff done, but he does it his way, so don’t wait for the bullets to start flying before stepping in to help.”

III

As soon as Keeno and Jake had taken off to catch their flight to Shanghai, Kelly informed Ross Fletcher that they, the girls, were going home early to catch up on some “girl time.” Ross merely smiled, offering only his tacit consent. He knew they were exhausted and stressed.

All three girls jumped into Janene's car and headed over to her apartment. Along the way they picked up food and beer, then kicked off their shoes and sat around her apartment disengaging from life at the RCMP.

"This is therapy for what I like to call FOS." Kelly said as she inhaled on a cigarette.

Janene smiled as Katherine gave Kelly a quizzical look, "FOS?"

Kelly pointed at the ceiling with her beer bottle, "**F**ucking **O**ffice **S**yndrome. The symptoms are restlessness, irritability, mood swings, a feeling like you're about to explode if anyone says another fucking word to you, and, extreme horniness – although that last quality isn't necessarily shared by Janene."

Janene rolled her eyes.

"Honestly girl, you need to get laid." Kelly prodded her playfully.

"Back at ya!" Janene said with a wave of her hand.

"Whatever!" Kelly sat up on the couch and faced Katherine. "Word on the street is that Jake's got his eye on you."

"How do you figure that?" Katherine asked. She was stretched out on an armchair, staring at the ceiling.

"Simple, we know Jake."

"I know men too and he's not the first guy to fall in love with my breasts."

"Jake's not quite like that, I mean, he likes tits and ass, and I'm sure yours are high on his preferred list," Kelly continued, "but I think he's actually falling for *you*."

Katherine nudged herself up straighter and looked at the other two women, "I'm listening."

Kelly blew out a smoke ring. "Like Keeno, Jake doesn't do the girl thing very well. Both these guys flunked at Women 101, they're kind of retarded on the subject, but in spite of that, we still love 'em. They keep to themselves, they don't talk a lot, but when they do open up, they wear their hearts on their sleeve. Jake's interested in you, he just has no balls when it comes to sharing his feelings."

Katherine smiled as she sipped on her beer. "Tell me about it! Since we left Rankin Inlet, they haven't said a word about it. For them it was like a Sunday walk in the park."

"That is their life. Where others go to work 9-5, these two eat bullets for breakfast and enjoy it. Honestly, I've been working with them for six years and I still can't figure them out, or how they can live like this, but they do. That aside, I've never seen Jake quite this gaga about anyone since you came along."

"I like him," Katherine started to say. "He reminds me of a big dog. Friendly, furry and simple – no baggage; the opposite of most guys I've met who kept a closet full of personal crap hidden from me, until they felt safe about opening that door. Jake isn't like that, he's transparent somehow.

Janene was listening to their conversation, but she was thinking about Keeno. She tried to size him up in her mind and he certainly didn't fit the description that Katherine gave for Jake. On the contrary, Keeno was still a mystery to her, like a ball of string, the more you unwound, the more you found out. When he looked at her with his intensely dark eyes, it was like looking through a window into his soul, and it magnetized her.

While she didn't think for a moment that she would ever tame the unaccountable recklessness in him, she did see him as a depth of life to be delved into. She had been looking for a soul mate and Keeno McCole fit that mold as if he had been made exclusively for her.

IV

When Paul Chang arrived back from Toronto at the CJN Holding's headquarters in Shanghai, he was applauded by his peers for netting one of the largest orders the company had ever taken. The Canadians had signed on for two million doses of vaccines. It was a landmark order and would place CJN firmly in the international arena.

Fueled by a passion to move China into every facet of the corporate and business community on the planet, the Chinese government, namely the People's Republic of China or the PRC, had given unanimous green lights on financing and aggressively forwarding CJN.

In their PR statements about the corporate structuring of CJN, the PRC had announced that it would retain ownership of 51% of the company, allowing the private sector to engage in the rest. Although that rang as congenially capitalistic, the truth was that the Chinese government secretly retained 91% of the company, and did not intend on forsaking one iota of that pie. They had carefully set up front groups, or fake companies, that appeared to be privately owned, and channeled huge sums of money through these to "purchase" into CJN Holdings. One of the perks of being a communist country was that China's books were not transparent to the rest of the world, and neither were its complete motives.

The real vision that the PRC embraced was to achieve financial control, to become the alpha-wolf in the international pack, and to use that economic base to leverage China into the number one spot of global power.

Most people failed to see their systematic advance in this direction, blinded by the fact that China now provided the West with the lion's share of manufactured products at a labor price that few countries could compete with, especially considering that China retained over 1/6th of the world´s population within its borders. The proverbial apple was too good to let go of, and that is exactly what the PRC had been counting on.

Paul Chang went straight to a meeting on the fifth floor of the huge facility. When he walked in, there were three people present in the room including the President of the company, his secretary, and Malcolm McDonald.

"Tell us about the trip," the President said.

Paul gave the broad strokes of his meeting with the Canadian medical establishment and their final determination to purchase the vaccines from CJN.

Malcolm McDonald wasn't interested in the details of the transaction. He already knew that the Canadians were locked in, and considering their circumstances, they had no choice but to purchase the vaccine. He wanted to see if there were any anomalies which might indicate a further problem, a hiccup or a hole in the fence – or worse, another encounter with Keeno McCole.

When Paul was done, the President thanked him and sent him on his way. Malcolm leaned forward and clasped his fat fingers, interlocking them under his chin, "It sounds ok – but we must be careful, McCole and his people are probably still snooping around."

The President of CJN Holdings, Chiny Yao Tsu, or Jimmy, as his colleagues and superiors called him, carefully assessed everything that Paul Chang had just reported. Jimmy had to answer directly to his superior within the PRC. There was no room for error, and the stakes were very high for him personally if anything went wrong.

Jimmy nodded, "It seems like all is well so far."

"Yes," Malcolm stood up. "I should be going now, I have some business to attend to," he smiled with a leer.

"Does that business include a young Chinese girl?" Jimmy tipped his head.

"I have always appreciated the finer things here in China," he bantered, looking forward to an afternoon of unadulterated sex with his seventeen-year-old secretary. For a man such as Malcolm McDonald, who had an obsession for sexual escapades with young girls, China was a dream-come-true, because, with his wealth, he could buy himself into and out of anything.

Just days before, when it had become clear that he had been compromised and that Keeno McCole had not been killed in Trenton, New Jersey, as planned, McDonald had arranged for his agency to put a sniper in the building across from his, to take him out, and if that failed, he had four more trained mercenaries waiting to ensure that the job was done.

The fact that McCole hadn't died in the gun battle was unfortunate, and disturbing to him, leaving a lingering worry, a sort of haunting feeling that he could show up anytime. For that reason, McDonald had stayed under the radar and had maintained a handful of trained mercenaries wherever he went. If McCole showed up again, there would be no misses this time.

He walked to his office, leering at his secretary as he passed her, closed the door and sat down at his desk.

"We never finished our meeting McDonald," someone said from across the office. McDonald nearly jumped out of his skin at the sound of that voice, and a cold chill coursed through his body. He turned and looked at the man who was seated on a small couch. “You have a unique ability to survive and to show up uninvited, Mr. McCole.”

Already the sweat was starting to bead over his entire body as a sense of panic began to grow inside, forcing his heart to beat hard and fast.

“I’ve been told that a few times, thanks.” Keeno responded.

“Are you here to kill me?”

“I’m not a murderer like you, McDonald,” he flicked his gun at him. “Turn around, put both of your hands on your lap. If I see them move, I’ll shoot off a few pounds of that fat hanging from your lower chin.” He stood and walked over to the other side of the desk, the gun held loosely in his right hand but still aimed at McDonald. “Listen McDonald, I’m not interested in confessions about how many sixteen-year-old Chinese girls you’ve screwed or how many dead bodies you have in your closet. I want to know who's pulling your strings – that’s all,” he said as he stepped closer to him, the gun menacingly close to McDonald’s face.

McDonald lowered his eyes and stared at the floor with a small, nervous chuckle. “You are an annoying man, and somewhat of an enigma. You keep showing up at awkward moments, and I find you're casual propensity for flippant humor to be ill-placed.”

“I’ll take that as a compliment,” Keeno replied. “Now tell me who your puppet master is?”

“Your arrogance surprises me. You realize that you will not make it out of here alive this time. Didn’t you notice the team of mercenaries outside the building?” McDonald replied, trying to buy himself time in the hopes that someone might enter the office.

"Should I start shaking now?" Keeno said, while poking the gun into the blubbery folds that girded McDonald's waist.

"You taunt death with such casualness."

"Actually McDonald, I invite it for a cup of coffee every fucking day, just to show it who is boss."

McDonald's mind was racing for some answer to his dilemma.

"You still haven't answered my question – who's the geek pulling your cords, McDonald? Who do you report to?"

Keeno put the gun against his neck. "Since you're not going to talk right now, then you're coming with me. Get up! Tell your secretary that we're going for lunch," and he pushed the nozzle of the gun into the small of McDonald's back.

As they stepped out of the office, McDonald turned to his secretary, "Ming – we're off for a quick bite. Tell Alfred that our meeting is postponed."

She smiled and nodded, waiting until they were out of sight, and then she made the call.

V

Something was definitely wrong – reports of flu illness were escalating again, dramatically. In the last twelve hours alone, hospitals were overwhelmed with people showing up at their doors for help. One report from a Dr. Putnam caught Katherine's attention.

She picked up the phone and called Trillium Hospital, and was soon speaking to Dr. Putnam.

"Dr. Putnam, my name is Katherine Riggs. I teach in the department of microbiology and viral studies at U of T."

"Yes?"

"I've just read your report from yesterday concerning the observations of a new strain of virus. Can you tell me if this was corroborated by more cases since then?"

"Yes – in fact, our hospital has had close to 1300 people walk through our doors since last night, all of them manifesting far more serious flu symptoms. The latest vaccines from China are not even making a dent on this new virus."

"You're sure of this?"

"Yes. We just got those new vaccines and it doesn't even slow this strain down. I've had my lab working on it for hours now and my technicians are pretty sure it's a mutant strain."

"Are you saying that it is self-mutating, on its own?"

"I am. In fact, from the tests I just received about an hour ago, the new strain is a combination of two of the earlier strains that hit the city. This new one seems to take several days to mature and reach its peak potency before it has a radical effect on a human body."

Janene and Kelly overheard her call and were sitting with a look of shock on their faces when Katherine hung up the phone. "You gotta be kidding... there's a new strain of virus?" Kelly asked.

Katherine nodded her head. She suddenly felt exhausted just thinking about it.

"What do you think?" Janene asked.

"We never considered the possibility of mutation."

"You mean, self-generating?" Janene asked.

"Yes. When we tested the other strains, we never anticipated they'd mutate, but if it's true and if it's a stronger virus, we're in big trouble."

"Ugggh," Kelly shook her head. "This is a nightmare!"

VI

Keeno directed McDonald down a back stairwell and out to a loading bay behind the main facility. Several workers having a smoke looked up at them. "Wave and be convincing," Keeno poked the gun into him. McDonald threw up his hand and gave his best Colgate smile.

Twenty minutes later, they arrived at the Crowne Plaza.

Keeno didn't have a plan, in fact, he was flying blind at this point, but an old adage came to mind which seemed to justify his rationale: *keep your friends close and keep your enemies closer.*

He wasn't letting go of McDonald this time. In fact, he was going to keep the fat man on ice, until he figured out a way to leverage some useful information out of him.

He keyed the door to his hotel room and was pushing McDonald into the room when something slammed into the side of his head with a crunch.

The last thing he remembered was the floor coming up at him and his world going black.

VII

The press conference was a literal shooting gallery, with the Prime Minister of Canada as its one and only target. The moment that René Norman announced that he, and five other members of his cabinet, had vetoed the emergency health bill, the press avalanched him with questions.

What should have been a ten minute press conference, ended up going for over an hour, and though prompted by his Press Aide to end it off before more collateral damage could result, René Norman still opted to let it run its course.

When it was over, he headed for his office, feeling like he had just stepped out of a boxing ring after ten rounds of repeated shots to the head and body. He was looking forward to sitting down, alone with a cup of coffee, but unfortunately, that was not going to happen. Standing by his office door was the Canadian Health Minister with a somber look on her face.

"Jacqueline?"

"We have a problem, sir." The look on her face was not at all reassuring.

"Come in."

He sat down and waited for the bad news.

"It seems that we have a new virus outbreak in Toronto, far more lethal than the other three combined. This one is causing a much more serious and disturbing infection in the lungs, and to date, none of our medical people or the hospitals are able to find a vaccine to abate it, not even the new vaccines we just got from this Chinese company" she paused. "There are already an additional 11,000 cases of this new virus just in the past ten hours. Toronto hospitals are overwhelmed, and worse, the number of possible mortalities with this new strain seems to be 25% higher than with the others."

René leaned forward with shock on his face, “Are you telling me that 25% of the people infected could die?”

Her eyes said it all. Norman slumped back in his chair. The bad news was overwhelming. He let out a deep sigh.

Jacqueline looked contrite.

“Relax Jacqueline… this is nothing that you could have predicted or prepared for. It’s not as if we’ve ever had this circumstance before. What do you recommend?”

“Immediate lock-down and quarantine of Toronto; including martial law to protect the rest of the country and our neighbors to the south. No one goes in or out right now. We have to contain it before the WHO declares Canada the source of a pandemic. I have teams of the best scientists flying in from Winnipeg, Vancouver, Edmonton, Montreal and Calgary – not to mention from every major university. We’ve already negotiated with the owner of Roger’s stadium to use it as an emergency field hospital to deal with the overflow. It’s centrally located so people can get there for treatment and vaccinations.”

“What are the chances that this same Chinese company has a vaccine for this virus?”

“We don’t know yet. We’re flying some samples of this mutant virus over to Shanghai as we speak.”

“What help do you need?”

“A prayer,” she smiled.

“Ok – do what you think is right.

When she had left, he picked up the phone and called Ross Fletcher.

“Ross?”

“Sir?”

“Are you guys any closer to nailing these people?”

"I have a team in China now. We think this Chinese company is involved in the plot and that they're playing both hands in the poker game."

"This is a nightmare. I just announced to the nation that I vetoed this bill, and now there is a new virus outbreak. At this rate, I'll be amazed if I'm not assassinated by tomorrow."

"Sir, we have to ride this out. I assure you we are not stopping until we get our man."

"I know that Ross, but I'm on the front lines and the troops are firing the bullets at me right now."

Ross let out a deep sigh, seeing the PM's position. He was taking the brunt of the public angst and the media's shit.

"Ok Ross – keep me in the loop."

"Yes Sir."

VIII

Jake had been crouched in the same position for nearly two hours. His legs ached, his knee joints were screaming, and worst of all, his bladder was about to explode, as he needed to take a piss in the worst way.

He checked his cell phone again; no call from Keeno in the last hour. That did not bode well. Although Keeno wasn't notorious for regular reporting, Jake had developed a definite sensitivity for his partner's world, and something did not feel right.

When they had split up some hours before, Keeno had told him to get inside CJN and see what he could find out, while he snooped around elsewhere.

Jake had squeezed himself behind two large pipes that ran vertically up the wall from the ground floor to the vaulting ceiling above. In front of him was a narrow metal catwalk that girded the massive, football field size facility below, and from which one could see more or less everything.

Only two people had passed by him on the catwalk, so he often took the liberty of craning his neck out from behind the pipes and glancing down at the activity below.

Knowing little to nothing about drug production facilities of this nature, the plant simply looked like a sprawling mass of boilers, tubes, pipes, and a covey of technicians and engineers flipping knobs as they monitored vats of gook. It wasn't very revealing, and in all honesty, Jake didn't have the slightest idea what he was going to find that would be of any use in their investigation.

Once again, he craned his neck around the pipe and looked down the catwalk, just in time to see four men approaching from the left. They slowed their pace, stopping not more than ten feet from where he hid. "Looks good," the closest man said with a distinct accent. "How long before you can have the new vaccine ready?"

"Approximately twelve hours. The process involves time for the vaccine to mature and stabilize before we can move it into packaging containers and ship it to Canada."

"Good, because by that time the new virus will be categorically a disaster for Canada and even America," the first man said. Jake couldn't make out any faces, as all the men were facing away from him, but he knew that voice from somewhere, it sounded familiar to him.

"We've seen the statistics," another one remarked with a Chinese accent.

"Pretty astounding that the mutant virus started up that fast," the first man said, and then waved a hand with casual indifference. Jake immediately recognized the gesture. He had seen that before and in tandem with the sound of that voice, his mind was struggling to formulate the answer.

"As long as the new vaccine works, that's all that matters. When I return to Canada, I will set the wheels in motion to get the emergency health bill pushed through."

"And your Prime Minister?" one of them asked.

"He's history. I'll be moving into power soon, and then we'll see a new Canada that will open the door to the RFID program, believe me," he said as he continued to stare down at the facility below.

Finally, he turned to face the others, and as he did Jake's jaw dropped. He pulled out his cell phone, clicked on the camera and gingerly positioned it where he could snap off several photos of the four men. "Jesus!" he muttered to himself and pulled back just as the foursome walked past him.

He waited until they had disappeared through a door, then slipped over the catwalk and slid down a pipe to the floor below. When he got outside the plant, he desperately wanted to call Keeno, but Mother Nature played her ace-card first, and the pain in his bladder won the battle. Jake ran for the nearest tree.

IX

Neil Hamilton and his team pulled into the parking lot at CJN Holdings in two unmarked cars. He immediately caught sight of several men stalking the front of the building. He knew the signs: short cropped hair, furtive looks and loose fitting jackets concealing guns – hired mercenaries.

Neil instructed his men to stay in their vehicles. He was pretty sure that Keeno and Jake were somewhere inside the facility. It was just a matter of sitting it out.

Nearly two hours into their surveillance, he caught sight of Jake Williams skirting the far end of the parking lot. Neil nodded to the other two drivers and they followed his car out of the parking lot and down the road, where they stopped out of sight of CJN.

Moments later, Jake showed up, "Keeno's off the grid, something's wrong. He always answers when I call, except when he's in trouble."

Jake got in the car and they sped off for the Crowne Plaza Hotel in downtown Shanghai.

Keeno couldn't remember a time in his entire life when his head pounded as badly as it did at that particular moment. In fact, he hadn't even tried to move his body or open his eyes yet because the pain throbbing from his cranium was taking the breath from him.

He tried to think back to what had happened, and all he could remember was pushing McDonald through the door of his hotel room, reaching for the light, when something struck him on the head. The rest was a complete and utter blank.

Slowly, he opened his eyes. The room was dark except for a small bed lamp to his right, but it may as well have been a knitting needle being jabbed straight into his retina – the pain was so tangible. He gasped and raised his hand to block it out.

As consciousness slowly came back to him, he acclimated to the light and realized that he was lying on the bed, in his hotel room.

Suddenly, there was a pounding at the door. "Keeno?" someone yelled. The pounding continued.

"Hold on!" He eased himself to the door and opened it. Neil Hamilton walked in with several agents and Jake on his heels.

"You look like shit, man. What happened to your head?" Jake asked.

One of the other agents turned on the lights, "Oh crap – that hurts," Keeno said, shielding his eyes and turning away. He walked over to the bed and sat on the edge, fighting the urge to suddenly throw up.

"What happened?" Neil asked.

Keeno shook his head, battling the nauseous feeling growing inside. "No idea. I woke up a few minutes ago. Someone whacked me when I came into the hotel with McDonald."

"You had McDonald with you?" Jake said.

"Found him at CJN, but he wasn't talking, so I brought him back here until I could squeeze something out of the fat lard."

Jake looked at Keeno's head injury. He had a purple colored lump across the left side of his head. It looked nasty.

Neil had one of his men call room service to get coffee, some food and pain killers up to the room. Meanwhile, Keeno called Ross Fletcher and explained their current situation.

Ross remained calm throughout Keeno's explanation, and then he spoke.

"Just relax, Keeno. Are you sure you don't have a concussion?"

"My head feels like someone's jack hammering my fucking brains from the inside."

"Stick by Homeland Security for now. If Jake hasn't already told you, he just called me about twenty minutes ago and sent us some pictures he took. He overheard a conversation at CJN with Carrie Levine, head of the Canadian New Democratic Party. Levine was talking to some guys at the CJN Holdings. Tom Sneider, from FAB-MED, was there too. Levine is involved in this virus attack up to his head and is planning a political shakedown in Canada to put himself into the PM seat. And, if you didn't hear it already from the girls, there's a new mutant virus on the loose in Toronto."

"How bad is the new virus?" Keeno asked as he rubbed the sides of his temples and then popped a couple of pain killers.

"Over 13,000 reported sick with this new one. The Minister of Health has already ordered a federal quarantine on Toronto. It's a total lock-down. The American's are going crazy because the same virus is now starting to show up across the border."

"Deaths?"

"Almost 1500 in the last day or so."

"Fuck!" Keeno said.

"Jake can show you the photos he took of the guys that Levine was talking to. We matched the pictures to one of the PRC's inner circle boys, plus the President of CJN."

Keeno's head was still pounding so he took another two pain killers.

"Ok...anything else I should know?"

"We studied all the stuff you brought back from Rankin Inlet. This God Chip is off the grid, meaning, they are years ahead of everyone. There is case history after case history in those files showing the damage they caused to people, small or large. This Chip is a walking time bomb." Ross said.

"How do they get that much power into a chip?" Neil piped in.

"They use satellites to amplify the signal. A radio signal wouldn't be strong enough," Ross answered. "According to the records we analyzed, they strategically place the chips on each side of the body and create a polarity of carrier waves between the chips, strong enough to damage organs in between."

"Like a microwave," Neil commented.

"Exactly," Ross confirmed.

Keeno cracked his neck, relieving some of his pain.

Ross continued, "According to Jake's latest info, Levine is using this entire virus attack to leverage his party into power. He's going to discredit René Norman and the Conservative Party, call for an emergency electoral vote, and bring in a new Prime Minister – namely himself. Whoever is behind this is using Levine to accomplish their ends."

"Can't we meet with the other NDP leaders and expose Levine?" Jake asked.

"We could, but if we move on that too fast we could blow our ace," Ross answered. "We know something that these guys probably think we're in the dark about. Also, keep in mind that while most of the NDP probably know nothing about this, Levine has to have a handful of assets working with him from within the party ranks. Snakes usually come in clusters."

"And our boys can't figure out a vaccine for this new virus?" Keeno asked.

"No, and if CJN has a vaccine already, then we have no choice but to use it, otherwise we're committing a lot of people to death, and putting both Canadian and American economies in jeopardy, not to mention the collateral damage to the international markets which would be rocked if North America stumbled and fell."

There was a long silence as Keeno tried to concentrate through the pain in his head.

"What do you want to do?" Ross asked.

"I'm gonna have some more coffee. Meanwhile, we'll go over it at this end and get back to you with our suggestion."

Ross agreed and hung up the line.

Neil Hamilton set up a watch, keeping a team of his guys posted on the hotel floor and in the lobby.

Meanwhile, they hashed out a plan, and by 11:30 p.m. they had called it in to Ross Fletcher and Richard Jacobs at Homeland Security. When the call was done, Keeno took a shower, then lay on his bed and was fast asleep in seconds.

Jake was sitting in the living room with Neil.

"You guys are tight," Neil said, as he drank down the last of his coffee.

"We've been through a few things."

"That's an understatement. Jumping out of planes over the Yukon Territory, not to mention parachuting onto a passenger boat under Niagara Falls and taking out two gunmen – at night time no less – how many people have that on their record?"

"Yeah, good times," Jake paused, "but I just don't get it, Neil; why is Keeno alive? Why'd they slug him over the head, take McDonald and just leave him here?"

Neil shook his head, "I've been asking myself the same question all night."

Jake stared out the window looking down into the streets of Shanghai, "I've got a bad feeling about this."

X

The plan was that Jake would stay in Shanghai along with Neil Hamilton's team. The RCMP would send out more people to join up with Jake, and between the two agencies, they would execute the mission. Meanwhile, Keeno would head back to Toronto.

Jake wasn't exactly happy about the arrangement for two reasons: he didn't like being that far from Keeno's back, and he wasn't big on Shanghai. He had trouble negotiating the language, the streets were incessantly crowded, and the smell of fish was everywhere, contrary to his palate which was fine-tuned to hamburgers and pizza.

Keeno's flight back to Toronto was uneventful, as he spent most of the time sleeping off the pain in his head. When he landed at Pearson Airport, he called Janene, and then jumped in a cab to their familiar hangout on Bay Street. She was standing outside the coffee shop waiting for him when the taxi pulled up.

Although she wanted so badly to comment on the dark bruise on his head and the bags under his eyes, she didn't. They spent the time romancing over cups of coffee, and then headed back to the office.

When they arrived in CIC, Ross Fletcher was seated with his Operations Officer at the conference table. "Welcome back," he said with a reserved smile. In his usual style, Ross treated the life and death episodes of his team as matter of course. He knew better than to make an issue over how close death had come to visiting his people. His philosophy was simple: *keep them looking ahead, not into the past.*

"What's the damage report?" Keeno asked as he sat down at the table and leaned into Janene.

Ross smiled at finally seeing some intimacy surfacing between the two.

"Since you left Shanghai, infections have escalated to 28,000. Hospitals are channeling the overflow of flu cases to the Rogers stadium for help. The effects are now starting to tsunami across the financial high ground, coast to coast," Ross answered.

"Looked pretty empty coming from the airport," Keeno commented.

"The city-wide curfew went into effect, not to mention the fact that police and military have locked down the freeways and are monitoring who is coming in and out. A lot of people are being sent back home to prevent more potential infections."

Keeno stared blankly, thinking to himself that this reminded him of some horror film he had once seen.

"The Department of Health has negotiated with CJN in China and they are expecting an antivirus to arrive here within twenty four hours."

"And the Americans?" Keeno asked.

"Their President has already seen the astronomical figures on this side of the border, and has called for a lock-down of three border cities where this virus has popped up – Buffalo, Detroit and Rochester. Meanwhile they're waiting for the same antivirus to arrive from CJN."

"And Carrie Levine, is he still shooting his mouth off about saving Canada from the Conservative Party?"

"He's all over the press and his popularity ratings are rising, while the Conservative Party is headed for the pits. Levine is high profiling the massive financial debacle in Toronto and the rest of the country. People are scared shitless that they're going to lose their jobs, their savings and their pensions. They're worried that the healthcare system is going to collapse. The bottom line is the Prime Minister is dodging bullets all day," Ross answered.

"Do we know who is backing Levine?"

"No. Their whole operation is clandestine, and we're walking on egg-shells in that department because we don't want to tip them off that we know about Levine. We're hoping that he might lead us to the people behind this. Levine is smart, but he's not smart enough to pull off this operation, and more importantly, he doesn't have the finances to do it."

Keeno stared at the table, "So, all we have is a big conspiracy, but not a single fact that we can stick to anyone's forehead to crack this wide open?"

"Right," Ross confirmed, "and another conspiracy theory will just wash through the media like shit through a goose, since 9/11 and the terrorist-on-every-block propaganda campaign, have calloused people on the subject. If the Prime Minister tries to hold off the attack using conspiracy as his platform, he'll be bowled over and he will lose his credibility."

Keeno let out a deep sigh, "Fuck, we're still behind the 8-ball."

XI

When Keeno woke up the next morning he laid unmoving, just staring at the ceiling. It was easier not to move, as his body hurt in too many places. Next to him Janene was still fast asleep. He listened to the quiet rhythm of her breathing and couldn't stop thinking about the night that had just passed. In spite of the knot on his head and the recent wounds to his body, all of it seemed to have evaporated when they had unleashed their passions on each other during the night.

When they arrived at the office that morning, Kelly was already there, as usual, planted in front of her computer with a cigarette burning in the ashtray next to her. Today her hair was a hue of pink and green. On anyone else the combination might have looked ridiculous but on Kelly it actually looked good.

"Doctor Phil just called for you. He insists that you go down to the medic wing for a checkup," Kelly announced with a drone. Then she turned to look at Keeno and Janene with a big smile on her face, "But then again, I'm sure EVERYTHING is in good working order," she leered at Keeno.

Keeno shook his head at her, "You're just jealous because you haven't been laid in decades," and he walked out the door.

"How would you know, you hypocrite!" she yelled after him as he disappeared through door, then turned and smiled at Janene, "So….?" she pried with wide expectant eyes.

Keeno went down to the medical wing and walked right in on Harry, the RCMP's resident doctor. Harry, also jokingly known as "Dr. Phil", had the honour of treating RCMP agents for all manner of light wounds endured in the field. Keeno had been a regular customer of his for years, so much so, that usually after every outing, Harry was calling him down for a checkup.

"How you doin' today Keeno? Any bullets I can remove? Or how about some shrapnel, or a nice slab of C-4 that hasn't exploded yet?" he joked.

"Sorry to disappoint you Harry – but nothing new that I know of. Been an uneventful week," he joked.

Harry chuckled, "*Uneventful* and *Keeno McCole* don't belong in the same sentence. Let's see..." and he pressed the palm of his hand against Keeno's skull right where the blow had landed. "Nice little bruise you got there."

"Yeah and it friggin hurts too," Keeno yelped.

"It should because it looks to me like someone dropped a tree on your head."

"It felt like it – believe me."

"I don't know Keeno, but there could be a fracture in there, and if so, we need to make sure it isn't going to hemorrhage or leak something."

"I'd hate to lose my brains."

"Indeed – probably not much left of them anyhow. Lie down here," he pointed. "We're going to do an X-ray and I'll do that left arm as well to make sure we got all the lead out of it since you've managed to get it shot up a few times."

"Keeping track, eh?"

"You have no idea. Makes my day when I can pull another slug out of you. I have a running bet with some of the guys on how many slugs you'll come back with each time. I'm getting pretty good at my predictions, even made some good money on you too," he smiled.

"The gambling Dr. Phil – a new low!" Keeno chimed.

The x-rays took another twenty minutes to do.

"You're free for now. I'll let you know what I find."

"Thanks Doc." Keeno went back to his office and sat down at his desk. He swiveled in his chair and stared out the window.

As he watched two birds dipping and diving, his thoughts returned to Shanghai. It felt surreal to him that he had been unconscious for hours and should wake up alive in his hotel room. Something made no sense and he hadn't stopped thinking about it; why was he still alive? What was McDonald up to?

He continued staring out the window when his phone rang, "What's up, Harry?"

"You need to come down here," the doctor's voice was grave sounding. Keeno went straight to the medical wing and found Harry sitting at a counter with a computer in front of him. Harry pointed to the screen and as he did he put his finger to his lips so Keeno would say nothing.

On the screen were the x-rays he had just taken. He pointed to two small black spots in the x-rays, barely perceptible to Keeno, but obvious to the doctor. "There's a God Chip in your left arm and another one near your heart," Harry scribbled on a pad.

Keeno's eyes lit up. The question flashing through his mind at that instant was whether they had actually heard their conversation that night in the hotel room when they planned out their assault. If they did, then they knew everything and they would be ready for them. Jake and the team would be walking into a death trap.

"I should take these out of you before they use them against you," Harry wrote.

Keeno shook his head and wrote… "Not yet!"

Keeno stood up, the rage coursing through him like electricity. He felt defiled, like a rape victim. He went up to CIC where he found Ross in discussion.

Keeno took Ross to one side and started typing on a computer. "I'm chipped with two God Chips. That's why they left me alive in Shanghai."

Ross stared at the message for a moment, not knowing what to say. Keeno continued to type, "If the God Chip can pick up vocal frequencies then they may have heard our entire conversation in the hotel room yesterday. The operation might be compromised."

Ross began typing, "Any ideas?"

Keeno sat staring at the screen and then began typing, "No, but I think our best approach is disinformation. Obviously they wanted me alive for a reason, probably to see what they can find out – so let's give them some plausible info, make it convincing and maybe throw them off their game."

"What about Jake and the plan in Shanghai?" Ross typed.

"We let it roll," Keeno typed. "If we change it now, we could lose on both fronts. It's a gamble."

"How can we be sure they didn't hear everything through your chips?"

"We can't, but it's the best we've got right now. One way or another, it's time to bring these bastards down." Keeno looked over at Ross, his face was resolute and his eyes were burning with determination.

Ross's face grimaced as he typed, "If we leave the chips in you, they could kill you anytime they want to."

Keeno's jaw clenched as he typed, "I know."

"It's not worth it Keeno," Ross typed.

Keeno shook his head, "Of course it is," he typed. "It can buy us time. If we take the chips out now, then we have no ace over them. They will just cover their tracks until next time, and meanwhile a lot of people die. I'm done with this bullshit."

Ross leaned back in his chair wondering to himself if he was signing off on Keeno's death warrant by agreeing with his plan.

What Ross didn't know is that Keeno had already decided on an alternate plan. He was done chasing after ghosts and second guessing them. He was taking the battle into the open field, and was going to broadside these assholes, even if it meant dying in the process

XII

Tom Sneider hadn't heard from Jim Vaughn in days; and according to the bits and pieces of reports that he'd received, the RCMP had busted up the show in Rankin Inlet, and the whole area was now under the watchful eye of Canadian law enforcement agencies.

He had to assume that Vaughn was either dead or lying low. Since returning from his tour of CJN in China, Tom continued to think about the RCMP agent, Keeno McCole, who kept showing up at the wrong times and in the wrong places. Although he knew that Malcolm McDonald had chipped McCole and was monitoring his every move, he didn't harbor the same optimism that McDonald did. McDonald had insisted that there was more value in the surveillance information that they might get from the chips than in just outright killing McCole. Tom had challenged his logic, arguing that McCole had been trouble enough, but McDonald held seniority over him and he won that argument. But, Tom had also conceded to the man on the simple basis that it had been McDonald who mentored him, and who had helped put him into his current position, and later introduced him to the RFID program.

Being the most senior board member of FAB-MED, McDonald had watched the aspiring Sneider as he worked his way up the ranks of the company, and it was he who had seen Sneider's potential, and had him fast-tracked to the VP of Operations spot. McDonald had seen something in Tom that others had overlooked: his aggression. Tom was not a dedicated company man so much as someone dedicated to getting to number one. He wanted job security at the top of the food chain, and McDonald recognized the value of using that motivation when he invited him to participate in their plan. The words of McDonald's closing pitch still reverberated in Tom's head: "Think of it as a fast-track to your most wanted dreams. The RFID program will put you ahead of the pack, riding the technological wave that will change the world. Why spend the rest of your life trying to get there, when you can have it in less than a year or maybe two?"

Surprisingly, and in spite of everything that had gone wrong, the entire operation was still considered a success by the old man. The Canadian government had purchased a massive volume of vaccines, and the Americans were following suit. With the new mutant virus spreading like wildfire in Toronto, it was just a matter of time before the emergency health bill was enacted, and with that would come the whole RFID program.

In spite of the old man's confidence in the plan, and McDonald's arrogance, Sneider was still uneasy about the RCMP, especially McCole, who had an uncanny ability to haunt them. Yet, the very idea of becoming the alpha-wolf in the new RFID industry, which his company would help to herald into the medical field, resonated strongly enough in his head to overcome his other concerns about the matter.

Chapter 8

I

Malcolm McDonald was feeling quite satisfied with himself. In the past forty-eight hours he had managed to turn a very nasty affair to his advantage, and in so doing, had maintained the confidence of the old man who saw the virtue in his impromptu plan.

When Keeno McCole had marched him out of his office at CJN, with a gun to his back, Malcolm had told his secretary that they were going out to lunch, and had asked her to inform Alfred that their meeting was postponed. Unknown to Keeno, "Alfred" was a code word, which meant that McDonald was in trouble.

The secretary had waited until Keeno and Malcolm had disappeared down the hallway, and then she called the head of the special mercenary team, waiting outside the building. The man quickly dispatched three of his hired guns to follow the RCMP agent to the Crowne Plaza Hotel. When they arrived at the hotel room, the mercenaries knocked McCole out cold with a cudgel to the side of his head, dragged him into the room, and then dropped him at the feet of McDonald.

After his momentary elation that the mercenaries had finally done something right and that he was safe, McDonald's first impulse was to kill Keeno on the spot. Yet, as he stood there looking down at the unconscious man, he realized that there might be an advantage to keeping him alive a while longer.

An hour later, a CJN technician arrived at the hotel and implanted two God chips into Keeno, one in the left arm, the other next to his heart. McDonald decided that he would activate the chips once he knew that McCole was back in Toronto, at RCMP HQ, where he could listen in on their plans and gain valuable information that could make sure that he stayed ahead of them at all times. Besides, with the size of that lump on his head, he didn't expect Keeno to be waking up any time soon; and if he did, and if he continued to snoop around CJN, he'd make sure that Keeno experienced an early, very painful and fatal heart attack.

II

Jake spent the next day waiting for word back from Keeno who had taken a very early flight back to Toronto. He had not been able to shake the haunting feeling that had started after finding Keeno in the Shanghai hotel room the day before.

His cell phone buzzed, "Doing ok?" Keeno SMSed.

"Oh yeah," he typed back, "I love eating duck and rice every day, friggin' awesome!"

"Stay cool. Your team is arriving soon. Kelly will send details."

"Can't wait to kick some ass," he SMSed back.

Sitting there chewing on his white rice and boiled duck combo, he thought about Katherine Riggs. *Now there*, he thought to himself, *was an interesting combo: a university professor with a pair of legs to die for, yet entirely capable of pulling the trigger and shooting a man in the back of the head.* Not that Jake was complaining, she had saved his life.

Since their first meeting, he hadn't been able to take his eyes off her. Inside of that beautiful body was someone that might even rival him. Most other women he'd been with had given up on him early in the relationship. He couldn't blame them – his line of work didn't exactly instill them with a sense of security, or the notion that he was a good long term investment.

Nevertheless, Katherine had a mystic appeal that magnetized him.

He flipped open his cell phone and looked again at the photo she had taken of herself sitting in the bath tub with a filmy layer of bubbles over her ample breasts. She had an inviting smile on her face, and her message read, "Waiting!"

"Just my luck," he mused to himself as he forced another forkful of rice into his mouth.

III

Before going home that night, Keeno and Ross spent two hours rendering a fake conversation, every word of which having been carefully hashed over in silence using the computer. It was designed to feed McDonald's arrogance and to lull him into a false sense of security, hopefully paving the way for Jake's operation to succeed. If he was listening through the chips inside Keeno, they hoped he would feel confident that the RCMP was off the scent.

Their tactic followed old military and counter-intelligence tricks. In the face of enemies who held the stronger ground, one tactic was to make them feel confident and give them the impression that one was weak, meanwhile preparing an attack to their flanks, hitting them when and where they wouldn't expect it.

By midnight, Keeno was exhausted. He had never experienced having to muzzle everything he spoke about. Ross had briefed his Operations Officer, Janene and Kelly on the situation, so they knew not to speak about anything critical in Keeno's vicinity.

Janene had stayed clear of Keeno all night, knowing that he was trying to navigate his way through rough waters.

She smiled at him as he stepped into their office, "How's my hero?"

"Oh, just peachy, thanks!

"You need some sleep."

"I know," at which they left the office arm in arm. When they arrived at Janene's apartment, Keeno eased into her bed and fell sleep. She watched him for a while, wondering to herself what Keeno was up to. Over the years working with him, she had come to see a certain subtlety in his body language; when he was upfront, his eyes were sharp and clear, almost translucent to her, but, when he was off in another world – some secret place to which Keeno McCole disappeared when he didn't want anyone else to interfere, his eyes became different, more solemn, lacklustre and less dynamic. Not to mention the fact that he was quiet. She was desperately in love with this man, who headed anti-terrorism and who, incidentally, had two lethal chips inside his body.

She lowered herself next to him and edged up against his body. The only thing she could do at this point was to rely on Keeno's sense of survival – yet she wondered, how many lives did the man have left in reserve.

IV

Carrie Levine, NDP leader of Canada, had bought into the grand scheme months before, after a series of secret meetings with Malcolm McDonald, and finally a meeting with the old man himself, at which time the deal had been consummated.

Their relationship was based on a mutual ambition for aggrandizement. Levine was not in it for the money – he wanted to be the Prime Minister of Canada. Since achieving his status as head of the NDP party, he had formulated countless plans to vault himself into the PM seat, but his personal popularity ratings never made the grade. In fact, his lack of political acumen and tendency towards "low-blow" politics was losing him, and his party, any chance at being taken seriously in the next polls.

When Malcolm McDonald had first approached him, Levine had no idea how much research and homework they had done on him. McDonald knew every button to push, and he was able to tactfully and diplomatically steer him right down the golden path they wanted.

It was after these initial meetings, during times when his wife was conveniently out of town, that Levine found himself provided with sexually wanton women. They appeared and disappeared, but they satiated his craving for every kind of sexual act conceivable, and like a drug, he craved more.

McDonald enticed Levine deeper into the rabbit hole, with the tacit understanding that cooperation was essential at this point, otherwise the women could disappear, and worse, his sexual escapades might leak to the media.

Levine played his role like a choir boy at Mass. He could not afford exposure of his darkest secrets, as that would ruin him, yet, they still offered him the vehicle to his ambitions, and that was the carrot that most appealed to him.

The financial debacle in Toronto was now having a domino effect across the nation. Levine rode that wave, attacking René Norman and his party through every media portal, and the public opinion was on his side.

Normally a nation of calm and peace, Canada was now a maelstrom of ill winds slashing from Vancouver to Halifax – and Carrie Levine was harnessing that chaos to bring his version of a new order to Canada.

V

When Keeno woke up that morning, Janene was already up and had a pot of coffee brewing. Over coffee, she tried to probe him, but he was keeping his cards close to his chest and for good reason; no one, Janene in particular, would ever approve of what he was about to do.

Ross was already in the CIC when Keeno arrived to see him. "Got a minute?" he asked Ross, while directing him to a computer terminal, along with the Operations Officer.

Keeno spoke while typing. "Any new developments?" he winked at Ross. Ross took the cue and they engaged in a fake conversation. Meanwhile, Keeno typed on the screen.

"Maybe we can trace the signal and see where the chips inside of me are being monitored from?"

Calvin Cole typed, "That could be rough, since they're using satellite relay."

Keeno nodded and typed, “I’m pretty sure CJN is involved, but we need to pinpoint the signal exactly, otherwise I might be experiencing an early heart attack,” he smiled.

The Operations Officer stared at the screen for a moment and then typed, “Our Vancouver office has some kind of surveillance facility in Taiwan, maybe they can help?”

Ross nodded to Calvin and took the keyboard, “Good idea. Contact the Vancouver office and give them the frequency codes for the chips. See what they can do.”

Calvin disappeared and Ross continued to type, “We can’t wait forever to take those chips out of you, and keeping up this charade is pissing me off.”

“I know,” Keeno typed.

Ross leaned back in his chair and looked at Keeno’s face. He was worried about him. They were taking a tremendous chance with his life in the hopes that they could somehow either track the bastards or deflect them for a while, buying more time in the process.

Keeno said, “I’m going to visit Ralph Ketchler’s widow this morning. I owe her a visit. I’ll be back later.”

Ross nodded. He knew that there wasn’t much that Keeno could help with right now, and keeping him around the RCMP HQ with the chips inside of him was like broadcasting their operations to the enemy. But he had also decided that if nothing useful was coming from the ruse, then he was going to force the issue and get the chips removed from Keeno by that afternoon.

Keeno went to his office, picked up a few things from his desk, and then went over to Janene who was busy at her computer. He told her he was going to pay a visit to

Ralph's widow, and kissed her lightly. She smiled and watched as he disappeared out the door.

"Is he ok?" Kelly asked with a concerned look.

Janene let out a deep breath, "Hmm, something is off with him, I just can't put my finger on it."

"Maybe because he's got two chips in him."

Janene shook her head. "No, it's something else. It's just a feeling I have. It's like he's not telling us something."

VI

Nickie Simms reviewed the latest reports from RCMP CIC at the Vancouver station. Her first order of business every day was to see what new situations and predictions had surfaced the night before.

As the Operations Officer for RCMP Vancouver, which encompassed a large region in itself, Nickie was responsible for ensuring that the RCMP was right on the heartbeat of west coast Canada's crime and corruption.

Vancouver, Canada, picturesquely situated with the Pacific Ocean to its west and mountains to its east, was also one of the largest ingress points for drugs, human trafficking and contraband into North America from Asia. The RCMP in Vancouver devoted a large part of their time and resources to monitoring the criminal element that snaked its way from Asia through the most westerly port in Canada. Working closely with the American agencies that were up against the same situation in Los Angeles, San Francisco and Seattle ports, it was a full-time war against the Asian tide that hit the North American shoreline.

For this reason, the RCMP had established a remote office in Taiwan, where they would have a means to more closely inspect illegal shipping activities through electronic surveillance. Nickie had been the one who had lobbied the RCMP to establish the Taiwan operation, after spending several years on the streets of Vancouver. In those years, she had investigated countless drug and human trafficking operations. There had been times when they had found ship containers with hundreds of Asians crammed inside during a voyage across the Pacific. The conditions were so inhumane and barbaric that it was hard to believe that there were people on earth who actually did this for a living.

Naturally, an office right in Beijing or Shanghai, or even in Hong Kong, would have been far preferable, but the Communists were not very cooperative about having foreign intelligence snooping around in China, so they opted for an RCMP surveillance unit in Taiwan to monitor shipping lines, looking for the telltale signs of contraband and human trafficking. It was still like finding a needle in the haystack, but at least they had been able to stop some of the illegal flow into Canada.

Her phone rang.

"This is Nickie."

"Hey Nickie, this is Calvin, Ops Officer in Toronto."

"Hey Cal, long time no hear."

"Need a favor. You still got that remote office in Taipei?"

"Yes."

"I've got a transmission frequency for a chip. Can your guys in Taipei see if they can get a fix on the source signal? It's a Code 1."

"No problem. I'll let you know."

She went next door and got her shift officer to pull up the file that had just appeared from RCMP Toronto.

"Get it over to Frankie in Taipei and ask him to trace that signal if he can. Tell him it's Code 1 – Urgent."

VII

Since Ralph Ketchler's murder at U of T, his wife Betty had tried hard to accept the fact that her best friend and soul mate of some forty years was truly gone. It haunted her day in and day out to walk through the quiet halls and rooms of their home without his smiling face and bantering. She had grown so accustomed to having Ralph there every night, sitting in his chair with a paper, a stack of books, and a glass of brandy, that his absence was like a black hole through the center of her being. She felt empty, and life seemed shallow without him to share it with her.

When Keeno showed up that morning to pay a visit, Betty was happy to see him, truly happy. The impulse to shed more tears was heavy in her heart, but she felt that for Keeno's sake it was best to put up a noble front. She had come to learn the details of Ralph's death, and was very moved by the fact that Keeno had held him in his hands when he died. She had also learned from the police about the car chase, and about what Keeno had done to get to the shooter who had taken her husband's life. Keeno had told her none of these details previously, and she remembered that Ralph had once told her that in spite of Keeno's adventurous life-style, he rarely spoke about it to others.

She hosted Keeno with coffee and some of her homemade pastries. Near the end of their brief talk, she asked him the question that had been on her mind since he arrived: "Did you find who did this to Ralph?"

Keeno looked her in the eyes, "He won't be bothering anyone again," he said with finality.

Betty nodded as her eyes watered and tears rolled down her cheeks. "Ralph always said that you were a man of few words," she forced a smile.

As Keeno pulled away from Betty's house, he looked back at her in his rearview mirror. She seemed a shadow of the woman he knew from before, and it reminded him how important friends and soul mates could be to one another. He thought about Janene – was he committing her to the same life, of early widowhood, loneliness, a broken heart?

He went to a nearby electronics store, purchased a new cell phone so that no one could trace him, and booked a flight to Ottawa using on-line ticketing so as not to announce his intentions to anyone.

Keeno's threshold of tolerance had long since been passed, and the fuse was burning at both ends now.

He could think of a dozen times in the past six years when criminals, wanna-be terrorists and others had tried to kill him. Sometimes the odds were against them, but each time his RCMP team had come out on top, with the bad guys either locked up or dead.

This time he felt defiled, degraded and humiliated. They had not only bested his team so far, but they had implanted him with the God Chip in the mix. It was demeaning to think that some fucking creep somewhere was monitoring him, following him, listening to his conversations, and that he was relegated to the likes of a prisoner under watch 24/7. On top of that, they had the ability to kill him in an instant.

At the age of four, Keeno knew his mindset and purpose. His father had helped to catalyze the process of sending him on the path he walked today. What motivated Keeno to live the life he did was not the fact that people committed crimes. He had no delusions about the fact that there would always be a certain element of society that was criminal. He was fueled by another passion altogether. He lived to give a message to criminals and terrorists alike – that there was nowhere they could hide, that he and his team would find them. His philosophy about anti-terrorism was a simple one: since terrorists dealt in "terror," then he would be their antichrist, their worst nightmare, the one factor that they should be worried about night and day. He wanted them to know that as long as his team existed, they would never succeed.

Now he was tired of the chase. He had taken enough bullets and enough bullshit from these people, it was time to turn the tables on them, raise the alarm and bring the fight out in the open.

In spite of the den of tigers he was about to walk into, Keeno was thinking of just one thing as he boarded the plane – Janene.

VIII

Frankie was slurping down his chicken and lentil soup when he got the call from RCMP Ops in Vancouver with the Code 1. He raced out of the small cookery, weaved his way through the ever crowded streets of Taipei, and arrived at his fifth floor office in the corner of the building where the RCMP had set up only one year before. He tapped his computer and pulled up the file just sent in from Vancouver, downloaded the contents and activated the frequency.

Frankie had dubbed the sophisticated machine "BOOBS." He fantasized that BOOBS was a beautiful, busty red-head, and he spoke to her as such as he worked.

It took several minutes to establish the metrics for the frequency that RCMP Toronto had sent him. BOOBS was designed to take a frequency and match it with other resonating wavelengths which were emanating from sources within her operating parameters and radius. She was linked to several satellites circling the globe, not limited to line-of-sight radio frequencies alone. Once she found precise matches, she assessed for anomalies and systematically eliminated the questionable ones until she had located the exact source of any frequency output.

If one thought of it in terms of a linear process, and indeed, if one actually listed out the sequence of actions that BOOBS engaged to accomplish the feat, it would fill hundreds of pages of single typed lines of code. In reality, she did the entire procedure in a matter of seconds, multitasking at a speed that defied normal mathematics.

Frankie sat there waiting for the ping – a sound and a notice on the screen that would tell him whether she had made a match or not.

Within seconds, she pinged.

“Holy shit!” he said out loud.

Someone in the other room looked up, “What?”

“We’ve got a live one,” he said, as he picked up the phone to call Nickie Simms at RCMP Vancouver.

IX

Jake had been instructed to meet up with the rest of the RCMP team at what seemed to be a low-profile establishment in downtown Shanghai. He wondered to himself, as he entered the club, why on earth Kelly had selected this place for the rendezvous, but as he passed by the sign on his way in, he understood better why the name

"Maggie's Place" would have disarmed her. It didn't exactly sound like a topless bar. In fact, it sounded innocent enough until you got inside and realized that the place was filled with nearly naked Chinese women wearing only G-strings and high heel shoes, serving up drinks and light food to a packed house of gawking male patrons.

Jake tried to avoid looking at the sea of naked breasts bobbing up and down at every turn. In fact, he was trying to be good these days since discovering Katherine. As he sat down at a table in the far corner, a topless cutie approached him, "Something to drink?" she asked with a thick Chinese accent, while jiggling her well-endowed breasts in front of his face.

"A beer."

Moments later, he was sipping on his beer when two members of the team arrived. They sat down and ordered drinks from the same busty lady. Within another thirty minutes, the entire team was present.

No words were spoken about their mission. They engaged in small talk, enjoyed their beers and the local sights, and then one by one they left the establishment.

Tomorrow they would hit CJN Holdings and Jake was looking forward to it. In fact, he was going to have a hard time sleeping tonight as the adrenaline pumped into his system in anticipation.

X

When Keeno's flight arrived at Ottawa's MacDonald-Cartier International Airport late that afternoon, there was a black Lexus waiting for him as he emerged from the airport terminal.

He was driven straight to the Capital building on Parliament Hill, and taken underground to a special parliamentary parking lot. The driver efficiently ushered him, by way of elevator, up to the large, posh reception area where a secretary greeted him by name.

A moment later, a door opened and the Prime Minister of Canada, René Norman, stepped out and invited him into his office.

"Make yourself comfortable, Keeno," he said, as he pointed to a small coffee table with two cups and a small carafe of coffee.

Keeno sat down and the PM followed.

"My secretary said it was urgent that you meet with me, and considering what you've been working on, I was more than interested in making the time for you."

René Norman sat back in his chair and studied Keeno McCole for a moment. He knew more about him than he was letting on. After Keeno had called his secretary to arrange the meeting, he had her pull up Keeno's RCMP profile.

"I came here because I know you have a press conference tonight and I would like to present your case for you."

The PM cocked his head and raised a brow, "You want to talk at my press conference?"

Keeno nodded as he sipped on his coffee. "It's not my forte, I assure you. Canada is under attack right now by an organized terrorist plot, a well-organized campaign designed to take you out of office, put Levine in power and give these people the open doors they need to implement the RFID program. We already know that their plan is to get a beachhead in Canada, and then use that to leverage the Americans to do the same."

"I know all of that – Ross has been briefing me. So what are you suggesting?" René asked as he watched Keeno.

"You can't go out and talk to the Canadian people about conspiracies or terrorist attacks – even if it's true. People don't buy conspiracy theories on a broad basis any more. After 9/11, the market is glutted with the subject. With that said, if you say anything about this, then Levine will nail the stake through your heart and you will lose your credibility. But, if I get up there and tell them what we know, from an RCMP anti-terrorism platform, then that would be believable coming from me, since it is my job. It would accomplish two things – it'd get the truth out there and shove a stake into Levine's heart, and secondly, it would expose the plot and maybe back these people down."

"It could backfire on us too?"

"It's a gamble for sure, but I think it's time to bite back."

"But what could you say that would spook them or get them to tip their hand?" the PM challenged lightly.

Keeno stared at his coffee cup for a moment, "You're going to have to trust me on this one. In the last two weeks they've tried to kill me three different times, and nearly succeeded. They want me dead, and if I show up on national TV and drop a few facts into the public domain, exposing their plot, it could piss them off – maybe even get them to make a mistake or two. All I need is for the snake to stick its head out and I will cut it off," Keeno said as he looked the PM in the eyes.

Norman sat there pensively for a while, thinking over Keeno's words. These were desperate times, and a rush on the ramparts was sometimes the only way to gain the advantage, so history reminded him at that instant.

"How close is the RCMP to dropping the net on these people?"

"We're not. We're still chasing ghosts."

"You're not being very reassuring."

"I'm being honest," Keeno said.

"Is this really such a good idea for the head of RCMP Ontario's anti-terrorism unit to go national, even global, when you don't have the answers yet?"

Keeno smiled, "Right now we're playing the role of sheep, surrounded by wolves. They have the upper hand, but I intend to force them to tip their cards. A little bit of Tsun Tsu strategy – we'll play the bleeding sheep and let them pounce. Beyond that, I think Canadians should know what's going on, and if I tell them, it saves you for the battle you're up against in the political arena."

Norman smiled. It was the one argument that could win him over anytime – honesty. But he sensed that there was something else Keeno wasn't telling him, he could see it in his eyes.

"The conference starts at 11 p.m. sharp. You will be first up."

Keeno nodded, almost graciously, but he was sweating profusely and could feel it under his clothes. If anyone had been monitoring his conversation with the PM, they would know of his plan, and if the God Chip worked, then they could kill him well before the press conference ever happened.

He had just taken a gamble. He had put all his money on one hand, and a lousy one at that, whereas McDonald and his peeps seemed to be holding all the aces.

But if there was one thing that Keeno had learned in his years of fighting crime, it was the fact that criminals always had a streak of stupidity and arrogance in them.

Eventually, they would slip, and he was banking on that happening soon. Short of spending endless weeks chasing after these guys while people died of the virus, it was the only card he had left to play in his otherwise empty hand.

XI

Malcolm McDonald rolled out of bed at 11 a.m. on Sunday morning with his head pounding and a consuming feeling of nausea. He had spent the whole night engaging in unadulterated debauchery with three sixteen-year-old Chinese girls. Their energy and his lust, combined with copious amounts of drugs, had kept him going until close to sunrise, when he had finally sent them on their way and then collapsed unconscious onto his bed.

He felt an anxiety. He had stupidly overslept. When he had left CJN the night before, he had instructed the night technician to SMS him the second anything important was overheard through Keeno's chip.

Unfortunately for him, in his drug and sex-dazed stupor, he had shut off his phone. Now, as he started it up again he saw several SMSs from the technician.

"Fuck!" he yelled, as he finished dressing and called down to the men standing outside his apartment building to escort him.

By the time he arrived at CJN's otherwise empty parking lot, it was nearly noon. "Play back the conversation from early this morning," he boomed at the technician as he stepped into CJN's control room. The man nervously fiddled with some knobs and put the conversation on the loud speakers.

Malcolm McDonald listened as Keeno and the Prime Minister of Canada conversed. When it was finished, he looked at his watch; it was just after noon local time, which was 11 p.m. in Ottawa, exactly when the press conference was supposed to begin. "Get the Canadian news stations on that screen there," he pointed to a monitor.

It was time to watch Keeno McCole die, he thought, *and this time he wasn't sending anyone else to do it. He would kill him in front of national television.*

XII

They traveled in four different vehicles – two with the RCMP team and two with the Homeland Security team. The plan was simple: get into CJN and secure incriminating evidence that could shut these people down, preferably something that showed the connections top to bottom.

They already knew that the facility would be closed on Sunday, so they weren't expecting any major opposition. What they didn't know was that Malcolm McDonald had already arrived at the facility just moments ahead of them and with him came a team of eight professional mercenaries.

Jake arrived at his position first, with another RCMP agent. They slipped out of the car and started walking along the fence line that surrounded the property.

The first shot that broke the morning silence sliced into the RCMP agent next to Jake, knocking him to the ground and spilling blood over the dirt and gravel. Jake dove to cover the man's body, pulling out his own gun to return fire, but there was no sign of the shooter anywhere.

"You ok?"

"Yeah I'll survive," the agent winced in pain. Jake tore off the sleeve of his jacket and wrapped it around the man's arm to help stem the bleeding, "Go back to the car."

"No way, I'll cover you," he said, with a look of determination in his eyes as he pulled out his gun.

"Stubborn asshole, you must be Canadian." Jake said. The agent smiled at the remark as he positioned himself on his stomach and aimed his gun towards the building.

Jake got up and bolted along the chain link fence when another shot struck the dirt by his feet.

On the other side of compound, the other agents heard the gunfire, saw Jake running and watched as two men appeared from the roof, aiming their guns at him. One RCMP agent snapped off a shot that struck one of the men in the back of the head. Neil Hamilton fired at the second shooter, forcing him to drop off the roof-top.

More shots suddenly rang out and pounded into the ground around the agents, and they dove for cover.

XIII

Inside the facility, Malcolm McDonald was hovering over the console, watching Keeno as he talked to the media at the Prime Minister's press conference.

He toggled the switch between his thumb and forefinger, increasing the amplitude between the chips inside of Keeno, and watched with pleasure as his face grimaced in pain. He was enjoying this, really enjoying watching him as he magnified the frequencies to induce the heart seizure.

Chapter 9

I

The call from the Vancouver RCMP station came just as Ross Fletcher was hoping for a miracle. The Taiwan office had traced the source-frequency for the chips to Shanghai. Within seconds they had their target – CJN Holdings headquarters on the outskirts of Shanghai. It was a dead match.

Since early afternoon that day, Ross had been climbing the walls. Keeno had disappeared off the radar. They had tried to track him through his phone, but he hadn't made any calls on it since early that morning. Janene and Kelly checked all his usual haunts and even inquired with Betty Ketchler, who assured them that he had left by noon that day.

Did this mean that Keeno was lying dead somewhere? Had McDonald activated the God Chips and killed him? One of his staff approached Ross, "Sir, you need to see this," she pointed to an HD screen on the opposite wall.

Ross turned to see live coverage of the Prime Minister's news conference. He stared at the screen as Keeno stepped up to the microphone. *So that's where Keeno disappeared to*, he thought. They hadn't even considered the possibility that Keeno would get on a plane

– it was so radical. He had gone rogue and was baiting the wolf to attack.

Ross watched in a sort of abject horror as Keeno introduced himself as the head of anti-terrorism, and it occurred to him that if he didn't act fast, Keeno would probably be dead in a matter of minutes.

"Get Jake on the line right away – flash Code 1 on his phone," Ross commanded. He was breaking all his usual protocols in calling an agent in the field. He had no choice – it was act or watch Keeno die.

Someone handed him a cell phone, "Jake's on the line."

"Jake – listen to me…"

As Ross explained to Jake what was going on, Janene and Kelly walked into CIC and froze as they saw Keeno speaking on live television.

II

Jake dove behind a small retaining wall just as another round of bullets chewed into it, exploding chunks of stone into his face.

Suddenly, his cell phone rang. Under normal circumstances he would not have taken the call, but the fact that his partner and best friend was half way across the planet compelled Jake to see if it was Keeno calling.

The Code 1 flashed on his digital dial. "Jesus – you gotta be kidding," he complained out loud as he flicked it open. Another bullet exploded into the wall near his head, sending a stone fragment into his eye. "Fuck," he yelled.

"Listen," Ross commanded, "Keeno's live on the air in Ottawa, doing a press conference with the PM."

"Great – really happy for him but I'm a little tied up right now, Ross." Two more slugs thundered into the retaining wall, splashing more rock bits into his forehead.

"No – you don't get it," Ross yelled over the din of crashing bullets. "Yesterday we found out that Keeno's got two God Chips implanted in him."

"What! So that's why McDonald left him alive in that hotel. That fat bastard is using him."

"Exactly, and we think that Keeno's convinced the PM to let him blow the whole show out into the open and bait McDonald to activate the chips."

"Why didn't you stop him before this?" Jake shot back as he peered over the jagged edge of the wall.

"Keeno went off the grid and got himself to Ottawa before we knew anything about it. The point is that he's about to commit suicide. If McDonald hears this conference, he'll kill him – I have no doubt about it.

"That sounds like something Keeno would do," Jake said, as another slug whizzed by his head.

"We tracked the signal for the chips to CJN – first floor. You need to get there before Keeno ends up in a body bag."

"Great, just fucking GREAT!" Jake said as he slipped the phone into his pocket. He wasn't ready to give a eulogy at Keeno's funeral service.

Jake dove over the top of the shredded wall, rolled twice and came up on his feet running straight for the nearest window. He let off several rounds into the glass plate, causing it to implode before he dove through the opening.

Two mercenaries suddenly dropped to the ground from the roof above and started running for the same window. One of them never made it, as a Homeland

Security agent unloaded three rounds into the man. The other mercenary speared through the window before anyone could get a shot into him.

III

The press conference was held in the largest facility on Parliament Hill, a room where former Prime Ministers had made history, a place where the ripples of reform and change had been set into motion for Canada. On this day, it would once again be the epicenter for the next tsunami to hit the nation.

The room was packed with Canadian media, as well as media from America, Australia, Britain, Japan and Germany. Canada had moved from being relatively low-profile in the world headlines, to being the apex of international news, as the epidemic in Toronto was causing a financial tidal wave that was now stinging the stock markets internationally.

At precisely 11 p.m., René Norman, the Prime Minister of Canada, stepped up to the podium: "Ladies and Gentlemen of the press, those of you watching this broadcast live, and those who will see it when you awaken, I welcome you. The outbreak of V-4, the mutant virus in Toronto, resulting in a lockdown and quarantine of that city and the resultant astronomical infection and death rate, has no doubt caused serious alarm and panic throughout the nation. I am doing this press conference to provide information concerning this matter, so that you, as Canadians, can understand our mindset."

He paused.

"First, please let me introduce Keeno McCole."

Keeno stepped up to the podium as cameras flashed and the crowd of reporters murmured over the sudden appearance of this mystery man.

"I am in charge of the RCMP's Ontario anti-terrorism branch. You don't hear much about us, because what we do is under the radar, as it should be. The less you hear of me the better, but in this matter of the Toronto situation, I offered to brief you on some details which the Prime Minister has conceded to."

He paused to collect his thoughts; Keeno had never been in this position before, speaking to live media on syndicated national television.

"The viral epidemic in Toronto was not a mistake," he began. "It was planned and caused by people who have an agenda. This virus attack was purposely designed to bring about a near collapse of our infrastructure, forcing the PM and his cabinet and the legislature of this country to pass the Emergency Health Bill, which would not only mandate national inoculation, but more importantly, would open the door to legislating an RFID program."

Keeno felt a slight discomfort in his side, a constricting feeling that caused him to catch his breath. McDonald was listening, which meant that time was no longer on his side.

"For the past three years, the people behind this attack have been running an illegal facility in Rankin Inlet, testing human implants of RFID chips, or Radio Frequency ID chips. They have developed an aggressive chip which, when planted in different parts of the human body, can be used to generate physiological conditions such as hemorrhaging, blood clots, physical pain, paralysis and even heart attacks. We have shut down their facility and taken documentation showing their research and the people who died at their hands."

The pain suddenly streaked through Keeno's body, shaking him to the core. It felt as if someone had just stuck a knife into his heart. He gasped and lurched forward against the podium. His world wavered and his face broke out in sweat as his skin turned white.

The PM, who was standing to one side, stepped up to Keeno to help, but Keeno motioned him with his hand. He focused his attention back on the room of cameras which flashed and buzzed as the media snapped off hundreds of pictures.

"I came here today, not at the request of the Prime Minister, but on my own, to tell you that Canada is under attack. Your Prime Minister is not to blame. These people have launched an organized assault designed to accomplish one thing – to pass legislation that would ultimately reduce you to human GPSs, controlled, regulated and nothing more than puppets to some master."

An agonizing wave ripped through Keeno at that instant. He felt nauseous and his world began to spin uncontrollably. He no longer felt any sensation in his arms and legs as the blood pooled to his heart, which was struggling to stay alive, to continue to beat in spite of the frequency pounding into it from the chips on each side of his body. The pain mounted to the point where it was unbearable. Keeno tried to say something more, but the words never came out as his heart gave up the battle and he toppled forward against the podium.

The PM and another man caught him before he struck the floor.

The press conference erupted into a melee of voices. Cameras zoomed in on Keeno as a paramedics team rushed in and moved him to a nearby room.

In the RCMP CIC in Toronto, everyone watched, transfixed, as Keeno spoke. When he suddenly collapsed to the floor, Janene's world caved in. Her body began to shake and the tears pooled in her eyes.

"Come on," Kelly wrapped her arms around Janene, and tried to nudge her out of the room, but she resisted, her eyes still glued to Keeno's lifeless form as people carried him away from the press conference.

Then she dropped into a chair and the tears poured out.

IV

Jake landed on the floor and skidded on top of some of the glass shards from the window he had just shattered. He felt the glass biting into his leg and hands, but he simply didn't have time to do anything about it. He was thinking about what Ross had just said. Jake knew Keeno better than anyone in the world, and years of surviving in the field with the man had taught him all the nuances of his partner. Where others would view his act of standing up in front of the media as suicidal, Jake understand Keeno's mind. He was pushing the envelope. He was pissed off and tired of being screwed with, and now, he was bringing the fight to him, even if it meant dying in the process. He knew that Keeno was not suicidal. He was impetuous, obstinate, wild and unaccountable at times, but there wasn't a streak of suicidal tendency in him. Keeno was doing what he did best, stepping outside the box and kicking ass.

Nevertheless, Jake was worried – *had Keeno pushed it too far this time?* he thought.

He jumped to his feet and ran through the open door, turned down a hallway nearly colliding with a small oriental man who stood there in abject terror as Jake waved his gun in the air. “Where’s the RFID lab?” he yelled.

The man’s eyes reactively followed the gun. Jake grabbed him by the arm and squeezed it to get his attention, “Where is the fucking RFID lab?” he screamed at him. The small Chinese man pointed nervously down the hall, but as he did, Jake caught some motion in his peripheral vision, and turned just in time to see one of the mercenaries aiming his gun at him.

He grabbed the technician with his left hand, shoving him to the floor, while letting off three rounds at the mercenary. Two bullets flashed by Jake’s head, missing him by millimeters, while another one slammed into his left thigh. Jake yelped in pain, trying as he did to pull the Chinese guy out of harm’s way, but the man was already dead with a bullet lodged in his forehead.

“Shit!” he yelled, and aimed his gun for another shot at the mercenary, but too late. The mercenary had his gun trained on Jake’s head and was pulling back on the trigger. It was the second time in less than a week that Jake Williams had looked down the barrel of a gun. The first time, Katherine had miraculously been there to bail him out, but this time he didn’t see any redheads with a great set of legs and a smoking gun.

He watched as the shooter’s gun exploded, but something about the sound was wrong. There was a double report. The bullet intended for him, skimmed by his forehead so close that he felt the heat-burn as it grazed his skull. He watched as the shooter’s chest exploded outwards in a shower of red that spattered the walls. His limp form plopped forwarded, and standing behind him was Neil Hamilton of Homeland Security.

"You ok?" he yelled at Jake.

"Yeah, just a flesh wound," he lied and then he turned and hobbled towards the glass doors at the end of the hallway.

Jake lifted his gun and fired two rounds into the thick glassed security door until it shattered. He pushed open the door and hobbled into the room, blood coursing down his leg as he did.

Malcolm McDonald stood on the other side of the room hovering over the console like a vulture guarding its meal. Beside him sat a technician, his eyes bulging in horror at the sight of the gun that Jake aimed at them.

Malcolm showed no apparent fear. He managed a look of smug arrogance with an air of dismissal about him. He also had his fingers on a dial and that worried Jake.

In truth, Malcolm McDonald was shaking inside. He had underestimated these people. He had never expected them to find out about the chips implanted in Keeno, and he had made the error of letting down his guard.

Now, as he stood there with the agent's gun trained on him, he realized that the RCMP had played him the fool. They had made him feel over-confident, making it sound like the RCMP was nowhere near cracking the case. Last night he had gone home with three young Chinese whores – certain that all was well.

"This dial," he eyed Jake dispassionately," is one unit-frequency from ending Keeno's life. If he isn't already dead from the heart seizure I just induced, this will finish him off for sure," he smiled. "You really don't want to shoot me because I will end it before you can get a shot off."

Contrary to the stereotypical "bad guy," McDonald's face wasn't twisted into some evil or maniacal grin. His eyes were not dark and sinister. His lips were not curled upwards with saliva running down his chin, as if he were savouring the moment. The man looked calm, and it pissed Jake off that he was casually taking Keeno's life with such monotony. *Keeno deserved better – certainly better than this fat piece of shit*, he thought.

McDonald smiled subtly at Jake, confident that once again he held the upper hand.

Jake looked down at his feet. He had never been good at diplomacy or tact. In fact, his best asset was his bullheadedness and his tendency to shoot first and ask questions later – if at all.

At that instant, he did something that Malcolm McDonald, in all his arrogance, would not have predicted. Jake's gun-hand flashed up with such speed that McDonald didn't have a chance to react. The bullet streaked across the space between them, punching a hole through McDonald's right eyeball and blowing out the back of his head. Blood and goop cascaded over the console and onto the technician next to him.

McDonald's body crumpled to the floor, and as it did, Jake's rage exploded over the thought that Keeno was dead. He unloaded his clip into the wall-to-wall console. The room erupted in a shower of computer parts flying into the air, followed by a wave of sparks and smoke as pieces began to flame under the onslaught. A terrified technician was lying on the floor as parts rained down on him.

Jake finally leaned back against the wall and slid to the floor. His leg was aching from the bullet lodged in it, but the pain was paled in comparison to the realization that Keeno might actually be dead.

V

The Prime Minister reluctantly left Keeno's side, as a team of paramedics tried desperately to save him. Keeno had stopped breathing, that's all that they knew so far.

Seeing Keeno suddenly turn pale and then topple to the floor, had shocked the PM, and then the sight of his motionless body lying on the floor had filled him with anger. Realizing that the entire nation was waiting for him to speak, he collected himself and stepped up to the podium.

Although he had no slightest idea that Keeno had just experienced a massive heart attack, caused by two God Chips implanted inside of him, the PM was moved by Keeno words, and in knowing the sacrifices the man had made in just the past week attempting to stop this very terrorist attack on his nation.

"I am not without the deepest sense of shock and grief over what we have just witnessed," he paused to hold back a wave of emotion. "I can only say this to you, and this is as unrehearsed a speech as I will ever give, I will not relax our assault on these people and I will not give in one iota to their attempts to make us compromise our country and our freedom. The RFID program, whether for medical reasons or not, will never see the light of day as long as I am your Prime Minister. If it is your choice to reduce yourselves to becoming human GPSs and being bar-coded like someone's property, then I implore you to find yourself a new Prime Minister. But on my watch, freedom is still the pillar that supports the structure of our country and I will do everything in my power to protect that."

He stepped off the stage and walked briskly to where the paramedics were hovering over Keeno's unmoving body, and for the first time in his life he felt completely powerless.

VI

"Jesus, Jake, what a fucking mess," Neil Hamilton said. McDonald's body was lying in a pool of his own blood and the control console was a smoking disaster.

The agents poured into the room and started to recover what information they could find from the damaged system. Fortunately, there were stacks of CDs to one side that had not been damaged by Jake's assault. They also found a complete record of all the research.

The agents combed the offices for evidence, and struck pay dirt when they found Malcolm McDonald's laptop, which contained names and information related to the attack in Canada.

Jake was still leaning against the wall, trying to negotiate the pain in his leg and the growing pool of blood that had collected on the floor, when his cell phone buzzed.

"What's up?" he said, recognizing the code.

"Jake, it's Janene," her voice was quivering and he couldn't tell if she was happy or crying.

"What's happening?" he asked, though he dreaded that she might be calling him with bad news about Keeno.

"Keeno's alive. They thought he was dead but they just got his heart going again. They're rushing him to the hospital."

Jake listened to her cry on the other end of the line and he felt a sense of tremendous relief. “You have no idea how good it is to hear that,” he said.

“Whatever you did over there, thank you.” she said.

By the time they got back to Shanghai, the chartered plane was already fueled and ready for take-off and the Canadian team was aboard. Neil Hamilton shook hands with Jake and told him to say hi to Keeno for him.

When local police arrived at CJN Holdings, they found the bodies of the contract killers, Malcolm McDonald, and a technician. One other technician was found huddled in a corner of an office, otherwise unharmed. The Shanghai police would inevitably take the easiest road in their investigation, not wanting to high-profile a company with connections to the inner circles of the PRC. With eight dead mercenaries they would also want to avoid any confrontation or media involving underworld contract-killers.

They would never know that the RCMP and American Homeland Security had just pulled off a successful assault in their country.

VII

The meeting had been scheduled at a remote lodge, just east of Webster, New York, outside of Rochester. Three men were in attendance. It was a private lodge, where no one else could hear or see them, miles from any local towns and nestled on a small plot of land facing Lake Ontario. They had set up several electronic scramblers to hide their conversation from any surveillance, and naturally, a few hired guns were outside keeping watch.

"The setback with our operation in Rankin Inlet and in Shanghai is a minor one," the old man assured them. "The RCMP has thrown a wrench in the works, but they haven't stopped us and nothing can be traced to us at this time," he spoke confidently while swirling the Jack Daniels in his whiskey glass.

Normally, the old man was to be seen in expensive suits, but today he looked substantially less threatening and formidable in a pair of blue jeans, a plaid shirt and a light vest.

Things had not unfolded entirely as he had expected, but all was not lost. The incursion they had made with the viral attack in Toronto was the first blow, which would open more doors in the future. He was confident that it was only a matter of time before everyone bent to the pressure and the public demand for the technological perks of RFID chips, and true to his own philosophy – he would never stop until he succeeded with his plans.

Harold J. Rosenfeld, the "old man," sat smiling and watching Tom Sneider. Tom had wanted to bail out of the operation after they learned of McDonald's death weeks before, but Rosenfeld had assured him that their tracks were covered. He also tactfully waved the carrot in front of Tom's face, reminding him that this was still his fastest road to power in the pharmaceutical industry. Tom had taken the bait.

The third man in the room, Carrie Levine, was seen by the magnate as nothing more than a stupid, power-hungry politician with megalomaniac goals of becoming the Prime Minister of Canada. He had no morals, no fiber or ethical constitution whatsoever. He could be bought off at any decent price, and would, by his nature, usher in any program that HJR wanted or needed, providing there was enough money showing up in his accounts and enough promiscuous women appearing in his bedroom. Levine would still be useful to Rosenfeld, which is why he had invited him here for this meeting.

"Our next phase will have to wait until the press has calmed down on this recent incident with that RCMP officer. Everything we have accomplished in the research of our RFID program is well documented. We are preparing new plans that will eventually popularize the chips and bring about the acceptance of this technology," he said, with certain smugness. "It's just a matter of time."

The door to the lodge suddenly burst open and in walked two figures. HJR stood up as he recognized the first of the two men, "You!"

Keeno smiled, "Sit down, asshole," he glared into the face of the old man.

Jake stepped up next to Keeno. His leg was still stiff and sore where the bullet had been lodged weeks ago.

The room suddenly filled with RCMP agents, all of them pulling out guns and leveling them at the three men.

"You are all under arrest for planning and engaging a massive terrorist plot against Canada and the United States, and for the deaths of nearly 5500 innocent people. You are also indicted for your involvement in the illegal research facility in Rankin Inlet, and for the illegal implantation of RFID chips in no less than 450 local people, eight of whom died as a direct result of that experimentation," Keeno said, with a look of cold contempt in his eyes.

"You can't get away with this," HJR said as he stood up again. He had never been verbally assaulted by anyone in his life. Keeno stepped forward until his face was inches away from the old man's: "Believe me, pops, if it was my choice I would have put a cold bullet through your scrawny fucking skull two minutes ago and walked away from this cabin, saving the Canadian tax payers a lot of time and money. But," he sighed with mock disappointment, "some people convinced me that we should make this a painful process for you and drain some of your millions and give it back to Canadians."

The RCMP agents handcuffed HJR and Levine and dragged them out of the lodge. Tom Sneider sat there, his eyes flitting nervously back and forth.

Keeno dropped down in the leather chair across from him, "So, Tom, we meet again. I did promise you when this all started that I'd get some hard evidence on you."

Tom's eyes were a mixture of confusion and hate, flipping back and forth between the two emotions uncontrollably.

Keeno leaned back in the leather chair, "I am reminded of a conundrum someone told me. If you take every person currently living in China, line them eight across and had them start walking in a straight line, how long would it take for them to pass by you?"

Sneider stared at Keeno and then shook his head, "Who gives a fuck!"

Keeno smiled, "It was just a little bit of rhetoric, Tom. The answer is that in the lifetime of one man, you would never see 1.4 billion people walk by you, and on that note, that's about how long you're going to spend behind bars – a lifetime."

Tom stared at the floor, "You can't arrest me. The RCMP has no jurisdiction here."

"No, he can't, but I can," a voice said from the doorway, and in stepped Richard Jacobs, head of Homeland Security. "Take him," Jacobs said over his shoulder. Three Homeland Security agents filed past him, cuffed Sneider and dragged him from the room.

Richard Jacobs and Jake Williams sat down in the leather chairs across from Keeno. Keeno picked up the bottle of Jack Daniels Whiskey, poured out three glasses and passed them around.

"Cheers, gentlemen!"

VIII

Larry Egens pulled into FAB-MED's parking lot at 7:25 a.m. When he stepped out of his car, Keeno McCole was leaning against a car with a smile on his face.

"Hey Larry."

"Keeno, how are you?" he said, as he went up and shook hands vigorously.

"Little sore, but good. How 'bout you?"

"Really good. I got a call from the Board of Directors last night; they asked me if I'd be interested in a job as the VP of Operations."

Keeno smiled, "You taking it?"

"I think so."

"You deserve the promotion Larry."

"Thanks. Want to come in for a coffee?"

"No, I'm going for breakfast and then catching a flight somewhere."

"You came here just to see me?"

"Yes, if you hadn't helped us, we would never have nailed those guys. You saved a lot of people's lives and I wanted you to know that personally from me."

They shook hands again and Keeno watched Larry disappear inside the building, then he headed to the same Denny's restaurant that he had been at many weeks before when the investigation had just begun.

Within seconds of sitting down, a waitress was standing next to him pouring him a cup of coffee.

"Can I help you?" she smiled.

Keeno looked up at her and his jaw dropped. She was wearing a Denny's waitress outfit, her hair was styled, she had make-up on and she looked very pretty indeed. It was the same young girl who had asked him for money weeks before outside of Starbucks, whom he had protected from the two bimbos who had stolen the money from her.

"It's you? You work here now?"

She smiled, "Yup! I decided to change my life. I wanna thank you for that."

"Whatever I did, you're welcome," he said with a wide smile.

"You stuck up for me that day, gave me back some pride."

"Glad for you, really!"

"So what's your order today?"

"The Grand Slam, eggs over hard."

"No problem, this one is on me. Besides, I still owe you twenty bucks," she said as she walked away.

IX

On the day following the watershed press conference held by René Norman and Keeno McCole, Canadians went into an uproar. Emails, letters and phone calls poured in to electoral representatives. There was a literal national meltdown over the news of the conspiracy that had been levied on the nation.

National news covered Keeno's live heart attack that had been induced through the chips in his body. The next day, there was a tidal wave of media coverage as the

RCMP released video footage taken of the surgical removal of the God Chips from Keeno, who had insisted that the only way to convince everyone that his heart attack had not been staged was through total transparency. The world needed to see the truth, and the video footage was incontrovertible evidence of the fact.

Money poured in from every province of Canada to help put Toronto back on its feet again.

The President of the United States declared, in his own press conference, that his nation would help in the debacle that had resulted in billions of dollars of loss to Toronto and Canada.

Other nations, such as England, Sweden, France, Germany, Italy, Australia, Japan and many more, decried and condemned the act and offered their support. It was an international stand against terrorism and saboteurs of any kind.

In consequence, there was no vote put to the polls in Canada. Within seventy-two hours, surveys revealed that 82% of Canadians were in total support of René Norman and his Conservative Party remaining in the driver's seat.

Although the WHO, the World Health Organization, had no jurisdiction or say in China, they were forced by the international outcry to direct a maelstrom of questions at the Chinese government for their alleged involvement with CJN and its connections to the virus attack. The PRC's public relations machine, however, denied any knowledge of the matter, saying that CJN Holdings was not run or administered by the government – which of course was a blatant lie. In their PR statements, they also said that any illegal activities would be severely and summarily dealt with.

The PRC engaged a mock raid of CJN, arresting its principal people, and one week later released their findings. Those involved were sentenced to execution. The speed of justice was tantamount to the necessity to close off any further suspicions, speculations or questions from the international community.

Naturally, once a few heads had been put on the pike by the PRC, most people turned their heads the other way. Most, that is to say, except for the Royal Canadian Mounted Police and Homeland Security, both of which had established special task forces to launch investigations into the People's Republic of China's activities overseas. The Canadian and American law enforcement agencies were not fooled by the PRC's theatrical pose.

As for the emergency health legislation, René Norman tore that bill up in front of Canadian Parliament. A unanimous vote had been cast in favor of not only throwing it out, but also of fully supporting the committee he had formed to investigate and research the full scope of RFID chip implants, in order to inform Canadians and the world of their true potential, good and bad.

Only one week after the V-4 vaccine had been received in Toronto, the epidemic had stemmed and was on a nose dive. Martial law and the lock-down quarantine on the city had been lifted. Toronto resumed normal operations, and in true Canadian style, the citizens simply snubbed their noses at their recent misfortunes and went about their lives.

The documents found in Malcolm McDonald's computer had proven most useful and had revealed other people associated with the conspiracy. Once all the dots had been connected, twenty-nine major players had been indicted and arrested between Canada and America.

The ensuing trials were made public and carried out efficiently and at maximal cost to Harold J. Rosenfeld's financial empire. HJR and Carrie Levine were admitted to prison following their sentencing, and Harold J. Rosenfeld's dreams of becoming the most powerful man in Canada and controlling "the masses" through RFID chip implants disappeared with him into his jail cell, where he became the wealthiest life-term prisoner in Canada.

Tom Sneider underwent similar litigation in America, and was admitted to prison within several days of the Canadians.

Finally, when the Inuit's of Rankin Inlet realized what had really been going on at the research facility, they took matters into their own hands. The locals arrived one morning, encircled the facility, with men and women hefting fully-loaded guns so that no one could interfere, and proceeded to tear down the structure with bulldozers until there was nothing left but an open field. In its place, they planted a large stone engraved with the names of those victimized and murdered at the hands of Ackerman and his team.

The following week, a large package arrived in Toronto at the Bank of Montreal building, addressed to the Board of Directors of Harold J. Rosenfeld's banking institution. Naturally, the suspect package was opened by security personnel, revealing, to their shock, a full five pounds of bear shit, packaged and sealed, with a note which read:

IF YOU COME TO OUR TOWN AGAIN, THIS IS WHAT WILL HAPPEN TO YOU. SIGNED – THE PEOPLE OF RANKIN INLET

The story was leaked to the media, and Canadians across the nation cheered for Rankin Inlet.

X

The skies were a perfect ocean-blue, with not a cloud to be seen anywhere from the island of Aruba. The sun caressed the beaches from early morning until sundown, and the air was warm and soothing – particularly if you had several wounds healing as a result of bullet holes, knife cuts or chip implants.

Even the lump on Keeno's head was nearly gone. When he looked in the mirror, he wasn't shocked to see his battered body anymore. It all seemed to be healing up very well, and the Caribbean sun was giving his skin a new hue and glow.

Keeno leaned back into the pearly white sand, closed his eyes, and listened to the surf and the gulls squawking in their seemingly endless search for something more to eat.

He felt something soft and warm pressing down against him, and opened his eyes to see Janene straddling his stomach. She was wearing a rather skimpy two-piece bathing suit that favored her ample curves and her suggestive, well-shaped breasts. Keeno smiled up at her.

"Nice view."

She looked down at her breasts. "You wanna see them?" she teased and reached around to her back with one hand. Keeno took a deep breath, and, seeing a few scattered people here and there, he gently grabbed her hand before she managed to untie her top. "Frankly, I'd love to see your breasts right now, but I'm not interested in sharing them with the rest of Aruba."

She tilted her head in mock disappointment, "Party pooper."

He had settled back into the sand and closed his eyes again, when he felt something else settle on his chest. Opening his eyes, he saw a cup of coffee and a bag of pastries sitting there – precariously ready to topple over at his slightest movement.

Jake was standing there, with a pair of swimming trunks on and Katherine by his side. She too was wearing a two-piece suit. They were hand in hand. "Found a coffee joint down a ways. Enjoy!" Jake said, as they walked off together.

Keeno reached for the coffee and took a sip as Janene slid down next to him. He leaned over and kissed her. "Hmm, nice lips, but shitty coffee! I wonder if they have Starbucks in Aruba," he said jokingly.

His cell phone rang, and he flicked the cover open to read a text message.

"Don't tell me, Ross wants you to call him?" she said half-jokingly.

"Actually, yes. He says that something really big has come up and needs me to call him." Keeno settled down next to Janene and closed his eyes.

"That's it? You're not calling him?"

"Can't waste this sun. I'll contact him later today."

Janene smiled. This is what she loved about Keeno – he never tried to fit in; he was born to stand out and that's how he lived his life!

THE END